# THE FIFTH COLUMN

a Novel

by
George Meech

iUniverse, Inc.
New York   Bloomington

The Fifth Column

iUniverse books may be ordered through booksellers or by contacting:

iUniverse
1663 Liberty Drive
Bloomington, IN 47403
www.iuniverse.com
1-800-Authors (1-800-288-4677)

ISBN: 978-0-595-49164-3 (pbk)
ISBN: 978-0-595-50325-4 (cloth)
ISBN: 978-0-595-60990-1 (ebk)

Printed in the United States of America

**To Joan and John**

Special thanks to Patricia Anderson, PhD, for all your help

Visit www.georgemeech.com

Also by George Meech:
"The Mating of Mata"

# CHAPTER ONE

THE DAY THE nightmare began started out like most of the others—with a whisper instead of a shout.

It was colder than I expected for the last weeks of February. The clouds had opened up and it was raining, but there was still the odd trace of the night's dusting of snow on the lawns. The morning drudge had commenced as it always did—with me strapped in behind a steering wheel, waiting in traffic as the people of Vancouver moved about and made their way to their offices or factories. A little more than an hour spent gazing past the hypnotic back and forth of my windshield wipers at cars filled with half-wakened faces sipping lukewarm coffees. Sixty-plus minutes of long lines and short tempers and gearing myself up for another day on the job.

I'd killed my first twenty minutes at the office writing a piece on the previous night's murder in the Surrey district. The city had grown an ugly face, and an act that used to warrant half the front page was now relegated to a handful of sentences on page three or four. But that was back when the annual body count in this town was a single digit number. These days, the announcement that another bloodied corpse had been abandoned under the Port Mann Bridge stirred about as much emotion in the people of this burg, as the promise of a tax cut made by one of our empty-headed political windbags.

It's funny how quickly your life can change. In the blink of an eye, white can become black, and right can become wrong. It's still hard to believe that it all started with a phone call from an old woman who was preparing herself for death.

⌘

1

I slouched down in my chair, fingered my lucky green tie, and flung my old grey hat onto the coat hook at the end of my cubicle. There was a time when men were men and they weren't fully dressed unless they had their hats on. Mine was a magical piece of felt. I only had to hold it in my hand to bring back the memories of my younger days, and I could still hit that coat hook from ten feet away. A lot of water had trickled under the old bridge in the time I'd spent pounding a beat. Hunting out news for the *Vancouver Tribune* had been my duty, my honour, and my passion for almost thirty years. I'd seen a lot of changes take place, for better, and for worse.

The world had become different, and the newsroom had transformed right along with it. The days when hard-driving reporters sat hunched over manual typewriters were history. The zing of carriages being hammered back and the clatter of tobacco-stained fingers punching out real stories on real keys were gone. Now I had to put up with the irritating tick of carefully manicured digits on plastic computer keyboards and the equally annoying whine of a bank of networked laser printers. The constant jangle of a score of ringing telephones was a thing of the past too. What once was Bakelite, heavy and black, was now plastic as well. You couldn't slam a receiver down in anger now if your life depended on it. And that nerve-grating electronic pulse tone: Who of sound mind could have come up with that? The newsroom had lost its character.

I could never figure out what had happened to the fever that used to saturate this room—the intensity that often came accompanied by voices raised in anger and even the occasional swinging fist. There was always a spark in the air, regardless of how badly it smelled in here. Back in the days when the bottom drawer of every desk held a bottle of six-dollar Scotch, you could always tell when a guy was on to something big. The smell always gave it away. The number of cigarette butts heaped in his ashtray, the stench of cheap booze drying in a dirty coffee cup, or that special fragrance that can only come from a shirt that's been worn for three or four days straight. Now we had flowers, for Christ's sake, and whipping out a cigarette in here was worse than pulling out your dick.

It all began to go downhill when they hired that first woman. When I was in my prime, a skirt had to have a bucket and mop to set foot in here, and that's the way it was meant to be. It was the seventies that did us in. The whole world started going for a shit back then. Nowadays, more than half the people in this room shaved their legs, not their faces. My only saving grace around this joint was that at least now my bottom drawer held a much better brand of whiskey. The desk to my right, along with a collection of potted plants, had a picture of a kid and a cat on it. What kind of reporter could put up with a cat?

I knew why management had assigned the two cubs to me. I was the best this paper had seen in ages. Retirement wasn't that many years off, and it only made sense that I pass my experience and my wisdom down the line. But why on earth a woman? Wasn't having Jimmy Olsen at my side enough? This was a man's world, and one that I had to fight to preserve. A reporter had to be as tough as nails, and have no fears or boundaries when it came to telling a story. I just didn't see the point. It made no sense to me at all. Was there really a need to drag Lois Lane around with me, too?

# CHAPTER TWO

I PUSHED OPEN the door to the meeting room and headed straight for the coffeepot. I dropped my briefcase to the floor and rested my mug on the counter. I glanced down the throat of the once white ceramic cup. Months away from its last good scrubbing, it had coffee stains that would most likely have to be sandblasted off. Extra taste, I said to myself as I poured my fifth of the day.

The digital clock on the coffeemaker read 8:55. The next hour would be devoted to coaching my apprentices and keeping my caffeine levels high enough to get me through to lunch.

The door swung open and the whirlwind of misdirected energy that was Amanda Southfield blew in.

"Whew," she said as she deposited her purse and briefcase on the table, "it was touch and go this morning. It was my turn to drop Rebecca off at daycare, and the traffic is horrible."

I nodded.

"I saw Grant chatting up that new mail room girl in the underground," she said.

"Hmm," I mumbled. "What's her name? Petunia or something?"

"Petra. She does tend to get your attention, doesn't she?"

I grunted. They couldn't possibly be real.

"He shouldn't be long. I know how much you hate it when he's late."

I nodded again and took a few more hits of caffeine.

Amanda shuffled and rearranged her notes. I could count on one finger the number of lessons the woman hadn't bucked me on. It was the only thing I'd managed to teach her about this business without a fight: From the top of her no-nonsense haircut to the tip of her sensible shoes, the woman was at least organized. There was no denying her intelligence, but it didn't matter much. The way I saw it, with her

4

penchant for a classic business suit over a brightly coloured blouse and skirt, her modest use of makeup, and lack of any jewellery at all—with the exception of the plain gold band on the fourth finger of her left hand—she'd be much better off teaching third graders.

Grant Shaw sauntered in. He tossed his briefcase onto the meeting table and hunted his mug out of the cabinet over the sink. The clock on the coffeemaker now read 9:04.

⌘

It's a thin line that separates confidence from arrogance, and Grant walked it well. Athletic and well dressed, he had the type of chiselled features that set him apart from the others in the newsroom. His presence alone was enough to elicit answers. Although, I had to admit, his skill with a pen did not yet match the woman's, the day would come when I could comfortably pass the torch to him. Unlike his female counterpart, there was definite potential there. Like taking a slab of raw granite, I could chip away until I had a carbon copy of myself. The woman, on the other hand, was destined to fail. There was no way she could balance a career as demanding as this with the task of bringing up a small child and managing a household for herself, her husband, and that stupid cat. I could see it. The world would be on the brink of disaster, and she would have to run off to watch little missy be a porcupine in the kindergarten play.

I looked down at my notepad. "OK," I said, "let's get started. I want to ask you both a question. What do you think our job is here?"

"Our job," Amanda said, "is to report the news. To inform the people of Vancouver about events taking place in this city, this country, and around the world."

"Is that all?" I asked. "Don't you think we're as much a part of creating history, as we are about reporting it?"

Amanda tapped her bottom lip with the butt of her pen and carefully chose the words to respond. "In some cases," she said after a moment's pondering.

"Explain," I said.

"If we're reporting on a plane skidding off a runway in Halifax, or a car crash in a Paris tunnel that claims the life of a princess, then no, we're not creating history."

"And?"

"If something that we write sets off a chain of events, then yes, we can create history."

Grant turned and faced me. "Like that series you wrote on Chris McDermott and Alan Ball," he said. "You certainly created some local history with that one."

I couldn't suppress the grin. "I did," I told him. "There's no room in this province for a dirty politician. It's our job—no, it's our duty—to root out people like Chris McDermott, and put a stop to them."

"But only when you have hard evidence."

I turned to Amanda. "And just what do you mean by that?" I asked.

"Chris McDermott," she said. "I'm not disputing that some things *may* have gone on that weren't totally aboveboard, but I think you blew that property deal way out of proportion."

"I did like hell. Sometimes you have to be creative. There's always a story; sometimes it just boils down to the way you word the facts. Politicians are privy to certain bits of information. They shouldn't be allowed to capitalize on that. They shouldn't be able to profit from insider knowledge."

"I agree," Amanda said. "But McDermott and Ball had been partners in various land holdings for years—long before McDermott was elected to public office. That property was purchased when an expansion of the rapid transit system was nothing more than a twinkle in the city planner's eye. I don't see anything sinister about adding to a portfolio you already own.

They weren't trying to hide anything. Can you give me one good reason why they shouldn't have bought that land? It was listed with the real estate agency for months. Anyone could have snapped it up. If you had some extra cash, don't you think it would have looked attractive?"

"That's beside the point. A person that holds the public's trust has a duty. That deal never should have gone through. Besides, I was told that McDermott might have learned as much as three years ago that the property in question was being considered for the placement of the new station."

"That's right. I'd almost forgotten about your unnamed reliable source."

I leaned back and scratched at an itch on my belly. "I'd watch your tone, if I were you."

"I think what you did was wrong. I think McDermott did a good job representing the people of that community. Look at the improvements that were made. The neighbourhood police station, the new library—"

"And the new rapid transit terminal," Grant interrupted. "That's the whole issue in a nutshell. Chris McDermott is as cold and as calculating as they come. Terry exposed corruption. That's part of our job."

Amanda glared across the table at Grant. "Corruption?" she said. "There'd been talk of the Skytrain going through that neighbourhood for years. It was public knowledge. There was no corruption anywhere."

"The people of this city didn't seem to think so," I said.

"You have to give McDermott credit," Amanda replied. "It was a pretty unselfish thing to do. Stepping aside, resigning an elected position after that many years, rather than have every accomplishment you've made picked to the bone."

"Get out while you can get out clean, is more like it."

"I know one thing," Amanda said. "With the weight of the *Vancouver Tribune* newspaper on your back, you don't have a lot of choices."

"Chris McDermott wasn't the biggest fish I've ever fried."

Grant smiled and nodded his head. "The Cottonwood scandal. The man was a thief. You nailed his ass good."

Amanda leaned on the table. "I still think what you did to Chris McDermott was wrong."

"All I did was tell the truth."

"But you told it in a way that led people to believe that McDermott had done something inappropriate."

"So?" I said. "The truth is the truth. What people make of it is up to them."

"Telling half the truth is just as bad as telling a lie," Amanda mumbled.

"Keep up the good work, Scoop," Grant said as he flashed me a thumbs-up.

Amanda rested her elbows on the table and let out a groan. "If you wanted to find some real skeletons," she said, "you should have looked in Alan Ball's closet."

I raised an eyebrow.

"You know exactly what I mean. The man gives me the creeps. Look into his eyes. That guy's got more secrets than Pandora's box. The only reason you went after McDermott was because it was the easiest path to follow. A politician makes a better target than a businessman."

"So what?" I asked. "An elected official always makes for good cannon fodder."

"You and your so-called reliable source destroyed Chris McDermott for the sake of a story. Ask yourself this: What did this man have to gain by telling you that McDermott was dirty? That is, if there really is such a man."

I stared the woman down. She just wasn't getting it. What was wrong with the young people of today's world? When I was her age, it didn't take me long to figure out that in order to get ahead in this business, sometimes you had to be ruthless. An exposé like the McDermott-Ball piece was a battle—me versus them. If I omitted a few of the details, then so be it. Grant was catching on, but the woman would never understand—not in a million years.

Our eyes remained fixed. Like every old bull, I expected a challenge, but who did this woman think she was? She refused to back down. I broke eye contact with her and looked down at my notes.

"That's enough about Ball and McDermott," I said. "I've run across something interesting." I looked in Grant's direction and smiled. "On Charles Wolfe, no less," I added.

Grant leaned onto the table and wrung his hands into a knot. "Charlie Wolfe?" he replied. "The man everyone in this city loves to hate?"

"I don't think everyone hates him," Amanda said. "What's he got to his credit? Six campaigns and six wins?"

"Seven," I said. "He's never lost an election."

The woman shook her head and leaned her elbow on the table and hooded her eyes with the palm of her hand. "You've had your sights set on him for a long time," she said. "What brought on this little vendetta?"

"He's an arrogant shit. He needs to be brought down a peg or two."

"You just like going after politicians," she said.

"What have you got on him?" Grant asked.

"A videotape," I said. "Of him taking a bribe."

"A bribe?" Amanda asked.

"Yup, I just stumbled onto it. It's from a surveillance camera in the parking garage at the Bayside Hotel. One of the parking attendants sold it to me."

"Sold it to you?"

"Yeah," I said, "I gave him ahundred bucks for it."

"And what's on this tape exactly?" Amanda asked.

I turned to her. "It's definitely old Charlie," I said. "He's facing right into the camera. The tape clearly shows him accepting an envelope and sticking it in his pocket."

"That's it?" Amanda asked. "Do you know who's giving him this envelope?"

"Not yet," I said. "You can only see the back of his head. I'll figure it out, though. I've made arrangements to buy the surveillance tapes from the entrance of the garage. Those will give me the license plate number of every car that parked there that day."

"What makes you think it's a bribe in the envelope? It could have been a party invitation for all you know."

Grant turned around in his chair. "Of course it's a bribe," he said. "Why on earth would Charlie meet up with some mysterious character in an underground parking lot to accept an invitation to a party?"

"You guys are unbelievable," Amanda muttered.

"You just wait," I said and waved my finger in her face. "I'll prove it."

Amanda closed her eyes and shook her head.

"That'll look good on you," Grant said, "having Charlie Wolfe's scalp hanging from your belt right next to Stanley Cottonwood's and Chris McDermott's."

# CHAPTER THREE

"Is this Terry Hartree?" the caller asked.

I shifted the phone to my left hand. "It is," I said. "Who is this?"

I listened to the sound of dead air for a moment.

"It's my birthday today," the woman said. "Be nice to me, I have a gift for you."

"What kind of a gift?"

"They call you Scoop, don't they?"

Habit made me open my desk drawer and punch the button on my telephone-recording device. I leaned back in my chair and readied myself for a game of twenty questions. "They do," I replied.

"Why is that?" the woman asked. "Is it because you clean up after your dog?"

"Listen, lady," I said, "I'm a busy man. If you don't get to the point, I'm going to hang up."

"I don't think you should do that. I have a pretty interesting story to tell you."

"And what would that be?"

"I've followed your articles for years. I was particularly impressed by your pieces on the Cottonwood scandal."

"You *have* been following my work. That was two or three years ago, now."

"Closer to four," she said.

"Cash was diverted into campaign funds. Money that was raised to fund amateur sports was used for Stanley Cottonwood's re-election crusade."

"I need to talk to someone who can tell my story to the world. I'm nearing the end of my life."

"Growing old is a fact we all have to face. That doesn't mean you don't have plenty of good years ahead of you."

"I'm dying. I have cancer. I waited a bit too long to see the doctors. It's spreading—quickly."

"I'm sorry to hear that."

"Guess what I was doing on the night the new millennium rolled in?"

"What?" I asked.

"While the rest of the world was waiting for their computers to crash, and for life as we know it to end, I celebrated the New Year by reading my oncologist's report. The news wasn't good."

"That's a shame."

"I've gone in and out of remission over the last couple of years, but the cancer is back with a vengeance. It's in my lungs now. There's nothing anyone can do for me. They give me a month—six weeks at the most."

"And you want to tell the world what it's like to be facing death?"

"No," she said. "It's more than that—a lot more."

"What?" I asked.

"I've committed some horrible crimes."

"What kind of crimes?" I asked. "I'm not interested in wasting my time listening to the ramblings of a serial shoplifter or someone who sneaks around and loosens the lids on the salt shakers at the old folks' home."

"Believe me. This won't be a waste of your time."

"Then tell me. What kind of crimes did you commit?

"Not yet. I know my story will be worthy of *your* time. What I don't know yet is whether *you'll* be worthy of my mine."

"I have a meeting to get to. When you're ready to talk, you've got my number."

I dropped the phone back onto its cradle, hit the button to end the recording, and gathered up my notes for the afternoon session with my cubs.

⌘

"So," I said, "Guess whose car drove into the parking garage at the Bayside Hotel ten minutes before our old friend Charlie was taped receiving that envelope?"

Amanda rolled her eyes away from me. I turned to Grant. "Simon Earling," I said.

"Jesus," Grant replied. "Doesn't he own Concordia Developments?"

I nodded my head and grinned.

"And weren't they just awarded the contract for the new addition to City Hall?"

I nodded again.

"Son of a bitch," Grant said. "Wolfe sat on the committee that decided who was going to get that job."

"Chairman," I said. "And the day after the meeting in the parking garage, Concordia announced that they will be the ones that will rebuild City Hall."

Amanda dropped her hand on the table. "Hold on," she said. "First of all, you don't know what was in the envelope. Secondly, you don't know if it was Earling who was in the camera shot with Wolfe. All you can see is the back of the man's head."

"The hairstyles are similar," I said.

Amanda groaned. "Perfect," she said. "In a city this size, that would narrow it down to what—a few thousand?"

"It was Earling," I said. "I feel it in my bones."

"But you don't have any proof."

I drew a breath and looked into Amanda's eyes. Again she refused to back down. The more time I spent with her, the more her outright defiance irked me.

"I don't need any more proof," I said. I leaned back in my chair and crossed my legs. "Look at it this way," I said. "William Jefferson Clinton. He instigated the largest deficit reduction plan in American history. He created six million new jobs and lowered his country's debt by hundreds of billions of dollars. That was what he was hired to do. But he was impeached. Do you remember why?"

Amanda lowered her eyes and blushed.

"For getting a blow job from a White House intern," I said. "And that, young lady, is politics. All's fair in love, war, and the battle between the press and those in public office."

"That's what's wrong with today's world," Amanda said, "and we newspaper people just keep stoking the fires. People just love a scandal. All anyone wants to hear about are the bad things. I'll bet if you lined up a hundred random American voters, every single one of them would know about Clinton's alleged indiscretion in the oval office."

I nodded.

"But less than half," Amanda continued, "would know how much he did for their economy."

"I'm going to get this Charles Wolfe character, and I'm going to do it with or without your or anyone else's blessing."

"And I suppose you have another reliable—unnamed—source hiding somewhere who's ready to reveal some damaging information on Charlie?"

"Maybe," I said. "They're not that hard to find—especially the ones with no names."

"And if worse comes to worse, they're easy enough to make up."

I glared at the woman.

"You're out to hang Charlie Wolfe. You're going to spin a story around this envelope thing, and you're going to make it look like Charlie was up to no good."

"All I'm going to do is present our readers with the facts. Charlie was taped receiving an envelope and Simon Earling was seen entering the same parking garage a few minutes earlier."

"Wait a minute," Amanda said and held up her hand. "It may have been Earling's car, but you can't prove it was Simon driving it."

"We'll let the people of this city decide that. Don't you think it's odd that Concordia was issued the contract for the City Hall reno a matter of hours later?"

"That doesn't mean Charlie met up with Earling or that he accepted a bribe."

"That, my dear," I said, "is not for you to decide. And that's the end of the discussion. I have assignments for you both."

Amanda let out a sigh and flipped open her notepad. Grant straightened his tie.

"Grant," I said. "I want you to handle the Independent Trucker's Association strike."

He nodded.

"There's a good story in there somewhere. I want you to dig. I want you to get into the mind of one of the truckers. These people have paralysed the docks. They are costing this province seventy-five million dollars a day. I want you to get to the heart of the dispute. I'm not talking about the politics, or all the rhetoric. I want you to get to the crux of the issue. The drivers are claiming it's the cost of the fuel, and the long waits at the docks that are killing them. I don't want to read all the bullshit from the union leaders or the businessmen. I want to know what it's like to be a trucker. I want you to grab people by the heart with this."

"Got it, chief," Grant said.

"And for you," I said and turned to Amanda, "the senior editor's wife belongs to a social club for ladies of Russian descent. They're having some kind of a tea this afternoon at the Trade and Convention Centre. He's asked me if we can do a human-interest piece. Get down there and see if you can find something to write about that's not going to bore the shit out of every subscriber this paper's got. It starts at three."

# CHAPTER FOUR

I PULLED OPEN my bottom drawer and rested my foot. I leaned back in my chair and read through Grant's assignment from the day before. It was light, a column and a half at best. I breezed through the copy and anticipated the hook. It never came. The words were basic. Structured and bland, the story had no feeling. It was a list of facts and figures, as dry as a box of soda crackers after a day in the hot sun.

A trucker could expect to pay up to three hundred and fifty dollars in fuel costs, for a day's work that might earn him three hundred. And a five-hour wait at the freight terminal was a deathblow to someone who gets paid for what they haul. It was concise, when *concise* was a word you'd use in place of *hurried*. There was no passion—nothing to relay the feeling that in fact, these people really had a bone to pick. Everyone struggles at some point. I tried to put myself in the shoes of the average readers: the plumbers, the cab drivers, the teachers, and the shopkeepers that read this paper every day. Everyone has had a tale of woe at some time, and can relate to the pain of others.

Grant missed the point entirely. I'd instructed him to get into the mind of a striker, to tell the story from the heart and soul of one of the sufferers. I didn't want facts and figures. If I wanted drivel, I could pick myself up a copy of the *Globe and Mail*. I was sure that Sharon Halter could bore me to tears, if that's what I was looking for.

I couldn't believe what I was reading. I knew the opportunity was there. There was enough going on at the docks for someone with a good nose to come up with award-winning material. I thought I'd done a better job with the kid. I glanced at my watch. Two hours till deadline. I had plenty of time to write some spirit into Grant's work. But first I had to give the woman's assignment the few minutes it deserved.

⌘

I placed Amanda's article back on my desk. I'd read it three times, and each time it stirred emotions I didn't like to admit I had. I'd sent her on a chase for the wildest of geese, to search out a story where I was sure one didn't exist.

Imagine, finding a woman like that at a social for Russian immigrants. Amanda had not only found a woman who'd grown up in the poorest part of the Ukraine, but had pulled a story out of her that was so moving it almost brought a tear to *my* cynical old eye. She told the tale of the woman's struggle to make it to Canada on her own at the age of twenty-three. Of the courage it took to leave her parents and her brothers and sisters and set out alone for a new world. As I read the words describing her backbreaking fourteen-hour days in the wheat fields of Saskatchewan, I could feel my own spine start to ache. The paragraph about the woman's trek to the West Coast, alone and afraid, in the freezing cold confines of an empty boxcar, made me shiver. The account of nights spent sleeping in parks, and of days devoted to collecting discarded pop bottles in order to put food in her mouth, caused hunger pangs deep in my gut. The story transported me back in time. I felt like I *was* that old woman.

Every sentence of the article was powerful; every word grabbed my heart. It's too bad, I thought, that Amanda has no respect for me. It's a shame that she can't listen. If only she could be a bit more like Grant, she might get somewhere in this world.

I tossed her article into the bottom drawer of my desk and reached for the phone.

⌘

"Terry Hartree," I said.

"Good morning," my mystery caller replied.

I laughed. "You again," I said. "Apparently you've decided that I *am* worthy of your time."

"I've narrowed the list down," she said. "I'm still not entirely sure about you."

"My tough luck," I said. "You're not that phantom jaywalker the police have been trying to stop for the last ten years, are you?"

"No. It's a little more serious than that."

I chuckled again. "What?" I asked. "You're not the person that soaped the windows of the mayor's house last Halloween, are you?"

"I've killed," she said.

I felt a chill run through my body. Her words had a haunting sincerity to them. I reached for my cassette recorder.

"I'm sure you must be taping this. Have you got your machine running?"

"I do."

"I'm a cold-blooded murderer," she continued, "and I don't want to go to my grave with this still on my chest. The guilt has been eating at me for years. I need to tell my story. The world has to know why."

"Who did you kill?"

"Not so fast. First, I need to know that I can trust you. There are other people involved. If they find out where I am, and that I've been talking to you, they'll kill me. And it won't be a pleasant death."

"Other people?" I asked.

"Yes, very powerful and very dangerous people. You'll understand once you figure out who the first victim was."

"The *first* victim? You're telling me there was more than one?"

"That's right. Once the killing started, it carried on for years."

"When can we meet?"

"Never," she said. "Even if I decide that you're the one to trust with my story, all of our conversations will be by telephone."

"No," I said, "I don't work like that. If you want to spill your guts about some murder spree you claim to have been a part of, then you'll do it face to face with me."

I listened to her laugh.

"We'll just have to see about that," she said. "I'm going to give you the biggest news story of the last forty years. Believe me, once you clue in to what's being handed to you, you'll dance naked down Main Street for a chance to break this story."

"Don't be so sure of that."

"It's between you and Sharon Halter of the *Globe and Mail*."

"Halter?" I asked. "Why would you want to get involved with that dingbat?"

"Dingbat?" she asked. "Wasn't she just short-listed for this year's Canadian Journalist Award?"

"Jesus Christ," I mumbled, "that woman shouldn't be allowed to cover anything more important than a Pillsbury bake-off. I don't know where she gets the nerve to call herself a writer."

"I guess the Journalist Association people made a mistake, huh?"

"It wouldn't be their first."

"Right, I hear they passed you over this year—again."

"They probably had to fill their quota of women, that's all. The piece I did on Alan Ball and Chris McDermott was ten times better than anything Halter's even dreamed about writing."

"Sounds like sour grapes."

"It's not sour grapes," I said. "It's the truth."

"It would be nice to go out with a bang, don't you think? How long have you got left before you retire?"

"I'll go when I'm goddamned good and ready."

"A Ceejay award would probably look pretty nice hanging in your den. You've never won, have you?"

"No."

"Didn't that Halter woman pick one up a couple of years ago?"

"She did," I said. "Her second."

"How's your knowledge of history?"

"It's as good as anyone's."

"It'll have to be better than that. You're going to have to spend some time researching."

"I've got people that can do that for me."

"No!" she insisted. "That will be something you will have to do alone. I don't think you understand."

"Understand what?"

"The type of people and situations you're going to be dealing with. I just hope you've got what it takes."

"Trust me," I said, "I've got the balls for it."

"You have to understand the rules here. Once you verify my story, you have to go public with it all at once. You can't let anyone know before that. That's why there can't be any researchers."

"But—"

"I'm telling you, Hartree. You can't breathe a word of this to anyone."

"And why is that?"

"I told you. These people are savage. If they even dreamt that you were on to them, they wouldn't hesitate to silence us both."

"Is that a threat?"

"It's a fact. You have to know what you're getting into. You'll understand soon."

"You're going to have to give me more than that."

"I will," she said. "Be patient. I've pretty much made my decision, but the final choice hasn't quite come down to you yet."

"I have two interns working for me. There's a young man, he's good, and he'll keep his mouth shut if I tell him to."

Silence again.

"Are you there?" I asked.

"OK," she said. "This story is huge; you'll probably need the help. You just make absolutely sure that your interns know the rules. No one can hear about this until the time is right."

"And who's going to decide when that is?"

"I am," she said. "I haven't got long to live. If you end up being the one, I'll make sure you have the whole story before I shuffle off this mortal coil."

"*For in that sleep of death what dreams may come.*"

"You know, *Hamlet*," she said. "It's my favourite Shakespeare play."

"Are you going to tell me your name?"

She paused for a moment. "No," she said, "not until the end. I have to protect myself. We'll use a code name for now. You can call me Dallas."

"Dallas?"

"Yeah," she said. "Deep Throat's been used already."

"Dallas?" I asked again.

"Yeah," she said. "You know, as in *Debbie Does*. I'll talk to you soon."

The line went dead. I ejected the cassette from my recorder and held it in my hand. Something about the way the woman spoke told me this was no prank. There was fear in her voice, but at the same time there was resignation. I marked the tape "call #2" and tossed it into my top drawer.

# CHAPTER FIVE

"THIS IS HOW we're going to hang old Charlie," I said.

Grant smiled and took a hit from his coffee mug. Amanda gave me an icy glare.

"We'll set the story up the day before they announced the winning contractor for the city hall project."

Grant turned to Amanda and grinned.

"We'll inform the readers that Charlie headed the selection committee, and that we've got him on tape receiving an envelope from a man in the parking garage at the Bayside."

Amanda let out an exasperated groan.

"Then we'll tell the readers that Simon Earling's car was seen entering the parking garage a few minutes prior to the time that Charlie was handed the envelope."

"But," Amanda said, "you still can't prove that Earling was driving."

I leaned over the table and turned to Grant. "Did you hear me say anything about Earling being in the car?" I asked.

Grant smiled and shook his head.

"That's as good as a lie," Amanda said. "You're leading the readers to a conclusion."

"They're perfectly capable of making up their minds for themselves," I said. "Any rational person would know that it wasn't necessarily Earling driving the car."

"Even if it was Earling in the car," Amanda said, "that still doesn't mean it was he that gave Charlie the envelope."

"That's true," I replied, "but we don't have to point that out. We have to assume that any clearheaded person would come to that conclusion."

"Have you talked to these men?" Amanda asked.

"Huh?"

"Earling and Wolfe. Has Wolfe got an explanation for the envelope? Did you ask Earling if he was at the Bayside that day?"

"Why would I do that?" I asked. "I've got them red-handed. Talking to them would just give them time to prepare an alibi. When this story breaks, I want to catch them off guard."

Amanda looked down at the table. "It's not right," she muttered.

"Well," I said, "if it will make you feel better—we might be pushing this story onto the back burner for a few days."

Grant's head jerked in my direction. "Back burner it?" he said. "Why?"

"I got an interesting phone call," I said, "from a woman who wants to confess to being party to a string of murders."

Grant's eyes lit up.

"She told me she has cancer. She wants to tell her story before she dies."

"Sounds good, boss," Grant said. "When do we start?"

"She didn't say much. She wouldn't even give me her name. She says there are some powerful people involved."

"A crank?" Amanda asked.

"I don't know yet," I said. "She's sounds educated; she quoted *Hamlet*. I have a feeling. I think there might be a story here."

"What's the next move?" Grant asked.

"Sit back and wait," I said. "She told me she'd call back."

"Terry Hartree speaking."

"Hartree," she said, "guess who."

"Dallas?" I asked and pulled open the drawer that held my tape machine.

"Got a fresh tape in that machine of yours?"

"Uh-huh," I said.

"Good. I've made my decision. You're the one."

"Was there ever any doubt?"

"It was a tough choice. Sharon Halter has some excellent qualities, but your series on that politician, McDermott, made up my mind for me."

"I'm glad you liked it."

"I need someone who's not afraid to take on powerful people."

"You've come to the right place."

"You wrote some things that weren't exactly true."

"What are you saying?" I asked.

"Admit it, Hartree. I'm no angel. I'm an old woman, and if I hadn't done the things in my life that I did, we wouldn't be talking now. Don't try and snow me. I haven't got the time or the stomach lining left. You lied."

"I may have been a little hasty with some of the comments I made. I could have spent more time verifying some of the statements made by my source."

"That's right," she said, "your unnamed source at city hall."

"And a very reliable source, too, I might add."

"Don't lie to me, Hartree. You manufactured the whole corruption scenario, and I think the reason you fabricated that mysterious source was so you'd have someone to shift the blame to if the story began to collapse around your ears."

"Don't shoot me," I said. "I was just the messenger."

"Don't bother trying to spin this one. I'm not going to waste time arguing with you. The fact is you destroyed a person's career. You took some vague information about a property deal, and you twisted it to look like something much worse than it really was."

"All right," I said. "I'll admit that I may have put a bit of a negative slant on things."

The laughter on the other end of the phone line turned to a vicious cough.

"You all right?" I asked.

"No," she said, panting for breath. "I'm coughing up blood. I think the doctors were being a little generous when they gave me a month. We have to get started."

"I'm ready," I said.

"It was late—the evening of August fourth. I remember it was very hot that day. It never really cooled off that night."

"August fourth," I said and made note of the date on my pad.

"Yes," she said. "Look at August fifth. The death wasn't recorded until early the following morning."

"August fifth," I repeated and scribbled over the date.

"My partners and I snuck up to the house."

"Where you committed the murder?"

"That's right. It was a cute little house. It looked kind of like a Mexican hacienda. There were wind chimes hanging in the yard. The sound still haunts me."

"And who did you kill?"

I heard nervous laughter again.

"What's funny?" I asked.

"We're not ready for names yet. I've told you the date, and I'll tell you that it was a woman that we killed."

"I need more than that."

"And you'll get more, but only after I've had the pleasure of teasing you a bit. Call it my last laugh."

"We haven't got that much time, remember?"

"I do remember," she said "only too well. You can't blame me for wanting to have some fun with you. Look at it this way: On one hand, I'm confessing to something that has eaten me up for over forty years. You must know that can't be easy. On the other hand, I've got one of the best news reporters in Canada at my beck and call. You're going to be my plaything, my monkey on a string. I plan on having some real fun with you."

"Listen, woman," I said.

"Dallas," she replied.

"OK then. Listen to me, Dallas. I'm nobody's toy. If that's the way you want to play this, then I think I should hang up right now and forget that I ever heard from you in the first place."

"Yeah?" she said. "Do you think you could do that?"

"You're goddamned right I could do it. Just sit back and listen while I drive this phone through the top of my desk."

"One thing before you hang up the phone."

"What?"

"Do you happen to have Sharon Halter's phone number? I know I have it here somewhere, but if you've got it handy, it would save me the trouble of having to look it up again."

My blood began to boil and I gripped the receiver of the phone like I had Halter by the throat.

"What's the matter?" Dallas asked. "Cat got your tongue, or old woman got you by the nuts?"

"All right," I said, "you can have your fun for now."

"You won't regret it. I told you, this is going to be the biggest story of your career. Maybe even the biggest news story in Canadian history."

"We'll see. If you keep playing games with me, you could die before we get off first base."

"Don't worry," she replied. The hacking returned with a vengeance.

I listened to her gag. The coughs sounded wet and painful; clearly they were choking her. I gave her a minute to catch her breath.

"I've written out my whole story," she said, wheezing between gulps of air. "I told you, I want the world to know. If I go sooner than I expect, the documents will be couriered to you. I've left instructions with my lawyer, but I have to warn you, if you don't rise to meet this challenge to my satisfaction, I'll have my attorney send the papers to the *Globe and Mail*."

"Halter?" I asked.

"That's right," she said. "I know you'll be diligent. I know more about you than you know about yourself. You couldn't stand the thought of this kind of feature being written by a woman. It would burn you up to be out-scooped by someone who sits down to pee. I'm going to hang up now. I'll call you in a couple of days to see how you and your two slaves do with the information you've got so far."

The line went dead. I shut the tape recorder off.

# Chapter Six

"WE'VE GOT WORK to do," I said. "I got another call from our anonymous serial killer."

Amanda readied her pen. "What did she say?"

I reached for the play button on my cassette recorder. "Listen to the calls," I said.

I turned the tape machine on. Amanda scribbled notes as she listened to the mystery woman lay out the rules. I let the tape run its course.

⌘

"What do you think?" I asked.

"You're right," Amanda said. "I think there's something there."

I let her comment hang in the air and turned to Grant. "And you?" I asked.

Grant scratched his head. "What's all this *sleep of death* stuff?" he asked. "That doesn't make sense."

"It's a line from *Hamlet*," Amanda said. "Act III, scene 1 of Hamlet's soliloquy, *To be, or not to be.* Ring any bells?"

Grant raised an eyebrow.

"Shakespeare's always been one of my passions," Amanda explained. "I couldn't get enough of him in college."

"Never mind that," I said. "It at least tells us that she's educated. What else did you pick up?"

"She knows journalism," Amanda said. "The Canadian Journalist Awards are not exactly front-page material."

"She's dying," Grant said.

I looked in his direction. He was grinning like he'd just found a cure for the common cold.

"When did you get the first call?" Amanda asked.

"Tuesday afternoon."

"Then she was born on February 20," Amanda said. "She said it was her birthday."

"What else?" I asked.

"She killed a woman," Grant said. "Cat fight!"

"She's frightened," Amanda said. "You can hear it in her voice."

"Agreed," I said. "Do you think it's death that she's afraid of?"

"No," Amanda replied. "She said she was diagnosed a few years ago. She would have come to terms with the cancer by now, I'm sure of it."

I ran my hand through my hair. "That's a good possibility," I said, "unless she's denied it until now."

"She said there were powerful people involved. I think that's why she's afraid."

"Yeah," Grant said.

"She also admitted that it was something that's been eating her up for over forty years. That would mean the killing took place back in the sixties."

I agreed with Amanda's observation.

"I think there's only one thing we can really be sure about at this point," Amanda said.

"What's that?"

"She's got a story to tell, and she wants *you* to relay it to the world."

"I guess we'll just have to wait for another call," Grant said.

"We can check with the Department of Vital Statistics," Amanda said. "They would have records of the murders committed back then."

"Exactly," I said. I turned to Grant. "Hop the ferry to Victoria. The Department of Vital Statistics is in the Parliament Buildings. I want you to start by getting any information you can on any woman murdered on August fifth, between the years 1960 and 1965."

Grant saluted.

"What about me?" Amanda asked.

"Investigating murder is a man's job," I said. "We'll find something for you to do later."

Grant packed up his belongings and headed out the door.

Amanda turned to me. "My article," she said, "on the Russian woman, what did they think of it upstairs?"

"Sorry," I said and shook my head, "maybe next time."

# CHAPTER SEVEN

"FIGURED IT OUT yet, Hartree?"

"Yeah, Dallas," I said. "I've figured it out. Grant got back from Victoria last night. He's checked the statistics for every August fifth from 1960 to 1965. There's no record of any woman being murdered on that day in the province of British Columbia. I'm starting to think I might be wasting my time with you."

"Sharon Halter wouldn't think so."

"Yeah?" I said. "Maybe you should run it past her."

"You know, Hartree, I thought you'd pick up on it faster than this."

"Pick up on what?" I asked.

"Listen to the clues. I never said anything about her death being recorded as a murder. I told you, it was the first of many. We were trained to make them look like accidents or deaths from natural causes."

"Accidents?"

"For the most part," she said. "There was one in particular that we weren't able to disguise—her boyfriend."

"Her boyfriend?"

"He was the real target. He was who we were ordered to stop. We killed the woman first to send him a message."

"This is starting to sound a little like a movie plot."

"He was a powerful man. We knew we couldn't get to him the way we got to her. We thought her death would open his eyes to the fact that no one is really safe."

"You keep using the term *we*. How many people were involved in this alleged killing spree?"

"We worked in cells. I never knew the people in the other groups. We kept it that way—for security reasons."

"Can you tell me how many people were in your cell?"

"Only three. He used the name Joker and she used the name Crystal."

"She?"

"Is that so hard for you to believe? That two women could be involved in the crime of the century?"

I laughed. "So, now it's the crime of the century, is it?"

"Crystal has been dead now for over thirty years. She always had a little trouble keeping her mouth shut. Death by misadventure was how the authorities explained it. I've always had my suspicions. Joker was the ruthless one. I'm sure he had something to do with Crystal's death. There was one person who had control over all of the cells. It would have been him who ordered Crystal's murder. We called him Mr. Smith."

I scribbled the name on my pad. "Mr. Smith?" I asked.

"Mr. Smith handled all the details. He coordinated the efforts of the cells, and he handled stuff like training and money."

"Are you saying you and your partners did this for money?"

"No," she said. "We were an elite group. We were well trained and well financed. But money wasn't the issue. You remember the sixties—they were difficult times. The world was on the brink of disaster. We did what we thought was right. We were young. We were easily influenced."

"Tell me more about this woman, the one you killed."

There was a lingering silence on the other end of the line for a few moments.

"I don't think so," she said. "Let's see how you do now that you're not looking in the wrong direction."

"Why don't you just tell me who she was? Why the games? You haven't got much time left."

"I've thought about that," she said. "It would be easy to send you the documents and let you inform the world. But I want you to dig. I want you to get a feel for the times and the situations we were involved in. I need the world to know more than just the answers to the puzzle. I need people to know why we did what we did."

"You want absolution."

"No," she said. "I've come to terms with the horrible things that I've done. Believe me, I've paid the price for my sins. I haven't had much of a life and I've shed enough tears to start my very own river. I've spent a lot of nights going to sleep wondering if Mr. Smith and his friends would come looking for me again."

"Do you think he's still alive?"

"No doubt about it. The Mr. Smith that ordered me to kill is probably long gone, but there's still a Mr. Smith out there. The face changes, but the evil that the name represents never does."

"Smith's a code name?"

"You're beginning to understand. You see, Mr. Smith is not one specific person. He represents a power. He's the personification of an evil—the evil that ruined my life."

I scribbled my thoughts on my pad.

"I thought I'd seen the last of him, but a new Mr. Smith has surfaced. He's here in Vancouver."

"You think he's coming after you?"

"No," she said. "It's the other way around—I'm going after him. As far as he's concerned, I'm out of the picture. I'll keep up the Dallas charade for as long as I can. I have the upper hand—for now."

"You do?"

"Mr. Smith is still out there, and he's still destroying people's lives. I have the chance to expose him and put a stop to him. That's where you come in. I just hope and pray that he doesn't find out that I'm a threat to him until it's too late—after I'm dead."

"I'm ready," I said.

"I have a plan. I know I can draw Mr. Smith out in the open. He has weaknesses, too. I've given this a great deal of thought. I've spent a lot of time preparing for this."

"What do you need me to do?"

"Follow the clues. First you need to find out who the victims were. That will give you an understanding of just how evil Mr. Smith really is."

"And then?"

"Once we have him totally exposed, we can strike. I can lure him into a position from which he can't run and hide. But first you need to know him intimately. You need to know exactly how he thinks and how he works."

"Tell me. Give me the names of the victims."

"Too easy. You have to follow the clues. I just hope you've got a strong stomach—and an even stronger heart."

"I can take anything you can dish out."

"There's evil in this world, Hartree, and it goes by the name of Mr. Smith. *How dangerous is it that this man goes loose.*"

"*Hamlet* again," I said.

"Very good," Dallas replied. "King Claudius is reacting to Hamlet's murder of Polonius. He's determined that Hamlet must be dealt with. You and I have a mission, Hartree. We won't just be exposing a man; we'll be exposing a wicked and corrupt strength."

I sensed desperation in her voice.

"Hartree," she said.

"I'm listening."

"I know who Mr. Smith is. He's shrouded himself in a veil of respectability, but he can't hide from me."

"Are you going to tell me?"

"I need you to confirm it—I have to be 100 percent sure. That's why I picked you. I need someone who's not afraid of powerful people."

I felt a surge of pride.

"Hartree," she said, "you're the only person that can help me put a stop to Mr. Smith. You're the only man I know who can get the answers we need."

"Tell me who you think Mr. Smith is."

"I will," Dallas said, "but only once you've put together the pieces of the puzzle. We'll confirm the facts together. It's for your own safety."

"My safety?"

"He has to be stopped. You can do it, I know you can."

I hunched over my desk.

"Mr. Smith destroyed me," Dallas said. "He's an evil that has to be brought to justice."

"You want revenge?"

"*Blood cannot be washed out with blood.* My life is over. I just don't want Mr. Smith to harm anyone else."

The desperation in her voice intensified. "One last thing before I go," she said. "You and your interns…"

"Yes?"

"You need to know."

"Need to know what?"

"The Mr. Smiths of this world are conniving and dangerous. Be very, very careful."

⌘

"Grant," I said, "I hope you enjoyed the ferry ride. You're going back to Victoria."

"Huh?"

"Back to Vital Statistics. This time, I want you to search for every woman that died on August fifth in the early sixties. We're looking for an accidental death that could really have been a disguised murder."

"You know," Amanda said, "I've been thinking this over. We could be making one very big assumption here."

I felt my blood pressure rise. Why couldn't this woman just shut up and pay attention to the voice of experience? "And what would that be?" I asked.

"Listen to the recordings again. Dallas hasn't said anything about the murder taking place in Vancouver, or even in the province of British Columbia, for that matter."

"And where do you think the killing took place?"

"I'm just saying it could be anywhere. It could have been Toronto, or Montreal, or Lethbridge, Alberta, for all we know."

"It had to have been Vancouver," Grant said. "Why else would she contact a reporter from the *Tribune*? She needs someone who knows the city."

"Why is that?" Amanda asked.

"Jesus," Grant replied. "You really are thickheaded. Why would she call a Vancouver reporter if the killings happened in Montreal?"

"You heard what she said in the last recording. She's been lying awake at night wondering if Mr. Smith would come looking for her after all these years. Listen to the woman. It sounds to me like they've been playing this cat and mouse game for some time. Don't you think she'd try and distance herself from the threat? Wouldn't she move to another city? And what about Smith? If he was the key figure in killings somewhere across the country, maybe *he* moved to Vancouver to hide from *her*."

"Don't be trying to throw us off the track," I said. "Grant's right. You wouldn't contact a reporter in Vancouver unless the murders happened here. There's too much researching to do. Can you imagine what we'd be up against if the murders had happened in Montreal or Toronto? How would we chase down the clues?"

Amanda threw up her hands in frustration.

I turned to Grant and pointed to the door. "Ferry," I said.

"I'm going, boss."

"And you," I said and spun around to face my female apprentice, "the mayor is giving a dedication speech at the new East Side Cultural Centre tonight. Get down there and ask some questions. See if you can dig up some interesting dirt."

# CHAPTER EIGHT

"It's Dallas," she said. "How are you and your interns making out?"

"We're not," I said. "Grant had a lot of records to search through. He had to spend the night in Victoria. He should be back sometime this afternoon."

"Really," she said. "That's too bad. I'd hoped we could move on today. I thought you'd have a name by now."

"You haven't given us much to go on: a day of the month, and the fact that it was a woman. Not exactly a good position in the starting gate."

"You can do it. I know men like you. It will come to you, in time."

"Are you sure about the date?" I asked. "It was a long time ago."

"I'm sure. I still mourn for her every August fifth. Of all the people who either lost their lives, or had them ruined over those few years, she was the one I felt the most regret over."

"Why?"

"She was a victim long before she ever crossed paths with us. She was in her prime—she was only thirty six—but she'd been passed around by the men in her life for years and years."

I jotted a note of her age on my pad. "We need another clue," I said. "My people are getting frustrated."

"Tell me about your interns," she said. "What are their names?"

"Grant Shaw and Amanda Southfield."

"Tell me about Grant."

"He's good. He's got what it takes to be a top-notch reporter. He reminds me of myself when I was his age."

"What does he do when he's not at work? What are his interests?"

"I don't know that much about his personal life. I've got better things to do. I know he considers himself to be somewhat of a wine connoisseur."

"A wine connoisseur?"

"Yeah," I said. "He spouts off every now and then about some fantastic wine purchase he's just made."

"How old is he?"

"Early twenties; they're both about the same."

I heard a sigh.

"I was in my early twenties then."

"What?" I asked.

"When we trained for the first murder—how to prepare a lethal dosage, and how to administer the solution."

"What are you telling me?"

"Nothing," she said. "Do you remember your twenties, Hartree?"

"Listen," I said, "I'm not in the mood to walk arm in arm with you down memory lane. I've got work to do."

"It was just a question. I just wanted to know if you were ever a happy person, or if you've always been this anal."

"I'm not anal," I said. "I'm just a little intense."

"We were all so young. It was one of the few times we met members from other cells. We all trained together. There were seven of us."

"Seven?" I asked.

I listened to Dallas cough. "Yeah," she replied as she caught her breath again. "We only spent a few days together. We called ourselves the Friendship Seven."

"The Friendship Seven?" I asked. "Nice name for a group of trained assassins."

"You know how young people think. Tell me about Amanda. That's a pretty name. What's she like?"

"Honestly?" I asked. "She's a mess. She's a waste of my time. She'll never make it in this business."

"Why do you say that?"

"She's a paradox—she's totally organized, but at the same time she's totally unfocused. She actually brought a diaper bag instead of her briefcase to a meeting last month."

"She has a family?"

"A husband, a little kid, and a mangy old cat."

"You don't treat her very well."

"I treat her the same way I treat everyone in the newsroom."

"You're not being honest again, Hartree. It's one thing when you lie to your readers, but don't lie to yourself. You don't like her. I can tell from the tone of your voice."

"She just doesn't have what it takes," I said. "I told you, she's a waste of my time."

"Is it because she's not a good reporter, or is it just because she won't put up with your crap?"

"What do you mean—put up with my crap?"

"I think you resent the fact that she's a woman who's got talent. Be honest with me. You feel threatened by her."

"That's ridiculous. How could I possibly feel threatened by her?"

"You know you're going to have to give up the chair at the head of the table one day soon. It would kill you to have to pass the torch to a woman. You'd be betraying the old guard."

"You're hallucinating," I said. "It must be the drugs."

"What are her interests?"

"What I know about her is about ten times less than what I know about Grant."

"If you had to buy her a birthday gift, what would you get her?"

I thought for a moment. "A book," I said. "She always has a book with her. You two have something in common: she reads Shakespeare."

The hacking started again. I waited until Dallas was able to continue.

"I have to go now," she wheezed. "I'm not feeling very well and it's time for my medicine."

"What about another clue?" I asked.

The coughing got worse. Dallas struggled to catch her breath.

"You've got your clues for today," she said. "Let's wait and see how Grant made out at Vital Statistics. I'll talk to you tomorrow."

⌘

Grant swung his backpack off his shoulder and dropped it on the table.

"How did you do?" I asked.

"I've got a few possibilities," he said. "Twenty-three women died in the province on August fifth between 1960 and 1965. I ruled out the ones that died from long term illnesses and the ones whose deaths couldn't be from anything else but natural causes."

"And?"

"That left me with four." He opened his bag and pulled out an envelope. "Here's the first one," he said and handed me a sheet of paper. "Mary Carruthers. She drowned in Cultus Lake."

I scanned through his notes.

"Next, we have Denise Lorne, killed in a car accident in Prince George along with her father."

I took the sheet of paper from his hand and placed it on the table in front of me.

"Shelly Kranz," he said as he read from the third sheet, "heroin overdose."

"Bingo," I said. I stood and grabbed the paper from his hand. "I got another call; Dallas told me how they trained for the first killing. She talked about how to prepare a lethal dose, and how to administer the drug."

"That's got to be her then. The only other possibility I came up with was an electrocution."

# CHAPTER NINE

"WE'VE GOT HER," I said.

"Finally," Dallas replied. "I told you that you'd figure it out."

"Her name was Shelly Kranz. She was found dead on August 5, 1960, in a rooming house on Davie Street in downtown Vancouver."

"Who?" Dallas asked.

"Shelly Kranz. The cause of death was massive cardiac arrest, brought on by an overdose of heroin."

"Go on."

"You gave it away when you told me about the training."

"Training?"

"Yeah," I said, "when you took your little jaunt down memory lane. You said you learned how to prepare a lethal dosage."

"I did say that."

"Kranz died of a drug overdose. The police thought it was self-induced. The death was ruled accidental. It was you who injected her with the drug, wasn't it?"

"What else have you learned?"

"She was a party girl. She had lots of boyfriends. Grant is out gathering information on her now. It won't take us long to figure out who the man you killed was."

"Just listen to the clues," she said. "They will lead you to the story."

"So you're confirming we've got the right woman? Did you kill Shelly Kranz?"

"All in due time," she said. "I'm not confirming anything yet. As long as you're sure you've got the right woman, it shouldn't take you long to figure out who the boyfriend was."

"And he was the real target. You told me that."

"Yes. The boyfriend was the target."

"Tell me more about Mr. Smith. Why did he want the boyfriend killed?"

Dallas paused. "It was a struggle for control," she said. "They were going in different directions. They couldn't share the power, so one of them had to die."

"Tell me more about the boyfriend. Let's get on with this."

"You're not ready to know about him yet. You haven't learned all there is to know about the woman. You have some surprises in store for you."

"So, I do have the right woman?"

"I told you. Her death has haunted me all these years. Of all the people that died needlessly, she was the one I mourned the most."

"So you're confirming it?"

"I need you to explain to the world why I would do such a horrible thing. *When sorrows come, they come not single spies, but in battalions.*"

"I need you to confirm it," I said. "Tell me that Shelly Kranz was the first victim."

"Just listen to the clues."

⌘

"I got another call," I said.

"Did you tell her?" Grant asked. "Does she know we've figured out who the woman was?"

"Listen," I said and turned the tape recorder on.

Amanda opened her notebook. Grant tightened the laces on his shoes. The tape proceeded to run its course.

⌘

Grant said, "More Shakespeare, right?"

Amanda nodded her head. "*Hamlet* again," she said. "*When sorrows come*, the king is speaking about Ophelia's grief over her father's death."

"That is one strange woman," Grant said and waved his finger at the tape recorder.

"She won't confirm that it was Shelly Kranz that she killed," Amanda said.

"It was Kranz all right," I told her.

"Then why won't she confirm it?"

38

"She's playing games," I said. "Everything fits—the date and the fact that she died from a drug overdose. It has to be Kranz."

"Everything fits if you're only looking at Vancouver," Amanda said.

"We're not just looking at Vancouver," I snapped. "We're looking at the entire province. Shelly Kranz is the only woman that died on August fifth in this province that fits with the overdose scenario. It has to be her."

"If the murder took place in British Columbia."

"Of course it took place in British Columbia," I said. "We've already decided that."

Amanda turned away from me. "*You've* already decided that," she mumbled.

I glared at the woman for a moment and then turned to Grant. "Find out everything you can about this Kranz woman," I said. "We're on the right track. Kranz *has* to lead us to the boyfriend." I turned to face Amanda. "You," I said. "I'm getting a little frustrated with your attitude. I think you need a break from this. I've been thinking about a series on retired local celebrities. Kind of a "where are they now?" sort of angle. Do you remember Kyle Osgood?"

Amanda nodded. "Lead singer of the Remains," she said. "They had a couple of hits in the late seventies."

"Right," I said. "He still lives in South Vancouver."

Amanda jotted a note on her pad.

"Hunt him down," I said. "Let's see if you can write something that's actually printable."

# CHAPTER TEN

"DO YOU KNOW the name of the man we shot yet?"

"No," I said. "And you never told me that you shot him."

"I didn't think it was necessary," Dallas replied. "I told you that it was the one murder we couldn't disguise. It was very public. Lots of people watched it happen. There's even a film."

"You filmed it?"

"No," she said, "it was just dumb luck. There was an amateur photographer nearby that day. He had his camera on. He caught the whole thing on 8 mm colour film."

"And you have this film?"

"No. But a man with your connections can find it. I know for a fact it still exists."

"After forty years?"

"Yeah, it's out there somewhere. There's no statute of limitations on murder. I'm sure the authorities still have it."

"And you're on this film?"

"No," she replied, "I was out of the camera's field of view. You couldn't see where the shots were fired from."

"Shots?"

"Yes—there were three shooters, a primary, and two backups. There was more than one cell on the job that day. You have to understand the amount of planning and training that went into this. Mr. Smith had to be certain we wouldn't miss."

"Let's get back to this Kranz woman. Her boyfriend was powerful enough for Mr. Smith to have you and your partners hunt him down in a public place?"

"I already told you how powerful the boyfriend was."

"How involved was Kranz with this man? Was he a casual boyfriend, a steady boyfriend, or what?"

More coughing.

"You're making some progress," she said. "You figured out the woman was killed with drugs. Now you know that her lover was killed by a gunshot. I've got to tell you, though, you've made some mistakes."

"I need to know more about the boyfriend. I remember what Canada was like in the sixties. I'm thinking that for this mysterious Mr. Smith to order a man's killing in a public place, he had to be some sort of a crime figure."

"You're on the right track. That just might be the key that will unlock the riddle. You know what Vancouver was like in the sixties."

"So he *was* a crime figure?"

No response.

"Is that it? Was he some sort of Mafioso or something?"

More silence.

"That's it, isn't it? Kranz died of a heroin overdose. I'll bet the boyfriend was some kind of a big-time dealer or something. You said Mr. Smith was a power, not a specific person. It was the Mafia, right? The boyfriend was a rival drug lord."

A struggle for breath.

"You called them cells. They were families, weren't they? You worked for a mob family, and Mr. Smith was the godfather."

"Some people said there was a link to organized crime, but you're getting off track."

"Then you'd better steer me back on."

"I shouldn't have told you about the boyfriend yet. You're dividing your efforts. You need to have a closer look at the woman."

"Shelly Kranz?"

"Do you have any friends on the police force?"

"I have lots of friends on the force."

"Good. The cop that was called to investigate the woman's death knew from the beginning that something wasn't right. We were young. We were scared. We made some mistakes that night."

"What kind of mistakes?"

"Simple ones. Look for a drinking glass."

"A drinking glass?" I asked. "You left fingerprints?"

"Just look for the glass. The cop knew right away."

"And this cop," I said, "I don't suppose you're going to give me his name?"

"His name was Jack—Clemmons—I think. He was a sergeant. The case destroyed his career."

"Because he wasn't able to solve it?"

"No," Dallas replied, "because he *was* able to solve it."

"You're not making sense," I said.

"Clemmons knew it was a case of murder. We were trained to make the killing look like an accident, but he knew it wasn't a suicide or an accidental overdose. I've told you how powerful these people were. Jack was up against a force he wasn't strong enough to fight. Lots of mistakes were made that night. Lots of lies were told as well. Jack knew."

"What happened to him?"

"He was fired from the police force. He wouldn't bend over and keep quiet about the inconsistencies."

"Inconsistencies?"

"Yes," she said. "The body was discovered shortly after midnight, but the police weren't called until almost 4:30 in the morning."

"Four and a half hours?"

"It gave certain people time to sweep the house. There were documents that had to be destroyed. There were things in that house that the public couldn't be allowed to see. Guess what the housekeeper was doing when Jack arrived?"

"What?" I asked.

The coughing started again, worse than ever before. The telephone line went dead. I glanced at my watch. Grant and the woman would be waiting in the meeting room for our morning session.

⌘

I switched the tape recorder off and looked over at Grant. "We're looking for a gangland execution," I said. "We need to find a connection between Shelly Kranz and organized crime. That will lead us to the boyfriend."

"You're still speculating," Amanda said. "Dallas hasn't confirmed anything yet."

I turned to her. "She did confirm it," I said.

"How?" Amanda asked. "By not denying it?"

Grant stood up from the table and began to pace. "It had to be a mob hit," he said. "Three gunmen—what else could it be?"

"Exactly," I said.

"What about this cop?" Amanda asked. "Dallas said he was fired from the police force because he figured out what was happening. Doesn't that sound a little far-fetched to you?"

"Why is that?" I asked. "Everything she's told us so far fits. She said we're dealing with a huge power. Don't you think it's possible that organized crime could have had some influential person on their payroll? Don't you think that a cop could have been sacrificed to save a crooked public official? Maybe it was a judge. Maybe even the mayor. Who knows how far this could reach?"

"You're just filling in the blanks," Amanda said.

I glared at her. Grant stopped pacing and crossed his arms across his chest.

"Of course we're filling in the blanks," I said. "How else are we supposed to figure this out?"

"That's not what I meant," Amanda replied. "You're not listening to the clues. Everything you've got hinges on this Shelly Kranz woman. Listen to what Dallas said. What do you think the housekeeper was doing? Tell me, what kind of a junkie—living in a rooming house—has a housekeeper?"

I looked down at my coffee mug. As much as I hated to admit it, the woman was right. I was rushing into this with my eyes only half open. I knew we had the right woman, but Amanda had made her point. Something wasn't right. Shelly Kranz was not just some junkie. Mr. Smith had ordered her killed for a reason. Someone had delayed advising the police of her death for over four hours, time to sweep her house. This Kranz woman was obviously in possession of something Mr. Smith needed to find. Dallas said there were documents. What kind of documents? Financial records, letters perhaps, or maybe some sort of proof that would put Mr. Smith in jeopardy? Maybe Mr. Smith wasn't the ultimate power; maybe he was following orders from someone even higher up. We had to learn more about Kranz. We had to find out exactly who this woman was. She would eventually lead us to the boyfriend. But Amanda was right; I had to start listening to the clues. I had to find this cop, Clemmons. I wondered, was he still alive after all these years? Did he just fade away into obscurity after he was fired from the police force? Did he become another victim of Mr. Smith's murder squad?

Dallas said they worked in cells. It was possible that Mr. Smith had Clemmons killed. Perhaps it was one of the other cells that did him in. Maybe Dallas doesn't even know. We had to focus on this man Clemmons. He knew the truth about Kranz. That was the key to the boyfriend. Find Clemmons, and dig up everything we can about Kranz. Then there was the drinking glass. Either Dallas or one of her partners must have left fingerprints at the scene of the murder. Did the glass still exist? Was it tucked away in some evidence storage locker along with the 8 mm film?

"Find that cop," I said to Grant. "Get down to the police station and pull in every favour owed to us. We need to talk to this man. He'll give us what we need on Kranz."

Amanda turned to Grant. "Let's go," she said.

I raised the palm of my hand. "Not you," I said. "There was a baby seal born at the aquarium yesterday. Get down there and see how the little guy is doing."

# CHAPTER ELEVEN

"I'm sorry, boss," Grant said. "I couldn't find any record of there ever being a cop on the Vancouver force named Clemmons."

I slammed the palm of my hand on the table. "Jesus Christ," I said. "How hard can it be to find out about a cop?"

"I'm telling you," Grant said. "There's nothing. I checked the name of every cop whose name begins with *C*. There isn't even a name that's close to Clemmons."

"Did you check the *K*s"?"

"Yeah," Grant said. "Nothing."

"Here's a thought," Amanda said. "Maybe you can't find a Vancouver cop named Clemmons because there never was one. The murder didn't happen in Vancouver."

"We've been over that," I said. "I'm not telling you again."

"You know," Grant said, "we're dealing with organized crime. Maybe the feds were involved. We could be looking for a member of the RCMP."

"Christ," I said, "I hope you're wrong. The way they transfer members across the country, we might never be able to find him."

"I have a contact down at E Division headquarters," Grant said. "He could tell me where to begin the search at least."

I rubbed my forehead with the palm of my hand. "Good place to start," I said.

"What about me?" Amanda asked. "Flower show? Ground Hog Day, maybe?"

I turned to her and grinned. "I hear that the baby seal is having some problems," I said. "Some kind of respiratory thing. Get on it."

⌘

Tape recorder running, I leaned back in my chair and raised the phone to my ear.

"Any luck finding the cop?" Dallas asked.

"No," I said. "There's no record of a Vancouver cop named Clemmons."

"What about the RCMP?" Dallas asked.

"Grant's still checking. It's a little tougher to get information out of the Mounties."

"I've been thinking," Dallas said. "It was a long time ago. I'm sure he was a sergeant, and I'm positive that his first name was Jack."

"What are you telling me? You're not sure about the cop's name?"

"It was Jack, for sure. There were a lot of people named Jack involved. I thought it was funny, back then."

"But you aren't certain it was Clemmons?"

"I'm sorry," she said, "maybe it was Clemson. It was a long time ago. Everything else I told you—"

"You're not sure about that either?"

"No. I am sure. Dead sure. He knew something wasn't right. We were scared. He talked to the media. He was quite vocal about his theory that it was no accident."

"You said he was fired."

"Mr. Smith had to silence him. Jack was smart enough to realize that his firing was really a warning. Back off—or else."

I laughed. "So, Mr. Smith orders a murder. Then, when the cops start figuring things out, he has the chief investigator fired."

"What's so funny?"

"It's more than just funny," I said. "It's ludicrous."

"Is it?" she asked. "You don't think that power like that exists in this world?"

I searched for words.

"Let's look at it under a slightly different light," she said. "You wrote a series of articles on Chris McDermott. You removed a respected politician with a handful of words. That's a form of power, isn't it?"

"Yeah."

"Imagine that you had a hundred times—no, a thousand times more clout. Don't you think it would be simple to make a cop disappear?"

I toyed with my pen.

"It's the age-old story. The caveman with the biggest club gets the food. The tallest kid in the schoolyard gets the best swing. The shark eats the tuna."

"Let's get on with this."

"I'm just trying to clue you in to the fact that if you have enough power, you get what you want."

"Now that we're on the subject of clues—"

"I know," she said. "I'm sorry that I'm foggy on the cop's last name. I'll give you something else."

"What?"

"Don't be so impatient. I'm feeling not too bad today. I think we should talk."

"I don't have time to chitchat."

"Ah," she said, "but you'll make time for me. I'm the one that's going to put your name in the history books."

I leaned back in my chair.

"What have you got your cubs doing today?"

"Jesus Christ," I said.

"Come on, humour a dying old woman."

"Grant's out trying to find a cop with no last name. The woman is down at the aquarium again."

"I read the story she did on the baby seal."

"You were one of the few. I'm surprised you could even find it."

"Why do you say that? Did you read it?"

"No," I said.

"Why not?"

"We're wasting time here. I've got better things to do than read some story about the birth of a seal pup that's buried on—what—page fifty?"

"That's the problem with you, Hartree. Everything has to be so intense. You should sit back and relax every now and then. Take a few minutes out and read something that will warm up that block of ice in your chest cavity."

"Sure," I said, "I'll put that on my list of things to do."

"I'll make you a deal."

"OK."

"I'll give you two clues, but you have to promise to read the piece on the seal."

I let out a sigh.

"Promise?" she asked.

"I promise."

"Right," she said, "there'll be a quiz, next time I call."

"I promise," I said, "I'll read the damned thing."

"The first clue comes in the form of a riddle."

"Great," I said.

"When you break a window to get into a house, where does the glass fall?"

"Christ," I grumbled.

"Got that, Hartree?"

"I got it."

"OK. Next, I want you to put yourself in Jack's shoes. I want you to close your eyes and pretend you're driving up to the house that morning to investigate a death."

"I'm listening."

"The house is full of people. There were doctors there; they claimed it was a suicide."

"Suicide?"

"Yes. That was the spin."

"You made it look like suicide?"

Dallas paused. "I was never able to figure that part out," she continued. "We were trained to make the overdose look accidental. All the clues we left were meant to make the police think she'd killed herself by mistake."

"Where did the notion of suicide come from then?"

"That's the confusing part. By the time Jack arrived, according to the police reports, everything we set up had been changed."

"Changed? By whom?"

"I don't know. We left an assortment of drugs on the table next to her bed. We wanted the police to think she'd taken a mixture of the wrong kinds of drugs by mistake."

"And?"

"When the story broke, it was reported that she had committed suicide. They claimed that the overdose was intentional. The bottles of drugs had been emptied. I never understood why they did that."

"Who?"

"I don't know that either. Mr. Smith ordered us to kill her. We were trained how to set up the crime scene to look like an accidental overdose. I told you we made a mistake with the glass. I guess whoever doctored the scene didn't notice either. But Jack knew; he spotted it right away. That and the suicide note."

"Whoever cleaned the house planted a suicide note?"

"No. That was one of the things that bothered Jack. Everyone was talking suicide, but there *was* no suicide note."

# CHAPTER TWELVE

"I'VE CRACKED IT, boss."

I looked over at Grant and smiled.

"Shelly Kranz wasn't a drug addict," he continued, "but she was well known to the cops."

I shifted in my chair and folded my arms across my chest. "What else?"

"She had a record. She was arrested in January of 1959 for possession of heroin for the purpose of trafficking. Guess who was arrested with her?"

"Who?" I asked.

"Angelo Buono."

"Who in the hell is Angelo Buono?"

"Buono was a drug dealer, big into heroin. He was connected to the Morazzo family in New Westminster."

"The same Morazzo family that now owns half of Sapperton? The grape importers?"

"Right," Grant said. "Only in the fifties, there was talk that they were importing more than just grapes. Another employee of the Morazzo family was gunned down in 1961. In the middle of the day, right here in downtown Vancouver. His name was Waugh—John Waugh."

"Jesus," I said. "Can we link Kranz to this Waugh character?"

Grant shrugged his shoulders. "I haven't been able to verify there was any connection. It makes sense, though. Kranz was arrested with Buono. It's certainly possible that she also knew Waugh."

"Possible," I said. "But can we establish a positive link?"

Grant smiled. "I can build a link," he said. "It was over forty years ago. I can dig up enough information to show that it was likely that they knew each other."

"And who would be able to deny it?" I asked.

"It's just too perfect," Grant said. "Dallas told us they killed the first victim with a drug injection. Kranz died from an overdose. Dallas also told us that the boyfriend was powerful, and that he was shot and killed in front of a number of witnesses. It has to be Waugh."

"Dallas had to have been working for the mob."

"Christ," Grant said, "no wonder she's scared."

"This could open the lid on organized crime in western Canada." I kept my voice even toned, but the fact was, I could barely control my excitement.

"What a story," Grant added.

⌘

"We've got them," I said. I listened to Dallas wheeze.

"It's about time," she replied.

I drummed the top of my desk with my pencil. "We know the woman was Shelly Kranz," I said. "She wasn't a heroin user, but she was deeply involved in the heroin trade."

"Interesting," Dallas said.

"The boyfriend's name was John Waugh," I continued. "He was shot and killed on the afternoon of May 26, 1961, in front of a restaurant on Homer Street in downtown Vancouver. There were witnesses to the shooting, but officially the crime was never solved. It was an obvious gangland hit."

"Did you find the film?"

"No," I said, "the murder is still on the record books as unsolved, but I couldn't find any mention of there being a film of the shooting."

"It doesn't matter now," Dallas said. "It was a long time ago. The names of the victims aren't important either. It's Mr. Smith we need to expose."

"That's right," I said, "we're getting there. We can link Waugh to the Morazzo family of New Westminster."

"The grape importers?"

"Right," I said. "Today they're a well-respected and influential family. But in the fifties, when Gino Morazzo started up the family business, there was talk that they were importing more than just grapes."

"I see," Dallas said, "and that's enough for you? Don't forget, in the fifties, any successful person whose last name ended in a vowel was automatically suspected of being involved with the mob."

"It all fits," I said. "The killing of Kranz by a heroin overdose, the fact that Waugh was gunned down in the street in front of a group of witnesses—"

"You're right," Dallas replied. "It fits."

"So," I said, "you're confirming it?"

"Ask yourself this. Does it fit because it's true? Or does it fit because you've made it fit?"

"Why are you being so evasive?" I asked. "Why won't you confirm anything?"

"I need you to be sure."

"About Mr. Smith?"

"Exactly," Dallas said. "I'm playing the devil's advocate for a reason. You seem to be more interested in uncovering dirt that happened forty years ago. Don't you understand how powerful Mr. Smith is yet?"

"So you're saying that the Morazzo family is still a threat?"

"Listen to me very carefully, Hartree."

"I'm listening," I said.

"Were you able to find Jack Clemmons?"

"No," I said, "I told you, it's like the man never existed."

"And why do you think that is?" she asked.

"I don't know for sure. Every trace of him seems to have been entirely erased."

"I told you. Jack was very vocal about his belief that the woman's death wasn't a suicide or an accidental overdose. Where did that get him?"

"You said he was fired."

"Right, and you haven't been able to find any sign of him?"

"No," I said, "I haven't."

"What does that tell you?"

I rubbed the corner of my lip with the end of my pencil.

"Talk to me, Hartree," Dallas said.

"I don't understand what you're getting at."

Dallas laughed. "I think you *do* understand," she said. "You'd better sit down and decide the real reason that you haven't been able to find any trace of that cop. Be honest with yourself for a change. Go over what I've told you again. Have another close look at this Shelly Kranz woman."

"Why?" I asked. "She's a minor character. It's the boyfriend we need to focus on. He's the key to Mr. Smith."

"You're right again. The woman will lead you to the boyfriend; the boyfriend will lead you to Mr. Smith."

"The Morazzo family."

"Be careful, Hartree. If you're not correct, or if you fail to take Mr. Smith out with your first shot, it could be the last story you ever write."

"I'm being careful," I said.

"Like Shakespeare said—*Come not between the dragon and his wrath.*"

"Then Kranz has to be the first step."

"If she's the right woman," Dallas said.

"I know she's the right woman."

"Are you ready for the quiz now?"

"The quiz?" I asked.

"The baby seal. You promised you'd read Amanda's article."

"Oh," I said, "I got too wrapped up in things. I just didn't have time."

"Read her story. I'll call you again tomorrow."

# CHAPTER THIRTEEN

I PLACED MY hands on the countertop and leaned my weight on my palms. I closed my eyes for a moment and pondered our next move. The coffeemaker hissed and bubbled as it churned out the morning's brew. I turned and faced Amanda and Grant as they huddled in discussion next to the windows of the meeting room.

"How's the baby seal doing?" Grant asked.

"Just fine," Amanda replied. "He's a little slippery, but you should know what that's like."

"Don't worry," Grant said, "the chief and I have just about got this murder thing figured out. You can carry on writing about your new friend, the fish."

"A seal is not a fish. It's a mammal."

"Whatever," Grant said.

"I guess I should congratulate you."

Grant's chest swelled.

"It sure didn't take you long to come up with an answer."

Grant smiled.

"I wonder how you're going to explain it if it turns out that you're wrong."

The smile on Grant's face disappeared. "I'm not wrong," he said. "You're just pissed because Terry gave the assignment to me."

"Who else would he give it to? You can't put something this important in the hands of a mere woman." Amanda glanced my way and then leaned in and whispered in Grant's ear. "How old was this Kranz woman when she died?"

Grant shrugged his shoulders.

"It would be part of the record. Didn't you check her date of birth?"

"Why would I? It was the date of her death that was important."

Amanda placed a hand on Grant's shoulder. "Good work," she said. "I'm almost positive that her year of birth would have been 1924. I guess there's no reason to muddy the waters with trivial stuff like verification."

"What's that supposed to mean?"

"Dallas told us that the first victim was thirty-six when she died; if Kranz was killed in 1960 that would make the year of her birth 1924."

"I guess it would."

"I really get a kick out of the way you add things up. I'm sure glad you're not balancing my chequebook."

"Everything adds up."

"Look," Amanda said in a hushed voice, "I'm sorry for talking to you like that. You don't know what it's like to be treated like an idiot every day. Hartree won't listen to anything I tell him. All you have to do is check the Kranz woman's date of birth. That will tell you if you have the right woman."

The time for idle chat was over. I filled my mug and called my cubs to the table.

⌘

"Did you read it?" Dallas asked.

"Huh?" I replied.

"Amanda's article on our new baby seal."

"Oh," I said, "right. I did read it."

"And?"

"It shows some promise. I would have worded it a bit differently."

Dallas chuckled. "You know, Hartree," she said, "you really are as miserable as they come."

"I'm not miserable. I'm just trying to be honest here."

"Honest?" Dallas laughed again. "You wouldn't recognize honesty if it snuck up behind you and bit you on the bum."

I let her insult go by without comment.

"I've been giving a lot of thought to this cop—Clemmons," I said.

"And?" Dallas asked.

"We can't find any trace that he ever existed. I have a theory."

"What would that be?"

"You said he knew the truth about the woman's death. If Mr. Smith had as much power as you say he had, do you think he may have given the order to have Clemmons killed too?"

"It's possible," Dallas replied. "When you find all the answers, you won't have any problem believing that Mr. Smith could order the death of a cop."

"Could it have been one of the other cells?"

"Maybe," Dallas said.

"Was there ever any talk of it? Did you ever have the suspicion that one of the other cells could have been ordered to kill Clemmons?"

"I told you. We rarely met up with members of any of the other cells. There's only the one time that really sticks in my mind."

"When was that?" I asked.

"The Friendship Seven. I told you about them."

"Right," I said. "When you trained for the first murder."

"Very good. You've been paying attention."

"Let's get back to Clemmons," I said. "Every record of the man's existence has disappeared."

"Are you finding that difficult to believe?"

"Not anymore. I've given this a lot of thought. It wouldn't be that hard. Over the course of forty years, files could be misplaced, records destroyed. If it was done discreetly over a period of time, it really wouldn't be that tough."

"You're right," Dallas said. "Memories fade as well. Most of the cops from back in the sixties are probably dead by now."

"But you do think it's possible. You agree that Mr. Smith could have waited until Clemmons was far enough out of the picture and then he could have ordered him killed."

"It's more than possible," Dallas said. "I told you how long the killings lasted. In addition to Crystal, Mr. Smith had a lot of key people killed."

"Who?" I asked.

Dallas paused. "Witnesses mostly," she said, "people that weren't really part of the murders, but who knew enough that they could have become a danger to us."

"I need some names," I said.

"I'll have to sit down and think. It was a long time ago. And I told you most of them were minor characters. All except Leon, that is."

"Leon?" I asked. "Who was Leon?"

Dallas sighed. "He went by a few different names," she said. "I knew him mostly as Leon, but sometimes he used the name Alex, too. He was one of the Friendship Seven. He was the oldest of the group; he was twenty-three. We all met in a bar one night. It was my birthday. I had just turned twenty-one. They threw me a party."

"He was a member of one of the other cells?"

"Yes."

"What happened to him?"

More silence.

"Are you there?"

"He had to die," Dallas said in a muffled voice.

I held the phone and tried to decipher the sounds coming from Dallas. It wasn't a cough, or a wheeze. It was a muted sound, softer and gentler than the hacking I was used to listening to. It sounded like she was crying.

"Dallas," I said, "are you all right?"

"Yes," she whispered, "I was just thinking about Leon."

"What happened to him?"

"Mr. Smith ordered him killed, too."

"At the bar?" I asked. "At your birthday party?"

"No," she replied in a hushed tone, "that night was wonderful. It was one of the best birthday parties I've ever had. We drank and we laughed—we were all huddled around a television set. There were a lot of people in the bar that night. That's when we decided to call ourselves the Friendship Seven."

"When was Leon killed?"

Dallas cleared her throat. "Not until shortly after the boyfriend's murder," she said. "Someone had to take the fall. Someone had to be set up to take the blame, and then they had to die before they could prove their innocence. I guess Leon drew the short straw. It was ironic."

"Ironic?" I asked.

"The owner of the bar, he was the one that was ordered to kill Leon. His name was Jack, too. I told you, I thought it was funny at the time. It seemed like every third person in this whole messy affair was named Jack."

# CHAPTER FOURTEEN

GRANT LEANED BACK in his chair and looked at his watch. "The woman's late," he said.

I glanced at the clock on the coffeemaker. "It's five after nine," I said. "We're not waiting any longer. Let's get started."

The door blew open and a bedraggled-looking Amanda rushed in. "I'm sorry," she said. "Rebecca is running a bit of a fever. I was late dropping her off at the sitter's."

I rolled my eyes and turned to Grant. "What have you been able to find out about the Morazzo family?" I asked.

"The Morazzo family?" Amanda interrupted. "What have they got to do with this?"

Grant turned to her. "We've established a link between the two murder victims and Gino Morazzo. We figure that he was the man calling the shots. He just might be our Mr. Smith."

Amanda spun around in her chair and faced me. "What kind of a link?" she asked.

"John Waugh—the man that was assassinated in downtown Vancouver—appears to have been a lieutenant in the Morazzo organization."

"How did you come up with that little gem?" Amanda asked.

"Waugh worked for the family. We know that for a fact."

"In what capacity?"

"Does it matter?" Grant asked.

Amanda turned to him. "Of course it matters," she said. "One minute he's unloading grapes off the back of a truck, and the next minute you've pegged him as some kind of Al Capone type."

"It was over forty years ago," Grant said. "We have to assume—"

"Assume nothing," Amanda said. "You can't accuse a family like the Morazzos of something like this."

"Look," I said, "we've figured out that Dallas was working for the Mafia. The killings were both mob related. We know that Mr. Smith was the godfather. We just have to prove it was Gino Morazzo who ordered the hits."

I could see colour flushing Amanda's cheeks.

"You guys are really making me angry," she said. "You're spinning this whole thing in the direction you want it to go. You're doing the same thing you did to Chris McDermott. What about the clues? Where is this cop named Clemmons? What about the housekeeper? What about the drinking glass? How come you can't find the film of Waugh's execution? Why did Dallas tell us about the glass from the broken window? All you have is questions. How about some answers?"

"The answers will come as we uncover more about the Morazzos."

"You two amaze me," Amanda said. "Dallas has given us some concrete leads to follow, and you're off trying to build a story based on dreams. The connection to the Morazzos is wishful thinking at best. You should spend a little more time trying to find Jack Clemmons."

"Clemmons is gone," I said. "We're never going to find him. Dallas confirmed it. I talked to her last night."

"What did she say?" Grant asked.

"She agreed with my theory that Clemmons was erased. We think he was killed by one of the other cells."

"My God!" Amanda said.

"Mr. Smith apparently had a number of witnesses and people that knew things about the conspiracy killed."

Amanda jotted notes on her pad.

"She told me about the meeting she had with the Friendship Seven."

"Friendship Seven," Grant scoffed. "What a thing to call a bunch of trained killers."

"She said it was her twenty-first birthday party," I said. "They watched TV and came up with the name for their group."

"Party on," Grant said and raised his fist.

"Her twenty-first birthday?" Amanda asked.

"Yes," I said as she made notes. "She said a man named Leon was part of the friendship group."

Amanda scribbled the name. Grant stood up and headed for the coffeepot.

"She told me the bar was owned by a man named Jack. Mr. Smith ordered Jack to kill Leon a short time after the boyfriend's murder."

"One of their own?" Amanda asked.

I leaned onto the table. "Dallas told me someone had to take the fall."

"What about Kranz?" Amanda asked. She turned to Grant. "Did you check her date of birth yet?"

Grant's eyes shifted away. "No," he mumbled.

"Date of birth?" I asked.

Amanda nodded her head. "If we knew her date of birth," she said, "we'd know how old she was in 1960 when she died."

I rested my elbow on the table and rubbed at my hairline with the palm of my hand. The woman was right. How could I have missed that? Dallas told me the first victim was thirty-six years old when she died. I turned to Grant.

"I'll do that this morning," he said.

Amanda's purse began to trill. She reached inside and pulled out her phone. She turned her back to me. "Amanda Southfield," she said.

I watched her squirm as she listened to the caller.

"I'll be there in twenty minutes," she said.

She closed her phone and turned in my direction. The look on her face was all the explanation I needed.

"Rebecca?" I asked.

"She's really sick," Amanda replied.

I pointed to the door. "Go," I said.

She smiled and thanked me.

"I read your piece on the baby seal," I said.

"And?" she asked as she packed up her things.

The words caught in my throat. Twice within a matter of days this woman had held me spellbound with her words. I'd had the pleasure of knowing plenty of good writers, but never one with so little experience that could take virtually nothing and turn it into a work of art. I could still picture that seal's eyes in my mind. Her description of the pair of ebony coloured orbs was some of the best crafting of the English language I'd read in eons. What could I say? I thought about what Dallas had said to me. I couldn't lie to myself. Amanda's article was good—damned good—and Dallas knew that when she coerced me into reading it. I swallowed a bit of pride and a whole lot of resentment. I nodded to her. "Not bad," I said as she headed for the door.

⌘

It was late, and the only sound that registered from my corner of the newsroom was the sound of dozens of computer fans humming in unison. I liked this time of night. I could sit and think without any distractions. It was the cleansing hour, the one time when I could be totally alone with my thoughts.

I opened the drawer that held my bottle of Scotch. I twisted the cap off and reached for my coffee mug. I drained the last remaining dribble of cold and bitter java into my throat and swallowed. I considered walking to the lunchroom and giving my mug a much-needed scrubbing. I laughed to myself and thought about the poor gnarled up old Scotsman, slapping labels on the fruits of his labour. I wondered what his reaction would be, seeing me taint his creation with the remnants of God only knows how many cups of coffee. I poured a splash into my mug. After all these years, what could one more assault on the pride of Scotland hurt?

I took a sip and leaned back in my chair. I stared up at the ceiling and pondered my next move. I felt my skin flush. I was still embarrassed about missing the Kranz woman's date of birth. Luckily, Amanda was focused enough not to miss an important detail like that. I knew Shelly Kranz was the Friendship Seven's first victim. Her date of birth would confirm it. I would have to try and force myself to give Amanda a little more credit. It was hard. I knew in my gut that she didn't have what it takes. This afternoon was a perfect example. We had leads to chase down, and clues to decipher, and she was off nursing a sick kid.

Dallas as much as told me that I was never going to find Clemmons. Christ, I couldn't find any trace of him ever walking the face of the earth. What chance did I have of finding him and squeezing him for more information on Kranz? A snowball's chance in hell—that was how much. I knew this Kranz woman was somehow important to Mr. Smith. She must have been close enough to him to know things about the mob—things that couldn't be revealed—information that couldn't be made public.

And what about Waugh? Dallas told me that the boyfriend was killed because they were going in different directions. She told me they couldn't share the power, so one of them had to die. Was that the story behind his execution? Was it a power struggle? Was Waugh trying to gain control of the family's business? How would I find out?

The Morazzos certainly wouldn't be keen on airing the family history. They were a powerful local family. They had both wealth and political influence. How was that wealth amassed? Did Gino Morazzo import more than just grapes? Was this just a rumour spread in the back rooms of neighbourhood pubs?

What about Leon? Mr. Smith had a member of the Friendship Seven killed to cover the tracks of the others. Dallas told me that one of them had to be the fall guy. How did the other members of the cells feel about that? Could I, perhaps, get more than one of them to open up about the killings? The murder of John Waugh was still on the books. If the reason that Leon was killed was to be the fall guy, then what went wrong? If he was set up to be the patsy, then why wasn't the case solved?

Who was this Jack character—the owner of the bar where Dallas celebrated her twenty-first birthday—was he the one that was ordered to kill Leon? If I could find him and link him to Gino Morazzo, he might turn out to be the final nail in the coffin. How hard could that be? Just find a bar owner named Jack. He's probably dead by now anyway. If I could locate even the history of such a man, it wouldn't be tough to build a story around him. After all, I was bullet proof—I'd taken out Chris McDermott easily enough. All it took was the suggestion of wrongdoing and statements that couldn't be proven false. All I did was put the seed of doubt in the public's mind, then stood back and let them do the crucifying.

I could do the same with the Morazzos, even if I couldn't find any record of this Leon fellow. Dallas told me he went by the name Alex, as well. He could have been using a dozen or more aliases. That was perfect. Find a skeleton in the Morazzo family closet and turn him into Leon the trained killer. Who would be able to deny it after all these years? With Grant's help, I could write a story that could bring the Morazzos to their knees. The Journalist's Association would be begging me to accept a Ceejay. I reached for the ringing telephone.

"Terry Hartree," I said.

"It's Amanda."

"Hi, Amanda," I said. "How's the baby?"

"She's comfortable, right now. I'm going to need to take a couple of days off."

"Fine," I said, "I figured as much. Grant and I are going to be busy on the Morazzo story. We won't need you."

"I'll check in from time to time," she said. "In case there's something you need me to do from home."

"We'll be fine," I said. "We'll see you in a day or two."

"Thanks," she said and hung up the phone.

# CHAPTER FIFTEEN

"DID YOU GET a birth date on the Kranz woman yet?"

Grant flipped open his notepad. "I did," he said. "June 16, 1923."

I looked up at the ceiling and closed my eyes.

"Thirty-seven," Grant said. "I figured it out."

I nodded. "Dallas is wrong."

"She must be," Grant replied. "Kranz turned thirty-seven a few weeks before she died."

I rubbed my hand over the side of my face. "I wonder what else she's been wrong about. Maybe that's why we can't find any trace of the cop. His name might be Lemmons—or Stemmons. Who knows?"

"It was a long time ago. Memories fade."

"One thing's for certain," I said, "Kranz was murdered and Dallas was responsible."

Grant nodded.

"I want to have the first part of the series ready for Saturday's edition," I said. "We'll get the front page with this. The pitch will be: exposing the Mafia on the West Coast of Canada."

"How do you want to lead in?" Grant asked.

"We'll start with a hook." I thought for a moment before continuing. "We'll tell the readers that we've uncovered a source. We'll let them know that this informant is ready to confess to mob killings that went on for years. We'll promise them the name of the godfather. We should be able to feed them details all week. We'll do the final exposé next Friday."

"We're going to need a week," Grant said. "We still haven't got the Morazzos nailed to the cross completely. Dallas still won't confirm that Mr. Smith was Gino Morazzo."

"She won't need to. There are other members of the cells out there. We won't name any names just yet. We'll tell the readers about Leon, and how the godfather ordered the murder of one of his own. If there are any surviving members of the Friendship Seven out there, maybe one of them will come forward."

"We can build that right into the article," Grant said. "We could put a sympathetic slant on the killers. We could focus on the fact that they were very young. That might motivate them to talk after all these years."

"I'm hoping that," I said, "and the fact that once Dallas sees her story on the front page, she might be a little more forthcoming with the names."

Grant turned to me and grinned. "This is going to be big," he said. "I'd start choosing a spot in your den for that Ceejay award if I were you."

I leaned back and gazed up at the ceiling. I held my arms out in front of me and spread them apart. "Already done," I said. "I've cleared a spot above the fireplace mantel. I can hardly wait."

"Congratulations," Grant said, "you've earned it."

⌘

"It's Amanda."

"Hi, Amanda," I said. "How's Rebecca?"

"She's much better. I'll be back to work soon."

"No hurry," I said. "Grant and I have been pretty much consumed by the Morazzo story. We've got a lot of facts to verify."

"Facts?" Amanda asked.

"Yeah," I said.

"Have you heard from Dallas?"

"No," I said. "I'm kind of expecting a call this afternoon."

"Good," Amanda said. "I've been doing some work at home. I've come up with a few interesting things on my own. I wonder if you could ask Dallas a question for me?"

"Sure," I said. "What did you want to know?"

"The drug," she said. "The first victim—I don't think it was heroin."

"It *was* heroin. The police report was quite clear."

"Just ask her. If what I think is correct, her answer will clear up a lot of cloudy areas for us."

"Well," I said, "I can ask her, but I already know the answer."

"Please," Amanda said, "before you put the story to bed. Just ask her what drug she used to kill the first victim."

# Chapter Sixteen

I PUNCHED THE button on my tape recorder. "How are you feeling today," I asked.

"Not too bad," Dallas replied. "The pain has been pretty intense the last few days, but my doctor changed my medication. I feel almost human today."

"That's good."

"Don't worry. I'll be around for the finale. I'm sure I've got a week or two left."

"Grant and I have started the first of the series of articles," I said. "We're still going to need more on the Morazzos though."

"I promised you," Dallas said, "before I die, you'll know exactly who Mr. Smith is."

"I already know," I said. "I just need a few more details to cinch the noose up tight."

"I have to tell you, Hartree."

"What?" I asked.

"You've handled this precisely the way I thought you would."

"You've made it pretty difficult. You've made some mistakes."

"Mistakes?" she asked.

"Small ones," I said. "The Kranz woman, she wasn't thirty-six years old when she died. She'd just turned thirty-seven."

"Really?" Dallas asked.

"Really," I replied.

"You know, Hartree, there never was much doubt in my mind that it would be you I'd end up telling my story to."

I laughed. "So all that talk about Sharon Halter," I said, "was just to stir me up?"

"You might say that," Dallas replied. "I have to admit, a woman wouldn't have come up with the answers that you and Grant came up with."

"Speaking of women," I said, "I haven't seen Amanda for a couple of days. She's home with a sick kid."

"Nothing serious, I hope?"

"No," I said. "The rug rat's got a cold—that's all."

"It sounds like Amanda's a good mother."

"I guess."

"Among other things," Dallas said.

I held my tongue.

"There's something on your mind."

"Not *my* mind," I said, "the woman's."

"What?" Dallas asked.

"This is going to sound petty this late in the game," I said. "Anyway, I already know the answer, but I promised Amanda I'd ask the question."

"What question?"

"She wanted me to ask you about the syringe. She wanted to ask what drug you injected the first victim with. I know it's a dumb question. We all know it was heroin."

Dallas didn't answer.

"Are you there?" I asked.

"I'm here."

"I honestly don't know why she would ask such a thing."

Silence.

"Dallas?" I asked. "It was heroin—wasn't it?"

"I never said anything about heroin," Dallas replied. "Go back and listen to the tapes."

"But it *was* heroin," I said. "The police reports confirm that Kranz died of a heroin overdose. Are you telling me that Mr. Smith managed to falsify that too?"

More silence.

"Answer me," I demanded. I could hear the sound of her breathing.

"Tell Amanda," Dallas said.

"Tell Amanda what?" I asked after a few moments of dead air.

"Tell her the drug was Nembutal."

The line went dead. I ejected the tape and labelled it "call #10."

# Chapter Seventeen

It was a rather cold morning. The walk in from the parking garage had chilled me to the bone. The heating system in the newsroom always did its best work in the summer months. I wrapped my hands around my coffee mug to transfer the warmth. I pushed open the door to the meeting room with my shoulder and stepped inside. Amanda jumped at the sound of the swinging door.

"You're here early," I said. "Making up for missing the last few days, are you?"

"I was here all day yesterday. I figured you and Grant would be wrapped up in your Morazzo story, so I spent the day by myself downstairs in the archives."

"The archives?" I asked. "What were you doing down there?"

Amanda fidgeted with her pen. I was staring at a different woman. She always was a bundle of energy hovering at the bursting point, but something about her manner was not quite the norm. She looked frayed. I knew that spending a few days with a sick child had to be stressful, but it was more than that. She was so high-strung, it was like I could see her nerve endings. Her eyes darted about the room, and if she shuffled through the stack of papers in front of her one more time, I was going to lose it. It was like she'd confronted a ghost. Her skin was pale and I could actually see her hands trembling. Too many days without sleep, I thought, too much coffee maybe. She'd looked at her watch at least three times in the last minute.

"Where's Grant?" she snapped.

I looked at her. Her brow was furrowed in anger and it almost felt like I'd just been barked at by a superior.

"Pardon me?" I asked.

"Grant. Where is that little prick? It's after nine. He's probably downstairs hitting on Petra again."

"Prick?" I said. "Did that word really come out of your mouth?"

"I've got things to tell you. I need to get started. I've been working on a theory of my own. Dallas confirmed my suspicions when she told you the drug they used to kill the first victim was Nembutal."

The door behind her swung open. Amanda nearly parted company with her skin.

"Where have you been?" she barked. "Don't we start these meetings at nine?"

Grant turned to me and whispered, "That time of the month?"

"Sit down and shut up," she said. "I've got some news for you two hot-shots. I want your complete attention."

I felt the hair on the back of my neck bristle. I couldn't believe this woman was speaking to us in that tone. It didn't take a rocket scientist to figure out she had something on her mind, but the insolence was almost too much to bear. It was bad enough that she was speaking to Grant like that. God help her if she spat any of that venom in my direction.

"Suppose you bring it down a notch," I said. "Tell us what you've got."

"Make yourselves comfortable," she said. "This is going to be a long story, and I'd like you to keep your mouths shut until I'm done."

I raised an eyebrow.

"Trust me," she said. "You can fire me if you don't like what I have to say."

I grinned. "Promise?" I asked.

She nodded. "Where's your story on the Morazzos?"

"The first part is in editing. We're dialled in for the front page on Saturday."

"Good," she said, "there's still time to kill it."

"Kill it?" Grant burst into laughter. "Kill the story that's going to earn Terry and I Ceejays?"

"Yeah," Amanda said, "the only thing you're going to win with that story is the moron of the decade award."

Grant rose from his chair.

"Sit down," I ordered.

Amanda took another look through her notes.

"Friendship Seven," she began. "What does that mean to you?" She looked up from her papers at me.

"That's what Dallas and her cohorts called their little group."

"Right," she said. "They were in a bar, on her twenty-first birthday, watching television. What was the date?"

"February twentieth."

"Right. On February twentieth, 1962, what was the world doing?"

I searched for an answer.

Amanda flipped a page of her notes. "Everyone was sitting in front of a television set watching John Glenn orbit the earth."

"Son of a bitch," I said. "You're right. I remember now; his space capsule was called Friendship Seven."

"Exactly, I'm guessing that's how they came up with their name. So, if Dallas celebrated her twenty-first birthday in February of 1962, how old was she when Kranz died?"

"Nineteen," I said after a moment of calculation.

"Sure," Amanda said, "I'll bet there were dozens of nineteen-year-old hired assassins running around back then. She told us the only time they ever got together with members from the other cells was when they trained for the first murder. How come she's meeting with the Friendship Seven group in 1962? Kranz died in 1960." She turned to Grant. "Did you find a date of birth for Kranz yet?"

"I did," he said.

"I did, too," Amanda said. "So you know that she was thirty-seven when she died. Dallas was very specific. She told us the first victim was thirty-six."

"Dallas was mistaken," Grant said, "that's all."

"You've got the wrong woman."

"We don't have the wrong woman," I said. "Dallas would have told us that."

"She did," Amanda said, "over and over again. She absolutely refused to confirm that Kranz was the first victim. The only reason you had for pursuing Kranz was that Dallas didn't deny it."

"Jesus Christ," I mumbled.

"It gets better," Amanda said. "I found your cop."

I stood. "You found Jack Clemmons?" I asked.

"Sort of—he died a number of years ago. But I did get his story."

"Speak up, woman."

"Sergeant Clemmons was called to the scene in the early hours of August fifth. I've got his notes as they were outlined in the news reports."

"Where did you get them?" I asked.

"Downstairs—in the archives. The answers were here in this building all along. There was an incredibly detailed account of the death that occurred on August fifth and the events that took place afterwards."

"I don't believe this," Grant said. "I searched every August fifth. You're telling us that I missed a death that was high profile enough to be covered by this newspaper and in that much depth."

Amanda stared at me. "Yup," she said, "that's exactly what I'm telling you guys."

"Bullshit," Grant replied. "I couldn't have missed something like that."

"You wouldn't have missed it—if you'd listened to me in the first place."

"Well," Grant said, "I'm pretty much done listening to you now. I think you've lost the fragment of a mind you had."

"Grant," I said, "try keeping that mouth of yours shut for a couple of minutes. Listen to what Amanda has to say." I turned to the woman. "Go on," I said.

"It's all here," she continued. "Just like Dallas said."

"Bullshit," Grant muttered.

"Sergeant Jack Clemmons was the watch commander that night. He received the call informing him of the death at 4:25 a.m. This information is straight out of the pages of the *Tribune*. Clemmons was told the body was discovered around midnight. You'll never guess who found the corpse."

"Who?" I asked.

"The housekeeper," Amanda replied, "a Mrs. Eunice Murray."

"Dallas mentioned the housekeeper," I said. "We never did get an answer as to what she was doing when the cop arrived."

"Well," Amanda said, "we've got one now. She was doing what any good housekeeper would be doing at four in the morning after discovering a dead body in the bedroom."

Grant shuffled in his chair. "What?" he asked.

Amanda turned to him. "Laundry," she said. "When Clemmons arrived on the scene, Mrs. Murray was doing the laundry."

It was all I could do to control myself. Her whole story seemed utterly ridiculous. There wasn't a chance we could have missed something like this.

Amanda scanned her notes. "This is right out of the official police report," she went on. "When Clemmons checked the woman's body, he made note of eight to ten bottles on her nightstand that had contained prescription medication. His report stated that every one of the bottles was opened, and that each one was empty."

"Dallas told us that," I said. "That was how they set things up."

Amanda looked up from her papers. "There was no syringe. You weren't listening to the clues. Dallas said they administered the drug. She didn't say they injected anything. Remember what she said about the drinking glass?"

"I do," I said. "One of them left their prints on a drinking glass."

"No," Amanda replied. "Dallas didn't say anything about leaving prints. Her exact words were: 'Look for a drinking glass.' She said the cop knew right away."

"Well, if they didn't leave prints on the glass, what was she talking about?"

"She said they'd made mistakes. Clemmons noticed it right off the bat. There *was* no drinking glass. How could a person swallow eight to ten bottles of pills without a glass of water?"

"Jesus," I said.

"It's all right here," Amanda said. "Front page of the *Vancouver Tribune*, August 5, 1962. I had archives print you off a photocopy."

She shuffled her papers again and produced the copy. Her hand trembled as she passed the reprint across the table to me. I felt a sickness in my gut. There it was, front-page banner headline—eighteen point bold type. Dallas was right. This was bigger than anything I could have ever imagined. The words blared at me. My eyes darted over the copy—the Associated Press release—dated August 5, 1962.

> *Blonde and beautiful Marilyn Monroe, a glamorous symbol of the gay, exciting life of Hollywood, died tragically Sunday. Her body was found nude in bed, a probable suicide. She was 36. The long-troubled star clutched a telephone in one hand. An empty bottle of sleeping pills was nearby.*

My mind raced over the conversations I'd had with the mystery assassin. I looked up at Amanda and said, "Dallas told us there was a film. You know who the boyfriend must be."

Moisture filled her eyes. In all the time I'd spent with her—through all the abuse I'd heaped on her and all the shit I'd passed her way—I'd never seen a tear even start to well. Her voice quivered as she struggled to force out the words. "People called him Jack, too," she said. "The thirty-fifth president of the United States, John—Fitzgerald—Kennedy."

# CHAPTER EIGHTEEN

I OPENED MY eyes. The pain in my head and the ringing in my ears reminded me of exactly how much Scotch I'd managed to slip past my lips the night before. My throat was dry and my mouth tasted like I'd spent the last few hours sucking on a dead carp. It was the first night I'd spent passed out in the newsroom in a lot of years. The smell coming from my shirt brought back a memory or two from my younger days. I would have to remind myself to pull out my driver's license and check my date of birth, before I pulled off a stunt like that again.

My neck hurt. The throbbing at the base of my skull felt as though an ice pick had been inserted into my brain stem. I thought about Mr. Smith, and then rubbed my hand over the back of my neck to make sure the source of the pain was just my imagination. I wiped at the crust of dried saliva on my cheek with my hand. The empty booze bottle lay amongst the papers on my desk. I picked up the dead soldier and dropped it into my wastebasket. The clang of the glass container smacking the bottom of the can echoed through my head. I pulled open my desk drawer and searched for my emergency stash of aspirin. Amanda had dropped a bomb of atomic proportions on me, a twenty-megaton reminder that I didn't always have all the answers. At least I'd managed to kill the story on the Morazzo family in time.

I steadied my hand and poured a healthy dose of aspirin tablets from the bottle. I needed water. My alcohol-soaked mind slid back to the woman's dissertation of the previous morning. I'd checked the facts myself yesterday afternoon. The records clearly stated the first thing that came to Jack Clemmons' attention early that morning when he looked over Marilyn Monroe's naked corpse. There were as many as ten empty pill bottles on her nightstand, and not a drinking glass or cup of any kind anywhere in the room.

I took a deep breath and stood. I leaned on my desk and waited for the flow of blood rushing into my head to give me some stability. I picked up my mug and turned in the direction of the watercooler. I took a step, and then paused to rest my hand on the partition of my cubicle to regain my balance. I tossed the handful of pain relievers into my mouth. The watercooler was a good thirty feet away, and I needed my hand free to help steady myself as I manoeuvred through the cubicles and make my way around the obstacle course of wastebaskets and chairs. I was still pissed at Grant, but only because it was easier to be mad at him than it was to be mad at myself. The woman had been right all along. I had to admit to myself that the lack of a *Y* chromosome didn't mean much when it came to the art of listening. She'd heard what Dallas was trying to tell me all along.

⌘

A miraculous little discovery, I said to myself, white powder, compressed into tablets—the saviour of all good reporters and connoisseurs of the art of fermentation everywhere. I snapped the lid back into place then stuffed the bottle of aspirin back into my drawer. I closed my eyes and held my head in my hands. The pain had eased over the last hour, and my half-embalmed body was beginning to show some signs of life. I had to push the grogginess from my head and focus.

The rumours of a love affair between Marilyn Monroe and both Jack and Bobby Kennedy were well documented, but never proven. Was it more than just gossip? Now the world could know for sure. After all these years, cancer had brought a confessor to my door. I tried to put myself in the shoes of the mystery caller. I could imagine the guilt that had eaten at her for almost half a century. What could she tell me about one of the most asked questions of the last forty-some-odd years? Mr. Smith had ordered the deaths of both Marilyn and JFK. What about Bobby? There were still questions about his assassination as well. Could they all be tied together? Was Robert Kennedy yet another victim of Mr. Smith's murder squad—was he really behind the Kennedy curse? I reached across my desk and picked up the ringing phone.

⌘

"Good morning," Dallas began.

"I know the real answer to the puzzle," I said.

Silence from the other end of the phone line.

"Are you there?" I asked.

A sigh.

"Dallas?"

"I can tell by the tone of your voice," she said, "you've figured out that Kranz was not the right woman."

"I have. Jack Clemmons, the lack of a drinking glass, August 5, 1962."

"I told you it would come to you. All you needed to do was to listen to the clues."

"This is hard to believe," I said. "You killed Marilyn Monroe?"

I listened to Dallas weep.

"Tell me about John Kennedy," I said.

Dallas fought for a breath. "Soon," she said. "I told you, the names of the victims aren't the issue here."

"I know," I replied. "Mr. Smith."

"You understand now. You and your interns—you have to be careful."

"But Mr. Smith, he must be an American. Are you sure he's here in Vancouver? He could still be in the United States."

"He's everywhere. I told you—he's a power—not a specific person."

"But you must have come to Canada for a reason. You must have thought you'd be safe here."

"Safer," Dallas said. "There's a difference. It was an escape. *To sleep, perchance to dream.*"

"Maybe Smith thought he'd be safer here, too."

"Lots of Americans fled to Canada in the sixties—you remember."

"The Vietnam war," I said, "the draft dodgers."

"It wasn't a war. It was an intervention."

"Right," I said, "an intervention that escalated into a war."

"And when did that happen?"

"Mid-sixties, after the assassination of JFK."

Dallas began to cough.

"How are you feeling?" I asked.

"Relieved," she said. "I don't have much time left. It feels good to know that I've finally shared my secret after all these years."

"We have to get moving. I have to have all the answers before you—"

I hesitated. Dallas finished my sentence for me.

"Die?" she said.

"Yes," I replied.

"It's time for a discussion about history. Remember—I told you your knowledge of history would be important."

I rested my elbow on my desk and let out a breath. "I remember the sixties," I said. "They were difficult years."

"Then you remember 1963."

"Vividly—the whole world changed on November 22nd."

"We have to go a little further back than that. Do you remember the theories that were thrown around after that day in Dealey Plaza?"

"I do. The CIA—the Mafia—the Cubans."

"Right. Mr. Smith knew that everyone that owned a pencil would be offering up a theory. That's one of the reasons he sacrificed Leon."

"Lee Harvey Oswald."

"Uh-huh, Mr. Smith spent years grooming him for his part—his involvement with the Russians, the Fair Play for Cuba organization, the CIA. He made sure that the conspiracy theorists had lots to work with."

"Jack," I said, "the owner of the night club?"

"Rubenstein, everyone knew him as Jack Ruby."

"Are you ready to tell me who Mr. Smith is now?"

"No. I told you. We're going to go through this from the beginning. I want people to know why. We'll start with Marilyn's murder."

"Do we have that much time?" I asked.

"I'm going to take you back to the Spanish Civil War."

"The Spanish Civil War?" I asked.

"The general's name was Mola. He ordered four columns of troops to capture Madrid from the nationalists. He had supporters loyal to his cause in the city. He called them his fifth column."

"The fifth column," I said. "That phrase went on to be used to describe a covert group working within a nation to undermine its strength."

"Exactly. You do know your history!"

"So you're telling me that Mr. Smith recruited a fifth column to wage war on the government of the United States from within?"

"We were young. Mr. Smith was clever. He knew that by inciting us to rebel against our parents and our teachers, he could eventually gain complete control."

"But," I said, "to kill a movie star?"

"I told you. She was a victim long before she crossed paths with us. We were told she kept a diary."

"The four-hour delay—that's what Mr. Smith was looking for in her house?"

"The Bay of Pigs, April 17, 1961, the CIA-sponsored invasion of Cuba. They were trying to overthrow Fidel Castro, the same way they toppled the government of Honduras a few years before. The rumour was that Marilyn knew more than she should have. She was in way over her head. The details were in the diary."

"What details?"

"It doesn't matter now. What's important is exposing Mr. Smith."

"We'll go public with your story—while you're still alive. You know who Mr. Smith is."

"I do," Dallas said. "But you have to figure it out for yourself. It's important that you follow the clues and find Mr. Smith on your own. If not, once I'm gone it will just be another matter of hearsay. What if John had an affair with Marilyn? What if she slept with Bobby, too? Was Leon part of a conspiracy? Were the Cubans or the Russians involved? Don't you see, they're just questions."

"Vital questions," I said.

"It's not the questions that are important. It's the answers."

"And you know the answers."

"I do. And you'll learn them, too. Just listen to the clues."

"What's the next step?" I asked.

"Marilyn," Dallas replied. "We'll look at the facts surrounding her death together. Just the facts, Hartree. Forget about the rumours and the *he said, she said* nonsense. Get a copy of her autopsy report, too. I have a doctor's appointment, I have to go. I'll talk to you later."

# CHAPTER NINETEEN

THE PAIN IN my head was just about gone, but I still felt like I'd been chained up and dragged behind a truck over a gravel road for a mile or two. I rubbed my hand over the stubble sprouting from my face. A rumble from my stomach reminded me that I'd gone far too long without food. I filled my coffee cup again. Grant and the woman would be arriving soon. I had to kick start my mind and achieve some sort of functionality. I was at a turning point in my life. I was hung over, and I smelled like I'd spent the night sleeping under a log in the park. I had to force the grogginess from my head. I had a Ceejay to win.

⌘

Grant strutted into the conference room and dropped his briefcase onto the floor next to his chair. "I still can't believe this," he said.

"It's the Crime of the Century."

"I should have never told Amanda about the birth date."

"What?" I asked.

"The birth date," Grant replied. "Shelly Kranz. It bothered me that Dallas wouldn't give us a confirmation. I told Amanda I was going to check Kranz's date of birth. I also told her I wanted to spend a day down in the archives. She just beat me to it, that's all."

I raised an eyebrow.

Grant held two fingers in front of his face. "I was this close," he said. "I should have kept my mouth shut."

Amanda walked into the room. I expected a strut from her, too, but instead of a swagger she hustled to her seat in her usual dishevelled fashion. She had earned the right to gloat. Instead of the ego-driven look of condescension that Grant was famous for, her face showed a quiet satisfaction. She'd done what a good reporter should do. She'd looked at the clues with an open mind and followed the trail to the answer. Dallas was right. Exposing Mr. Smith would put my name in the history books. That wasn't all; she was right about another thing, too. My cubs and I would have to be careful. Mr. Smith was lurking out there somewhere, and he was a very dangerous entity indeed.

"Dallas called again this morning," I said. I reached into my briefcase and pulled out my cassette recorder. "I told her we know about Marilyn."

"What was her reaction?" Amanda asked.

"She was relieved," I said. "She started to cry."

Amanda looked down at her notepad. "I can imagine how she must feel," she said. She looked up at me. "I wonder what it was like for her. That's quite a burden to be packing around for over forty years."

I nodded my head.

"What about the Kennedy assassination?" Grant asked. "Did she tell you who Mr. Smith is?"

"No," I said.

"She's playing with us," Grant mumbled. "That bitch."

Amanda turned and looked over at Grant. "She's been playing with *you* all along," she said. "Why don't you knock that chip off your shoulder and listen to the woman. She was used. She was steered into a position where she made a horrible mistake. She was hardly more than a child. Now she's trying to do the right thing. Cut her some slack."

"She's a killer," Grant said. "She doesn't deserve any slack."

"Grant," I said, "put a lid on it. She's starting to feed us information on the cells. She told me there was a fifth column operating in the States. Mr. Smith called the shots. He was the one that ordered the assassination of John Kennedy."

"Why won't she tell us who Mr. Smith is then?"

I hesitated for a moment and thought back to her phone call that morning. What Dallas had told me made sense. She needed me to search through the clues myself and come up with the answers. I had to find Mr. Smith on my own. For all I knew, the rest of the members of the Friendship Seven were dead and buried. If I learned the answers myself, I might be the only living witness to the events that took place over four decades ago. Dallas could put me there.

In Marilyn's house the night she died, and in the Texas School Book Depository the day the shots rang out across Dealey Plaza and around the world. We had to get to work.

"Grant," I said, "I want you to dig up everything you can on the day that Marilyn died."

I turned to the woman. She looked up at me and readied her pen on her pad. It was like she knew what to expect. I could tell from the look in her eyes. Another day's energy wasted on fluff while Grant and I took on the meat of the story. I felt a twinge of guilt. What conscience I had left reminded me that I at least owed the woman something for saving me from the embarrassment of running the story on the Morazzo family. "Wait," I said, "Amanda—you start working on Marilyn."

I turned to Grant. "And you," I said, "find me a copy of her autopsy report."

Grant nodded.

"We'll spend a few minutes listening to the last phone call," I said as I inserted the cassette into the tape recorder. I turned to Amanda. "She quoted more Shakespeare: *To sleep, perchance to dream.* You can explain it to Grant."

⌘

It's a difficult task—admitting that you're wrong is not something that anyone likes to do. With Grant and the woman off on their assignments, I had some time to collect my thoughts. I sat alone and stared at the blank walls of the meeting room and thought back on the events that had taken place over the last twenty-four hours. I'd gone out of my way to make things difficult for Amanda. I'd put up as many roadblocks as I could and I'd even gone so far as to sabotage her work in order to push Grant to the head of the class. I thought about Dallas, and about how she had read me like a book. She hit the nail on the head when she accused me of feeling threatened by my young female cub.

Amanda had a special talent, I couldn't deny it. She also had a strong sense of what was right and wrong. She could have sat on the information about Marilyn. Just a few more days, that was all it would have taken. She had the answer to the puzzle, and a little smoke and a couple of mirrors were all that she needed to keep my theory alive. I had put the facts together and had come up with the story I wanted to hear. The attack on the Morazzo family would have hit the streets, and I would have been the laughing stock of every journalist in Canada. I could only imagine what Halter's reaction would have been. I'd have ended my career by writing obituaries for the *Moose Jaw Free Press*. But everything changed yesterday morning. Thanks to Amanda, I'd need to set aside some time to work on my acceptance speech.

I gathered up my briefcase and headed back to the newsroom. I paused at the watercooler for another shot of life-giving fluid. I sat down at my computer and logged on to the Internet. I typed Marilyn's name into the search engine. I needed to do some research. I'd have some questions for Dallas the next time she called.

# CHAPTER TWENTY

"IT'S ME," DALLAS said. "How are you doing this morning?"

I rubbed the back of my aching neck. "I haven't slept too well the last couple of nights," I said. "I feel like a sack of shit."

"I know that feeling," Dallas replied.

"I've spent some time investigating. There's certainly no shortage of information about Marilyn."

"You'll have to be selective. There were lots of theories."

"How will I know?" I asked.

"I'm done playing games," Dallas said. "I've had my fun with you. Now that you know the truth about me, we'll have to concentrate on exposing Mr. Smith before I die."

"Are you scared?" I asked.

Dallas laughed. "Of what?" she asked. "Of death or Mr. Smith?"

"Both," I said.

"Death will be easy in comparison to a lifetime of trying to steer clear of Mr. Smith."

Silence for a moment.

"I've thought about dying," she said in a humbled voice. "I've had a hand in taking so many lives over the years. I've often wondered how I'll go. I've wondered if there will be a final retribution."

"A higher power?" I asked.

"Perhaps," Dallas said. "Maybe it will just be my final meeting with Mr. Smith."

"Do you still think he would come to Canada to look for you?"

"I told you. He's already here. He's everywhere."

"I've checked out your story," I said. "It's all very well documented. Jack Clemmons, the four-hour delay—"

"Everything I've told you is true," she said. "We have to work together. You and I are going to right a terrible wrong."

"We need to make some progress," I said. "Tell me about the morning of August fifth. The history books tell me you broke the window to get into Marilyn's bedroom. That's what the riddle was about. When you break a window to get into a house, where does the glass fall?"

"That's where the lies started. It's true, the bedroom window was broken. But not by us."

"How did you get into the house?"

"I told you how hot it was that night. Every bedroom window in Los Angeles was wide open."

"Then what was the point of the riddle?"

"Just to show you that we weren't the only ones that made mistakes. If the window was broken to get into the bedroom, why was the glass found outside on the lawn? There were quite a number of people in the house. It was even rumoured that the attorney general was there at one point."

"The attorney general?" I asked. "Robert Kennedy?"

"I said it was a rumour. That's what we have to do to expose Mr. Smith. We have to separate what we know for sure, from what is nothing more than hearsay. Let's look at it another way. We're going to play a game. It's called fact or fiction."

"Jesus Christ," I muttered, "not another game."

"Alan Ball and Chris McDermott—they bought a parcel of land together on the corner of Scott Road and Hillside Drive. Fact or fiction?"

"Fact," I said.

"Correct. Chris McDermott was in a position to know what was happening with the Skytrain expansion. Fact or fiction?"

"Fact," I said again.

"Good," Dallas said. "Now—McDermott had prior knowledge that the expansion of the rapid transit system would include the property at Scott and Hillside. Be honest. Fact or fiction?"

I hesitated for a moment. "McDermott *could* have had knowledge," I said. "It's certainly possible that some kind of confirmation could have been passed along."

"One word answers, please," Dallas said. "Fact or fiction?"

"Fiction," I grumbled.

"Alan Ball made a statement to the TV news people. He said that you were on some sort of a witch-hunt. That your only intention was to take down a political figure."

"Alan Ball's a big-mouthed asshole," I said, "just like Chris McDermott."

"Maybe Alan Ball's not the man you think he is."

"He's dirty—just like his partner."

"But you see my point. We can't expose Mr. Smith with half-truths. We have to sort out what's actually true, and separate it from what's rumour and what's only partially correct."

"I understand."

"Fact or fiction?" Dallas asked. "There were two doctors present at Marilyn's house along with the housekeeper."

"Fact," I said.

"Bobby Kennedy also made a visit to the house that night. Fact or fiction?"

"Fiction," I said. "It was never proven."

"Good," Dallas said. "You're beginning to understand. Now we can move on. This is what I want you and your interns to concentrate on. Have you got your tape recorder running?"

"Yes," I said.

"Good. I told you that we left an assortment of pills on her nightstand."

"You did," I said. "You also told me about forgetting to leave a drinking glass."

"And Jack Clemmons' report that the bottles were empty. Fact or fiction?"

"Fact," I said.

"I need you to get a copy of the toxicologist's report. It shouldn't be hard. There is plenty of written information available about the night of Marilyn's death. The report states that all but two of the bottles had pills in them. And that, my friend, is a fact."

"OK," I said, "I can verify that. Someone's not telling the truth."

"Next," Dallas went on, "I want you to look at the doctors' statements."

"The doctors?" I asked.

"Dr. Ralph Greenson and Dr. Hyman Engleberg, Marilyn's psychiatrist and her physician. Why do you think that two medical

85

professionals would wait over four hours to inform the police that Marilyn was dead?"

"I don't know."

"And another thing," she said. "Do you think that a doctor would be so emphatic about her death being caused by her own hand? There was no suicide note. Don't you think they would wait until the coroner had done an investigation? Only a thorough medical examination would reveal the true cause of death."

"I've instructed Grant to find a copy of her autopsy."

"Good," Dallas said. "We're going to need it. It was Dr. Engleberg that officially pronounced Marilyn dead. He was quite a remarkable man."

"Why do you say that?"

"His original statement claims that he was called at 3:30 that morning. He dressed, drove to Marilyn's house, examined her body, and pronounced her dead all in the space of twenty minutes."

"Twenty minutes?"

"Uh-huh," Dallas replied, "she was pronounced dead at 3:50. Check it out."

"I will."

"Now let's add another little twist to our game. We'll call it myth. When a person dies from an overdose of sleeping pills, they drift off to sleep and dream the dreams of the innocent until death comes calling. Fact, fiction, or myth?"

"I don't know."

"It's myth," Dallas said. "Normally, any kind of a drug overdose will cause a body to go into agonizing convulsions. There would most likely be vomiting as well. Don't you think it's odd that Mrs. Murray was washing bedsheets?"

"What are you telling me?"

"Jack knew right away that something wasn't right. He'd seen people dead from drug overdoses before. Marilyn's body was neatly positioned on the bed, face down, and arms at her sides. Everything in the room was organized and tidy. Nothing seemed to be out of place. Even the pill bottles on the nightstand were all lined up like little soldiers. Jack knew."

"The inconsistencies," I said. "You spoke about them."

"Right," Dallas said, "and there was one thing that Jack couldn't have known."

"What was that?"

"Only the three of us knew."

"What?"

"Marilyn died lying on her back."

I swallowed a lump in my throat. "More," I said. "Keep talking."

"I'll leave you with this," Dallas replied. "There were other members of the fifth column in the house that night, too. Crystal and Joker and I were just the instruments of death. Someone else had to make sure the stage was set properly. I think that's how the pills miraculously reappeared in the bottles. Mr. Smith couldn't allow the world to find out that her death was really a murder."

"What about the doctors? Were they part of this?"

"They were participants—but I don't think they were willing. Two very powerful forces clashed that night. I think the doctors got caught in the middle."

"There will be records. Tell me the names of the fifth column members."

"You haven't been listening. I told you, it was an army. I only ever met the Friendship Seven."

"Then how do you know—?"

"Trust me—I know. We were only ordered to administer the solution and set up the pill bottles. I didn't realize until we were actually giving Marilyn the drug."

"Tell me," I said.

"If something had gone wrong, if we'd been caught in the bedroom. We were expendable—just like Leon."

"You think Mr. Smith would have had you killed?"

"In a heartbeat. We were young and our heads were filled with lies. We thought we were playing a part in saving the world from nuclear war. Remember, it was only a few months after that that John Kennedy stood toe to toe with Nikita Khrushchev."

"The missiles of October," I said. "The Cuban Crisis."

"Mr. Smith convinced us that Kennedy was a war monger, and that he was leading the United States down a path to war with the Soviet Union. We believed him when he said that Marilyn's death would send him a clear message. We were so young and naive."

"They were tough times."

"So much distrust. Everyone was suspicious of everyone else."

"I remember."

"There were company men at the house that night, too."

"Company men?"

"Yes," Dallas said, "I'm certain of it. We always joked. You could tell an FBI agent from the shine on his shoes, and a company man from his haircut and his sunglasses."

"Company?" I said. "You mean CIA?"

"Lots of people knew about the diary. I think they must have been searching for it, too."

"Did it ever turn up?"

"There were rumours. The story was that the coroner's office had it. It vanished mysteriously."

"The CIA grabbed it?"

"We were young," she said, "but I never said anything about us being stupid. It was just a rumour that the coroner had possession of the diary."

"My God," I said, "you three took it?"

"Call it life insurance."

"Do you still have it?"

"I don't actually have it. It's secure—it's in a safety deposit box right here in Vancouver."

"You said that two powerful forces clashed that night. Mr. Smith and the CIA?"

Dallas laughed. "At one time," she said, "Mr. Smith *was* the CIA. But that all changed. Mr. Smith grew into something even more powerful and destructive."

"More powerful than the CIA?"

"Yes—a lot more—even with their friends."

"Their friends?"

"Sam Giancana and Johnny Roselli."

"The Mafia?"

"The cloak and dagger boys worked with the Mafia a lot, back then. Sometimes they found themselves both working toward the same goals. One hand washed the other. Take Cuba, for example. The mob wanted Castro out so they could continue with their gambling and drug rackets.

The CIA wanted Castro dead for obvious reasons. There was actually a CIA plot to use Mafia hit men to assassinate Castro."

"Jesus," I said, "can we prove that?"

"It's in the diary. In 1975, the Senate Intelligence Committee uncovered a link between the Mafia and the attorney general's office during the sixties. I know the CIA was mixed in there somewhere."

"But Mr. Smith was more powerful?"

"Much more," Dallas said. "You'll understand soon. I want you to study Marilyn's autopsy and the report from the toxicologists. I've prepared a list of questions. I'll call you in a couple of days."

"But . . ."

"No more today, Hartree. I said that I'll call you in a couple of days."

"But . . ."

"Don't be greedy. I'm about to give you your few minutes of true fame. *Life's but a walking shadow . . . that struts and frets his hour upon the stage.*"

# Chapter Twenty-One

"You look tired," I said.

Amanda glanced up from her notes. "I didn't sleep at all last night."

"Me either," I said.

"I may never sleep again. This whole situation is so unbelievable."

I nodded. "Who would have thought that one of the people involved in the Kennedy assassination would turn up in Vancouver."

Amanda lowered her stare. "It's all so horrible," she said.

"But Dallas is right; the world deserves to know the truth after all these years."

Amanda slowly raised her face. I could see the strain of the last few days in her eyes.

"Where's Grant?" she asked.

"He's rounded up Marilyn's autopsy," I said. "I've got him out looking for the toxicologist's report now."

"I've been reading everything I can get my hands on. There are lots of conflicting statements."

"I know. I've been searching too."

"The housekeeper, I've found documents stating that she discovered the body at midnight and others saying that it wasn't until 3:30 in the morning."

"I know," I said. "The doctors' statements are inconsistent as well."

"What do you think?"

"Dallas told me that Mr. Smith's men were there. I think the housekeeper and the doctors were threatened into changing their stories."

"The broken window. Dr. Greenson stated that Marilyn's bedroom door was locked, and he went outside and smashed the window to get in."

"Right," I said, "that's what Dallas was getting at with the riddle. The majority of the glass was found outside on the lawn."

"It doesn't make sense. If the window was broken from the outside, you would think that the glass should have ended up inside the bedroom. Did you run across the name Norman Jefferies?"

I nodded my head. "Mrs. Murray's son-in-law, he did odd jobs around the house. She called him over to replace the pane of glass."

"Why would she do that? The woman that she worked for was lying there dead. Why would she be concerned about a broken piece of glass? Why would the police stand by and allow evidence to be altered?"

"Unless the police officers were members of the fifth column."

"Dallas said they weren't the only ones that screwed up. Do you think they were trying to cover up the mistake of the broken window?"

"I don't know."

"Her last quotation," Amanda said, *"Life's but a walking shadow . . ."*

I looked up.

"It's not from *Hamlet*; it's a quote from *Macbeth*."

"What do you think she's trying to tell us?"

Amanda shrugged her shoulders. "There's always an underlying theme in Shakespeare's works. In *Macbeth*, it's greed."

"Mr. Smith," I said. "She's trying to tell us he was driven by greed."

"Maybe," Amanda replied. "I'll tell you one thing, though."

"What?" I asked.

"This Dallas woman is one smart lady."

"Especially with the inside knowledge that she has."

"Right," Amanda said. "I can understand why she waited until she was on death's door to tell the world who Mr. Smith is."

# CHAPTER TWENTY-TWO

I FELT A weakness in my arm as I pulled open my bottom drawer and leaned toward the record button on my tape machine. I'd managed no better than to toss and turn the last few nights and the lack of a good sleep was taking its toll on me. Too much time spent sitting at my desk. Too many hours spent staring at my phone, waiting for Dallas to call. Too many episodes of panic, wondering if Mr. Smith was lurking in the shadows of the newsroom, waiting for the opportunity to strike out and bury his identity for another forty years.

"How are you today?" I asked.

Dallas coughed. "I'm drained," she said. "I kept a journal through all those years. I knew there would come a day when I could tell the world my story. I've been going over my notes. I don't want to make any mistakes. We need to be certain of the facts when we expose Mr. Smith for the monster that he is."

"I'm ready," I said. "Where do we begin?"

"We'll start with the lies," Dallas said. "Then we'll move on to the medical evidence. Did you get your hands on the reports I asked for?"

"Done," I said. "I've got a copy of her autopsy and the toxicologist's report."

"Good. You may need the help of a doctor to decipher them."

"Handled," I said. "Everything's arranged."

"Mrs. Murray first claimed she discovered the body at midnight."

"Agreed."

"We also know that Jack Clemmons received the call notifying him of the death shortly after 4:30 a.m."

"Fact," I said.

"Marilyn was officially declared dead at 3:50 a.m."

"Fact," I said again.

"And Clemmons informed the L.A. County Coroner's Office after visiting the scene."

"Uh-huh."

"The coroner's office used the services of a number of mortuaries in the area. They worked on a rotation basis. The Westwood Cemetery was hired to collect her body. The owner's name was Guy Hockett. He and his son, Don, arrived at the house at 5:45 a.m. Sunday morning."

"August fifth."

"Right," Dallas said. "It was also their job to gather up anything pertinent to Marilyn's death. They took the pill bottles from the bedside table. Check it out."

"I will."

"Marilyn's body was taken to the Westwood funeral home. It was decided that a follow-up by the L.A County Coroner and the Los Angeles Police Department was in order. From there, her body was taken to the coroner's office on Temple Street."

"Uh-huh," I said.

"She was assigned a case number—81128. Her body was placed in crypt number 33 at the county morgue."

"To await the autopsy."

"Right," Dallas said. "That's when the cover-up really got going. Mr. Smith knew who to lean on."

"The coroner?" I asked.

Dallas laughed. "The list of names was long and distinguished," she said. "The coroner was just one of many."

"I've read the statements that the Hocketts gave to the press. Guy said that the body showed advanced signs of rigor mortis and he estimated the time of death to have been between 10:00 p.m. and midnight of August fourth."

"Right," Dallas replied. "Sergeant Clemmons put the time of death even earlier—at around nine. He also noticed signs of lividity on Marilyn's back. Do you know what would cause that?"

"I do," I said. "She spent time lying on her back after she died."

"So what does that tell you?"

"Her body was moved. Clemmons found her on her stomach."

"And does that jibe with the statements of Mrs. Murray and the two doctors?"

"Yes," I said. "They claimed that's how they found her—on her stomach."

"So you're saying that Mrs. Murray and the two doctors lied?"

I paused for a moment. "It's possible," I said.

"And what could be another explanation?" Dallas asked.

"That the body was moved before Mrs. Murray sounded the alarm."

"Exactly," Dallas replied. "You see, Hartree, that's what can happen when you tell the truth—but not the whole truth. It's not quite the same as a lie, but it is deception just the same."

"We could go on arguing this point for the rest of our lives." I caught myself. "Sorry," I said to her, "poor choice of words."

Dallas chuckled. "I've heard that about you," she said.

"What?" I asked.

"That sometimes the only reason you open your mouth is to change feet."

I felt the burn of her verbal slap across my face.

"Hartree," she said.

"I'm listening."

"Can you see what Mr. Smith has started here?"

I searched for words.

"The truth mixed with lies and half-truths. We have to sort out what is true, from what is only half true and what is an outright lie. If you follow the deception it will lead you to the answer."

"What's the next step?" I asked.

"Verify what we've talked about today. Then I want you to study the autopsy and the toxicologist's report. I'll call you in a couple of days."

"All right," I said.

"I also want you to start giving some thought to a motive."

"Motive?" I asked.

"I told you. Mr. Smith told us that Marilyn's death was necessary to send a message to the Kennedy brothers."

"Yes."

"The world was in a dangerous place in the sixties. The situation between the Americans and the Russians, the escalating conflict in Southeast Asia—"

"Agreed."

"Certain factions stood to benefit from John's assassination. He and his brother got in people's way. That's where you have to look. *Fair is foul, and foul is fair.*"

"Mr. Smith was after both the president and the attorney general?"

"Follow the clues. Look for the motivation. Was it money? Was it power or fame?"

"I always look at the money—that's usually the greatest motivation."

"Hartree," Dallas said.

"I'm here."

"You and your interns, you haven't said anything to anyone about me?"

"Not a word," I said.

"Good," Dallas replied. "You know what could happen to us?"

"I do."

"You have to keep this quiet. You'd better remind Grant and Amanda how vital it is that word of our conversations doesn't leak out."

"I will."

"I told you about Crystal."

"Your suspicions about her death?"

"Her mouth moved a lot faster than her brain. She said things about the Kennedy assassination."

"And you think Mr. Smith found out?"

"I'll call you tomorrow morning around nine," Dallas said. "I want to move on to the medical reports."

I listened to the sound of Dallas hanging up her phone. I took a sip of coffee and leaned over and shut my tape recorder off.

⌘

*Life is but a walking shadow.* I'd never been a huge fan of Shakespeare, but what Dallas was telling me was hitting home. Billions of people walk this earth for a brief moment in time and leave nothing but a shadow upon the stage. A certain few, however, leave a definite mark. The John and Bobby Kennedys of the world will forever be remembered, more for how they died than for how they lived and what they accomplished. Marilyn Monroe—from movie star to legend in the blink of an eye, on a hot August night. The Walter Winchells, the Edward R. Murrows, and the Walter Cronkites left their marks by reporting the news, rather than by creating it.

Could the name Terry Hartree become part of that list? I was being handed the ripest of plums: the opportunity to shed light on the greatest conspiracy of the twentieth century. I was the chosen one. A dying old woman had handpicked me to tell the story that an entire generation needed to hear. This was my shot at the title, my one last chance to add a Ceejay to my list of achievements. I couldn't share the limelight with Grant—and I wouldn't share it with Amanda. I had to take over the story. Mr. Smith was a dangerous force. That's it. That was how I could ease Grant and Amanda out of the picture and keep the glory for myself. I just couldn't put my cubs in jeopardy.

# Chapter Twenty-Three

I RUBBED MY fists into the sockets of my eyes. Four hours spent struggling through Marilyn's autopsy report had drained me. I stood and stretched my arms over my head. I grunted, and twisted my torso back and forth to stretch the muscles in my aching back. I looked over the piles of paper on my desk. I'd sorted through the medical terminology the best I could, had made notes, and divided the details into pertinent groups. Now I had to sit down and add the names of the people involved.

Deputy Coroner Dr. Thomas Noguchi was assigned the job of performing the autopsy; also in attendance were Dr. Theodore Curphy, the Los Angeles County coroner, and John Minor, the deputy District Attorney. Minor had a medical background. He was an associate clinical professor at the University of Southern California Medical School.

Noguchi's first task was to examine the body for needle marks. He literally went over Marilyn's corpse with a magnifying glass. Minor helped. Not even a hint of a needle mark was found.

I leaned back in my chair and stared up at the ceiling. How could Dallas have administered the drug? I added a note to the scribble of questions I was preparing for her.

Lividity was noted on Marilyn's stomach. That was no surprise. It would be caused because she was lying on her stomach after death had occurred. But signs of lividity were also spotted on her back. My mind flashed back to the conversations I'd had with Dallas. Dual lividity could only have been caused by Marilyn spending time on both her stomach and her back, after she had died. Dallas had told me that. She had said that only she and her two partners knew that Marilyn had died on her back. The body had obviously been moved. The report also indicated that bruising was found on Marilyn's back and hip. A bruise, I said to myself, is a sign of violence and inconsistent with a self-administered overdose. I stacked the papers on the initial examination together and started another pile.

The medical evidence was more of a challenge. A prescription for fifty Nembutal capsules was found on the table next to Marilyn's bed. Some reports claimed it was empty; some did not.

Noguchi started the autopsy by opening Marilyn's stomach. It was virtually empty. No visible trace of barbiturate capsules was found. That meant that she couldn't have taken the pills orally. Nembutal is packed in distinctive yellow capsules. Even if she had swallowed and digested the drugs, the bright yellow dye from the capsules would have lingered in the stomach. A smear from her gastric contents was examined under a polarized microscope. Ingestion of a large quantity of barbiturates would leave refractive crystals in the digestive tract. No such trace was found. Noguchi and Minor were unable to find any evidence that Marilyn's death was caused by the oral ingestion of barbiturate capsules.

The two men knew that only a toxicological examination of her organs would answer the question as to how the drugs had entered her system. If the pills were swallowed, they would first be broken down by the stomach and then absorbed by the duodenum, the first digestive tract after the stomach. From the duodenum, the drug would be carried by the blood to the liver, and then from the liver back to the blood and then to the kidneys. But no trace of the Nembutal was found in the duodenum either, no refractive crystals and no telltale yellow dye. Noguchi prepared brain tissue, blood samples, urine, liver and kidney tissue, the stomach and its contents, and the intestines for delivery to the toxicology lab.

I leaned over the stacks of paper and picked up the phone.

⌘

"How are you making out? Dallas asked.

I let out a long gasp of breath. "I had no idea," I said. "Not only is there not a shred of information that supports the suicide story, the medical evidence pretty much rules it out as a possibility."

"I told you," Dallas replied. "You know what has to be done."

I rested my thumb on my temple and ran my fingers back and forth across my brow. "Mr. Smith," I said. "The world has to know."

"There will be questions," Dallas said. "You'll have to be prepared. There are people who won't be happy when your story breaks."

"Speaking of questions," I said, "I have a few of my own."

"Shoot," Dallas replied.

"Dr. Noguchi," I said.

Dallas laughed. "You're not questioning his autopsy, are you?"

"No," I said, "the man's record is spotless. But in 1962, he was a junior member of the coroner's team. Why would he be assigned to such a high-profile case?"

"Let's think about that for a moment. If you were Mr. Smith, who would you want to see performing the autopsy?"

"I see," I replied. "He was hoping that Noguchi would turn out to be incompetent?"

Dallas coughed.

"Is that it?" I asked.

"Mr. Smith knew that even though Noguchi was a junior member of the staff, he was more than capable."

"Then what's the answer?"

"Think about it," Dallas said.

I tapped my fingertips on my desktop. "Maybe he figured that because Noguchi was low on the totem pole, he could be manipulated."

"Now you're getting somewhere. Smith is a master at the art of manipulation."

"But the evidence," I said, "the fact that there was nothing found in her stomach."

"Maybe it was pumped. Don't forget, there were doctors in the house that night."

"I checked," I said. "Even if her stomach was pumped, some trace of the drug would have reached the duodenum."

"Very good," Dallas replied, "I thought you'd miss that. Have you read the toxicologist's report yet?"

"No," I said, "not thoroughly."

"Do it. You'll be amazed."

"At the findings?"

"No," Dallas said. "At what was *not* found."

"I'll take it home with me and start reading through it tonight."

"Hartree?" Dallas asked.

"I'm here," I said.

"Are you absolutely certain that the news of your story hasn't leaked out?"

"What do you mean?"

"You haven't said anything to anyone about me?"

"I swear," I said, "not a word."

"And your cubs?" Dallas asked. "Are you sure they're being careful what they say?"

"I'm sure."

"I went out again yesterday," Dallas said. "I had to see my lawyer about some changes to my will."

"And?" I asked.

"It may have been a coincidence—"

"What?" I asked.

"A black Jaguar. The windows were tinted, I couldn't see the driver."

"That's it?" I asked. "You saw a black Jaguar?"

"Like I said, it may have been a coincidence. I saw it twice on the way to the lawyer's office—behind me—in the mirror."

"You're right," I said, "it's probably a coincidence."

"That's what I thought, too."

"Then why the questions?"

"This morning," Dallas said, "I saw the same car pulling away from a parking spot across the street from my house. Someone's watching me."

# Chapter Twenty-Four

IT WAS A miserable night. I drove up Richards Street and took my place in the lineup to the Granville Bridge. I made the turn onto Pacific and squeezed my way into the right-hand lane. It was raining harder than usual, and I turned my defroster up higher to clear the mist that was gathering on the inside of my windshield. My body was tired, but my brain was still in overdrive. The voice on the radio informed me that not only would the rain continue for two more days, but a cold front was moving in from the west. We lived in a rainforest. This was the Vancouver we all knew and loved.

I ran over that afternoon's conversation with Dallas once again. How could the story that Marilyn had taken her own life have survived for over four decades? There were a number of challenges to the theory, but each was quietly swept aside. The questions raised by the autopsy alone should have been enough to spark a full-scale investigation. There wasn't even a coroner's inquest. In the face of the medical evidence, how could the police, the district attorney's office, and the coroner have possibly come to the conclusion that Marilyn had died by her own hand? Mr. Smith, I said to myself, was a power that had to be neutralized.

A mass of red taillights lit up in front of me. I nailed my brake pedal and the nose of my car dipped as I came to a halt inches away from the back of a red Toyota. The rain pounded the roof of my car. Water drops the size of grapes splattered onto my hood and windshield. A horn blared. I glanced up and checked the clog of traffic in my rear-view mirror.

I sat in the lineup on the bridge and waited. The intersection at Granville and Broadway was most likely gridlocked, and I could probably expect at least a twenty-minute crawl to Sixteenth Avenue. The back-and-forth motion of my windshield wipers drew me into a trancelike state. There were so many questions, and at this point, so few answers. The fact that Marilyn was murdered was clear. The story of her suicide had been spun from the rumours of her troubled life as the reigning goddess of Hollywood. Her abuse of prescription drugs was common knowledge. But in the sixties, drugs like Nembutal, Sodium Pentothal, Demerol, and Phenobarbital were passed around Hollywood parties like after-dinner mints. The fact that she died from an overdose of barbiturates was firmly established; how the drugs made it into her system was not. A person who had downed fifty pills would certainly not get up from her final resting place and hide her drinking glass. Besides—the autopsy evidence couldn't be interpreted any other way. Even if her body had time to metabolize the drugs, there would still have been traces in her digestive system.

I had to change my focus. I still had the toxicologist's report to pick through, but I knew it would only confirm the fact that Marilyn had died by a hand other than her own. I had to concentrate on the motive. Dallas said that Mr. Smith was sending a message to the Kennedys. What kind of a message?

I squeaked through the yellow light at Broadway and straddled the crosswalk. I thought back to the issues the Kennedy brothers were faced with in the early sixties. The cold war was raging, and a hot war was brewing in Southeast Asia. The brothers had slapped the CIA in the face by refusing to provide American air support to the Bay of Pigs invaders back in '61. Was Mr. Smith working for the Cubans loyal to Fidel Castro? Dallas said he was a power—not a specific person. Communism was just one of the powers that the Kennedys had committed to fight against.

The traffic in the centre lane came to a complete stop. Two car-lengths ahead of me, a woman leapt from the driver's seat and frantically raised the hood of her car. She stood in the rain and waved the traffic around her stalled vehicle. I switched on my turn signal and forced my way into the left lane. I glared at her as I crawled past.

Back to the motive: Dallas had told me that there were company men in Marilyn's house the night she died. In February of '62, the Bay of Pigs disaster was still a festering wound in the CIA's chest. Was the red diary the reason that Marilyn was killed? Dallas said there were details in the log. Was there a link between the CIA and the Mafia? The truth about her relationships with the Kennedys, perhaps? Would the diary have exposed Marilyn's alleged affairs with both Bobby and

John? Was the CIA's intention to reveal the secrets held in the book? Were they out to even the score and embarrass the Kennedys? Would confirmation of the affairs not have demolished the brothers' wholesome family images? And if the scandal was brought to light, would Richard Nixon have been the first American president forced to resign?

I slid into the left hand turn lane at Sixteenth Avenue and waited. The light turned yellow, as I eased myself through the intersection. I glanced in my rear-view mirror. A car stole through the amber light and pulled in behind me. It was too dark and rainy to tell whether it was black or dark blue, but the chrome cat pouncing off the hood was unmistakable. It was definitely a Jaguar.

# Chapter Twenty-Five

**I missed Sandra.** Coming home to an empty house after a long day at the office was worse than torture. The trial separation had lasted longer than we'd planned and now it was looking more like a permanent thing. I longed for the smells most of all. Not just the smell of her perfume, but the smell of a real home. The aroma of her lasagne cooling on the top of the stove or her freshly baked cookies. Even that special trick she had for washing the towels—that trick that I could never quite get right. I glanced at the telephone. The last time I called her we ended up fighting again. I would have to try harder next time.

⌘

My steak had been tough and my peas mushy. I cleared my dinner dishes from the table and stuffed them into the dishwasher. I stood in my kitchen and listened to the sound of the rain on the roof. I leaned over the counter and pulled the curtains back. Lights from my neighbour's yard lit up the dark. I liked the night and the rain.

My mind wandered back to that November day in 1963. I remembered the look on my teacher's face. We all sat at our desks and watched as she spoke to our principal in the hallway. She was crying when she walked back into our classroom and told us that school would be closed for the rest of the day. I remembered the walk home, and finding my mother sitting alone in the living room. The curtains were drawn, and they were never closed during the day. The TV was on. I remembered the black-and-white images of panic in Dallas at a place called Dealey Plaza. My mother was crying too, and I don't think I had ever seen my mother cry before.

I turned and walked to the den. I stood and looked at the pile of papers on the table next to my chair. One last thing before I dove back into the medical reports. I was sure it was only coincidence: a Jaguar had followed me up Sixteenth Avenue for a couple of blocks. Big deal—there were lots of Jaguars in the city. I walked to the front window and cracked open the drapes. A Chevy and a Lexus were parked on the street to the east, and a Ford van to the west.

The first ring of the telephone actually made me jump. I was worn out and my nerves were frayed, but my startled reaction to the sound of the phone came unexpectedly. I pulled the chair away from my desk and sat.

"Hello," I said. I could hear someone breathing. "Who's there?" I asked.

More breathing.

"Hello," I said again.

Then I heard the click of the line going dead.

Wrong number, I said to myself. Why can't people have the courtesy to apologize when they make a simple mistake and bother someone in their home?

⌘

My eyes were tired. I glanced up at the clock on the mantel of the den fireplace. It was past eleven and time to hit the sack. The rain was still coming down in buckets, and I could hear a stream of water pouring from a plugged gutter on the house next to mine, and splattering against the ground. I'd given up on the reading an hour ago and had climbed into a fresh bottle of Scotch. With two good shots under my belt, I fixed on the blank spot on the wall above the fireplace; the space I'd cleared for my Ceejay award.

I thought back to my early days as a cub reporter. I remembered the day when the old boys in the newsroom decided that I'd run enough errands and fetched enough coffee and was finally ready for my first solo flight as a writer. I still had that article here somewhere. A few hundred words about the annual Remembrance Day ceremonies at Victory Square. I was so proud to see my first effort published—even if it was buried on page 22 and you almost needed a magnifying glass to spot it, it was still my first work in print. I idolized those men. One of them had actually been part of the D-Day landings on Juno Beach. These men had literally fought for the truths that they believed in. I wondered what they would think of me now. Would they be proud of the man they'd helped to shape?

My piece on the Cottonwood scandal and the Alan Ball/Chris McDermott series had changed the face of local politics in this town. Stanley Cottonwood was in jail and Chris McDermott hadn't even bothered to raise a hand in defence. The only response to my allegations was Alan Ball's feeble attempt to provide an explanation to the TV news. McDermott didn't even bother to show up for the press conference. The most ruthless politician this city had seen in years wouldn't even stand and fight. All Mr. Ball had to say was that McDermott was tired of living under a microscope, and that the two of them had done no wrong.

McDermott's resignation was the talk of the town. There was nothing the readers of this paper liked better than to watch a powerful person fall from grace. If McDermott was innocent, why was there no attempt made to address the charges of wrongdoing? Ball told the TV news that McDermott just wanted to get on with life, and put the whole incident to rest. That was when he accused me of being on a witch-hunt. He said that I'd fabricated the whole property deal into something sinister. Chris McDermott wanted no more of public life after that and had gone into virtual seclusion. A politician who was good for the people—maybe. A politician who was a little shady—perhaps. A politician who was vulnerable—most definitely.

The McDermott affair was minor in comparison to what I was working on now. Over the years, being awarded a Ceejay had become more than a mere goal: it had become an obsession. Exposing Mr. Smith would earn me a place in the history books, and I wouldn't have to resort to half-truths or innuendo. The facts were clear. Dallas would ask the questions—and I would find the answers. I'd gone over it a hundred times in my head. I'd stand on the podium, under the hot lights, in front of hundreds of distinguished guests. I'd take the award and shake hands with the presenter. I'd thank the old boys from the newsroom—and Sandra—in my acceptance speech.

I raised my glass and tilted my head back and drained the last bit of Scotch into my mouth. I closed my eyes, swallowed and pushed back in my reclining chair. I could only imagine what it would feel like to finally bring home a Ceejay. I'd have to do my best to mend fences with Sandra. I couldn't enjoy the most exciting night of my life without her by my side.

The phone rang. I opened my eyes and looked over at the clock. It was almost half past eleven. There was only one person that would call that late. I pulled forward in my recliner and stood. The phone rang a second time. Perhaps Sandra felt as bad as I did about the last time we talked. We'd fought over something stupid again—as usual. The phone rang a third time. Don't hang up, I said to myself as I leaned over my desk for the handset. I grabbed the phone and held it to my ear. Should I start with an apology, or should I just tell her how much I missed her? I heard a click and the line went dead.

# Chapter Twenty-Six

"It's me," Dallas said. "How did you make out with your reading assignment last night?"

"Not too bad," I said, "I have a few questions. A colleague of mine is making arrangements for me to meet with one of the pathology professors at the university. That should help."

"So, now that you've gone over the toxicologist's report, let's play another round of fact or fiction."

I groaned and shifted the phone to my left hand.

"Marilyn died from a massive overdose of barbiturates. Fact or fiction?"

"Fact," I said.

"She killed herself by swallowing a whole bottle of Nembutal."

I laughed, but not because it was funny. "Fantasy," I said. "There was no trace of barbiturates found anywhere in her digestive system."

"So," Dallas said, "someone injected her with the drugs?"

I paused. "I'm still confused about that," I said. "Enormous amounts of barbiturates were found in her blood and liver. We know she didn't swallow the pills, and administration by injection doesn't sound plausible to me either."

"Why?"

"There was no needle mark."

"There are places where a needle mark could never be found. What about her mouth? What about under her tongue?"

A shiver ran up my spine. "My God," I said. "You put the needle in her mouth?"

"No," Dallas replied, "it's just a question. I was only pointing out that there are ways to hide a needle mark. Your pathologist friend will tell you. A massive injection would have killed her instantly, long before any liver metabolization could have occurred. The drugs were absorbed into her system over a period of time."

"Then how?" I asked.

"Think about it," Dallas said. "There is one other method of entry."

I stared up at the ceiling.

"You're sitting on it," Dallas said.

I felt a queasiness in my gut. "Suppository?" I asked.

"Enema," Dallas replied.

I rubbed my hand over the back of my neck. "Jesus Christ," I mumbled, "how could you?"

"Let's get back to the evidence. The tox report discovered both Phenobarbital and chloral hydrate in Marilyn's blood."

"Agreed," I said as I scanned my notes.

"Do you know what chloral hydrate is?"

"Knockout drops," I said, "a Mickey Finn."

"It didn't show up until the blood work was finished. Chloral hydrate emits a strong odour of pear, but only when it's ingested orally."

"So?" I asked.

"Think about it," Dallas replied. "I told you there are places to hide a needle mark."

"An injection of chloral hydrate would have knocked her out immediately."

"Yes," Dallas said. "It was necessary."

"The bruising—she fought back?"

"The best she could. There were three of us, remember."

I looked over the page of notes I'd prepared the night before: "4.5 mg % Phenobarbital and 8 mg % chloral hydrate in her blood."

"We had to be sure," Dallas said. "We gave her a heavy dose of Mickey Finn."

"And the liver," I said, "13 mg % Phenobarbital. That's a huge amount."

"Many times the lethal dose," Dallas replied.

"Good God," I muttered.

"Did you notice anything odd about the tox report?" Dallas asked.

"I can't say. I'm not a doctor. There were things I didn't understand."

"Of course, but didn't you notice that the report was kind of light?"

"What do you mean?"

"The testing was only carried out on the blood and the liver."

"You're right," I said. "What about the other organs?"

"Dr. Noguchi had specifically ordered tests on the stomach and its contents, the kidneys, and the intestines. Did you see anything in the report on these organs?"

"No," I said, "I didn't."

"Lab analysis of the digestive tract would have confirmed Noguchi's findings that the Nembutal was not taken orally. If traces of barbiturates didn't show up in the kidneys, there would be no questioning the fact that Marilyn couldn't have swallowed those pills."

"So," I said, "why do you think the tests were not done?"

Dallas laughed. "It's not a case of what do I think," she said, "It's a case of what I know."

"Tell me."

"You can't test organ samples that you can't find."

"You're joking," I said. "They lost them?"

"I wouldn't say they lost them."

"Mr. Smith," I said, "he took them?"

"You still can't get your head around how powerful a force he controlled, can you?"

"My God."

"There was one clue to how the drugs were administered that didn't need a tox report."

"What?" I asked.

"John Miner noticed it first. I told you he had a medical background."

"What?" I asked again.

"The sigmoid colon," she said. "It was coloured purple."

"Purple?" I asked.

"It bothered Minor enough for him to send a copy of Marilyn's autopsy to a Dr. Leopold Breitnecker; he was one of Europe's foremost pathologists."

"And?" I asked.

"He also shipped a copy off to New York City's chief medical examiner."

"And?" I asked again.

"They both came to the same conclusion. That the discolouration of the colon was caused by an inflammatory response to barbiturates introduced into the large intestine."

"The enema." I said.

"Uh-huh."

# CHAPTER TWENTY-SEVEN

"I WANT TO bring you two up to speed," I said. "There have been some interesting developments over the last twenty-four hours."

Grant leaned back in his chair. Amanda opened her notepad.

"I've discussed the autopsy and the toxicology reports with Dallas."

Amanda looked up.

"There's no doubt in my mind—Marilyn Monroe was murdered."

Grant stood and began his pacing routine. "What about the Kennedy assassination?" he asked. "What did Dallas say about that?"

"We'll get to that," I said. "The first step is to establish a motive for Marilyn's murder."

Amanda rested her elbow on the table. "Dallas told us her death was meant to send a message to the Kennedys."

"Right," I said. "And she also told us that both John and Bobby were getting in people's way."

Amanda looked down at her steno pad. "I'm going to need a bigger piece of paper," she said.

"What?" I asked.

"Just think about the sixties. The Civil Rights Movement, the Cold War, the CIA, Vietnam, Cuba. Where do we start?"

"Exactly," I said, "and don't forget about Bobby's commitment to destroy organized crime."

Amanda let out a sigh. "It might be easier to make a list of the people that *didn't* want to see the Kennedys dead."

"The CIA," Grant added. "President Kennedy was threatening to rein them in. He thought they had too much power, and that they should be held more accountable for the things that they did."

I nodded. "Marilyn's red diary," I said. "In 1994, a CIA document surfaced that confirmed that they considered Marilyn's diary to be a major national security concern."

"It's hard," Amanda said, "sorting out the truth from the lies. I read that Marilyn had scheduled a press conference for August sixth, and that her intention was to reveal the contents of her diary."

I nodded again. "I read that, as well," I said.

"Who knows if it's true?" Amanda said and shrugged her shoulders.

"We have a lot of questions. We have to start coming up with some answers."

Grant raked his fingertips through his hair. "Dallas said there were CIA agents in Marilyn's house that night," he said. "I'm guessing that they had the most to gain by getting their hands on that book."

"Don't forget organized crime," I said. "It was common knowledge that Marilyn had connections to Sam Giancana and the leaders of the West Coast Mafia families."

"I wonder if there were details about the mob in the diary?"

I turned to Amanda. "That's a good question," I said.

"Marilyn could have been the common thread," she replied. "We know she was involved with both the Kennedy brothers *and* the Mafia."

"And what about the greatest motivation of them all?" Grant said. "Money."

"Money?" Amanda asked.

"Why not?" he replied. "You don't think that the president could have been killed in order to line a few pockets?"

"You think Dallas was lying? Do you think they killed Marilyn for money?"

"No," I said and turned to Grant. "You're on the wrong track. I don't agree with that at all. I'm sure Dallas was exactly who she said she was: a young person lured into a situation and convinced that what she was doing would save the world from nuclear devastation."

"Then who would stand to gain?" Amanda asked.

"Think about Kennedy's position on Vietnam," Grant argued. "Do you have any idea how many helicopters Howard Hughes shipped to Southeast Asia?"

Amanda tapped her pen on the table. "Thousands, I would think."

"Probably many thousands," I said. "Billions—maybe even hundreds of billions of dollars worth."

"You think Hughes Aircraft was involved in this?" Amanda asked.

Grant turned to her. "I'm just saying that a lot of big businesses stood to make a lot of money by escalating the war."

"And Kennedy was making moves to avoid a full blown war. He'd already started scheduling the withdrawal of the American troops stationed in Vietnam."

"Right," he said. "It's a motive."

Amanda rose from her chair. "We're losing sight of our objective, here," she said. "Our goal is to find out who the fifth column was taking their orders from."

"Exactly," I said. "We need to put a name to Mr. Smith."

"Dallas was right," Amanda said. "We already know who the victims were. That's not as important as exposing Mr. Smith and putting an end to him."

"And while we're on the subject of Mr. Smith," I said, "I've made a decision."

"What?" Grant asked.

"I'm going to ease you both out of the story."

Amanda leaned on the back of her chair.

"Why?" Grant asked.

"Things have happened," I said, "Dallas is worried that Mr. Smith might come looking for us."

"That's bullshit," Grant said. "What's he going to do—come and kill us all?"

I stared Grant down. I thought about my encounter with the black Jaguar.

"I've made up my mind," I said. "I'll use you both from time to time for research, but you have to be very aware of how dangerous this Mr. Smith is. Keep your mouths shut."

I closed my notebook, tucked it under my arm, and headed for the door. I paused and checked the pocket of my shirt. I turned and looked over the meeting room table for my missing pen.

Amanda leaned toward Grant and mumbled something I couldn't catch. Grant covered his mouth with his hand and whispered back.

I saw Amanda flinch. She looked in my direction as if she was expecting a reaction to Grant's comment. I wasn't close enough to hear their whispers. I could tell by the look on Amanda's face that whatever Grant had mumbled had struck a nerve. I could only hope and pray that he'd watch that mouth of his, and keep the secrets we shared. The wrong word to the wrong person could put us all in serious danger.

# Chapter Twenty-Eight

I WAS REALLY starting to hate mornings. I'd spent yet another night tossing and turning in my bed and every muscle in my body ached. For the first time in my life, my age stood out like the stain on my lucky green tie.

I'd arrived at the newsroom shortly after six, and even with a half-dozen cups of coffee in my system, I was still not completely awake. I needed a good sound sleep. My nerves were tattered, and I couldn't shake the feeling that someone was watching my every move. I had only seen the black Jaguar once. It was probably just a coincidence, but Mr. Smith lurked in the dark corners of my mind.

Grant hustled his way into the meeting room and took the seat next to Amanda at the table. I leaned forward and flipped open my notebook.

"I want to start zeroing in on Mr. Smith," I said. "We have enough information to start compiling a list of possible names."

Amanda took her notebook from her briefcase.

"Dallas has given us enough information on Marilyn's murder to start us off in the right direction," I said.

I watched as Amanda's gaze drifted toward the ceiling.

"What are you thinking?" I asked.

"Dallas," she said. "She hasn't really given us anything more than questions."

"I disagree," I said. "We've learned from the evidence that Marilyn Monroe was murdered."

Amanda nodded.

"We also know that there was a fifth column, and that a man known as Mr. Smith was calling the shots.

"As far as we've been told," Amanda said.

I glared at her.

Grant stood. "There's some kind of connection to the CIA," he said. "She told us that Mr. Smith *was* the CIA at one point."

I leaned back in my chair and tapped my pen on my pad. "Right," I said, "I think that's where we should start looking."

"I've done some reading," Amanda said. "Kennedy wasn't very happy with the CIA in the early sixties. They'd been linked to either plots or to the actual assassinations of a number of world leaders."

"Right," I said. "In addition to the plot against Castro, there were rumours that they had something to do with the deaths of a number of other foreign leaders, as well."

Amanda turned a page of her notebook. "The Congo's Patrice Lumumba, Chile's Rene Schneider, and South Vietnam's Ngo Dinh Diem."

"And Rafael Trujillo," I said, "from the Dominican Republic. We know that Kennedy wanted to put a leash on the CIA. Firing the director, Allan Dulles, was just a start."

"It's odd," Grant said, "that Dulles would turn up as one of the members of the Warren Commission."

"Right," I said and nodded my head. "I wonder?"

"I was thinking that, too," Grant replied. "Do you think Mr. Smith could have been powerful enough to have had Allan Dulles appointed to the Warren Commission?"

"It would make sense. If you wanted to put up a smokescreen, imagine the advantages of having a fifth column member sitting on that committee."

"Dallas told us that Mr. Smith was more powerful than the CIA—even with their influential friends."

"Sam Giancana," I said, "the alleged head of the Mafia in the United States."

"Right," Amanda said. "Do you know what happened to him?"

Grant turned in her direction.

"He was assassinated," she continued, "June 19, 1975, in his own home, the day before he was to testify before the Church committee."

"The Church committee?" Grant asked.

"Senator Frank Church," Amanda replied. "The Senate Select Committee to Study Government Operations; they were probing the CIA's alleged improprieties." She read through her notes. "The plot to kill Castro reads like a James Bond novel." She placed a finger on the page of observations and dragged it down. "Treating a box of his favourite cigars with botulism, contaminating his diving suit with a chronic skin disease called Madura Foot." She began to laugh. "Here's a good one," she said. "Constructing exploding seashells and placing them in a reef where Castro liked to dive."

"What?" I asked.

She looked up at me. "Yeah," she said, "the plan was to detonate them from a mini-submarine."

"Well," Grant said, "we can't realistically link Giancana's murder to the fact that he was about to testify before the Church committee. After all, he was a gangster. You know—live by the sword, die by the sword."

"You're right," Amanda said and turned in Grant's direction. "It could have been a mob hit."

"Exactly," Grant said.

"Do you know how he was killed?"

"No," Grant replied.

"He was shot in the head—with a .22 calibre pistol."

"So?" Grant asked.

"Think about it," Amanda said. "What kind of self-respecting Mafia hit man would pack around a .22? Don't you think something like a .45 would be more their style? A .22 is small—discreet—quiet. Don't you think that's more of a cloak and dagger kind of gun?"

"You're right," I said.

Amanda drew a breath. "I'll tell you what I think," she said.

"What?" I asked.

"I think that there were powers in the intelligence community that were way out of control. I think that the Kennedy brothers knew it, and that's why John was threatening to dismantle the CIA. Dallas told us that Marilyn's murder was meant to send a message. We know that the red diary contained details about the whole Bay of Pigs fiasco. We know that the CIA didn't have any reservations about assassinating Castro. We know that the Mafia was involved in the plot as well."

"And?" I asked.

"What if Mr. Smith was a power figure in the CIA? What if he recruited the fifth column members from within the ranks of the intelligence community?"

"But," I said, "Dallas doesn't fit that scenario."

"No," Amanda replied, "but Dallas was only a member of one of the cells. Who better to carry out the actual murders? Just like Leon—they were expendable."

"It makes sense," I said.

"That's where I'd start looking," she said. "Dallas told us that Mr. Smith *was* the CIA at one point, but that he'd grown into something more powerful."

I nodded.

"I think that Mr. Smith broke away from the intelligence community, and that the fifth column was recruited to carry on the fight against the Kennedys."

"Get to work," I said. "I want you both to put together a short-list of names." I looked at my watch. "Dallas said she'd call before noon today. I have to get back to my desk."

# CHAPTER TWENTY-NINE

"HARTREE," DALLAS SAID, "are you ready to get to work?"

"I am," I replied. "Where do we start?"

"What do you know about the Kennedy assassination?"

I leaned back in my chair and stared up at the ceiling. "I was quite young," I said. "I know the Warren Commission concluded that Lee Harvey Oswald acted alone, and that the three shots were all fired from the sixth floor of the Texas School Book Depository building."

"Correct," Dallas said. "That's the official version—in a nutshell. Do you believe it?"

I paused. "I guess," I said. "I know there were lots of conflicting theories."

"Mr. Smith made some mistakes that day. That's where we're going to start."

"What kind of mistakes?"

"Did you know that moments before the shooting started, the police lost one of their communications channels?"

"No," I said, "I didn't."

"They were using two frequencies that morning. Channel one was dedicated to routine police traffic and channel two was assigned to the Secret Service and the presidential motorcade."

"OK."

"Channel one was inoperable for nearly five minutes."

"It was?"

"The official explanation was that the microphone button on one of the motorcycles got stuck in the open position. Do you believe that?"

"What are you saying?"

"Nothing. Just that it's rather a convenient coincidence—don't you think?"

"It could have happened."

Dallas cleared her throat. "Sure," she said. "Those five minutes would have been crucial for the police. Imagine—bullets are flying—the president's been shot—and the police have no means of talking to one another."

"Mr. Smith, he arranged for the radio system to go down?"

"Wouldn't you if you were in his shoes?"

"It must have been total confusion."

"It gave us the time we needed."

"Explain."

"There were at least fifty witnesses that claimed they heard a shot from behind the fence on the grassy knoll. You've seen the photographs: people pointing—cops running up the hill."

"How did you manage to escape?"

Dallas laughed. "Easy," she said. "We rehearsed it down to the split second. I was wearing an ankle length wraparound coat. The moment after Crystal fired the shot, I opened my coat and Joker strapped the rifle to my leg. The gun was out of view in seconds. Then we just walked down the hill past the police officers."

"And none of them bothered to stop you?"

"Are you kidding?" Dallas said and chuckled. "The rifle was strapped to my thigh and my calf. I couldn't bend my leg."

"And that didn't look suspicious?"

"It was perfect," Dallas replied. "I had a cane and Joker was supporting my other arm. We just strolled right past at least a dozen cops and Secret Service agents. I don't think it occurred to them that two young women could have had anything to do with the shooting, especially once they saw that I appeared to have an injured leg."

"My God," I said.

"It was total chaos. Jamming that radio was the perfect way to create confusion. Too bad it came back to haunt Mr. Smith."

"What do you mean?" I asked.

"The transmissions over both radio frequencies were automatically recorded. The police ended up with a complete audio record of the entire event."

"The Warren Commission came to the conclusion that three shots were fired at the president. Are you saying the sound recordings dispute that?"

"That's your job to find out. Crystal only fired once. I told you already—there were three shooters. Not all of the shots came from the School Book Depository Building."

"Oswald?"

"I didn't say that. I just said some of the shots came from the building Leon was in."

"But Oswald's rifle was found on the sixth floor."

"Fact," Dallas said, "and three spent cartridges were found on the floor next to the window he supposedly fired from."

"Are you telling me that that the Warren Commission was wrong? Are you saying that more than three shots were fired?"

"Think about it," Dallas said. "Just because the police found a rifle and three bullet shells doesn't mean that Leon, or anyone else, fired any shots from the sixth floor of that building."

"But you just said—"

"I said shots came from the building—that's all."

"You told me that Oswald was set up to be the patsy. Are you telling me that he never fired at the president?"

"You've got work to do, Hartree."

"No kidding," I grumbled.

"We'll talk about Leon later. The sound recordings of the shooting have been analyzed using today's technology. That's where you need to start your search. Sound can be deceiving."

"And how will that help me find Mr. Smith?"

"You need to know how carefully the frame was built around Leon. Trust me—you'll have a much better understanding of who Mr. Smith is and how he works once you do some digging."

"I'll get started as soon as we hang up."

"You need to hurry."

"The cancer?" I said.

Dallas remained silent. I could hear short laboured breaths.

"Are you there?" I asked.

"The end is close," she whispered. "I'm afraid that the cause of my death might not be natural. That black Jaguar was outside my house again last night."

"Smith?" I asked.

"One of his operatives. Mr. Smith would never take the chance. Tracking people down was Joker's specialty."

"Your old partner?"

"We were close. I—"

"What?" I asked.

"I was about to say that I'd bet my life that it was Joker behind the wheel of that Jag."

# CHAPTER THIRTY

"I NEED YOUR help," I said. I looked at Grant and then turned to Amanda. "The Dallas police inadvertently made a five-minute sound recording of the shooting of the president."

Grant looked up.

"It's true," I said. "I checked it out this morning. One of the microphones on a police motorcycle malfunctioned. It stuck in the open position and transmitted the sounds from Dealey Plaza straight to the police recording machines."

"Jesus," Grant said, "do you think Mr. Smith had some kind of device to jam the police radio frequency?"

"It doesn't seem that sinister," I said. "The microphone button was stuck in the open position. It could have been a piece of tape."

"Or," Amanda said, "maybe it was just that—a malfunction."

Grant rolled his eyes. "Pretty convenient malfunction, don't you think?"

"Still," Amanda replied, "it could have been."

"It doesn't matter how it happened," I said. "Dallas told me that the recording has been analyzed with today's technology, and that it disproves the Warren Commission's findings that three shots were fired from the School Book Depository building."

Amanda scribbled some notes.

"I need you two to start digging. Dallas told us there were three shooters—a primary and two backups. She said that Crystal fired one shot, from behind the fence on the grassy knoll."

Grant leaned back in his chair and folded his arms across his chest. "The Warren Commission established that Oswald fired three shots from the window of the School Book Depository. If what Dallas is telling us is true, then there should be the sound of four shots on the recording."

I held up my hand. "We have to keep an open mind here," I said. "Dallas hinted that Oswald may not have fired on the president at all. Remember, the Warren Commission's decision was only based on the fact that they found a rifle with Oswald's prints on it and three spent shells on the sixth floor of the Depository."

"She's saying that there was a second gunman in the warehouse?"

I shrugged my shoulders. "She said there were three shooters. She didn't say that Oswald was one of them."

"Jesus," Grant said.

"Remember what she told us a few days ago. Mr. Smith needed someone to take the fall."

"Someone to cover the tracks of the others."

"Right," I said and nodded, "and that person had to die before he could prove his innocence."

Amanda stood. "Let's get to work," she said.

⌘

I sat in my cubicle and stared at the fabric-covered partition that separated me from the rest of the newsroom. My head was swimming; I pressed my thumbs into the sockets of my eyes and tried to rub the ache away. The more time I spent researching, the more my hatred for Mr. Smith intensified. The inconsistencies were piling up like garbage at the local dump. The smell coming from the pile grew more foul and putrid by the day, as lies and half-truths festered amongst the facts. Like cancer attacking healthy flesh, the lies would eventually vanquish the truth completely.

But Dallas had come out of hiding to set the record straight. Like a pair of skilful surgeons, together we could cut through the mire of falsehoods and resurrect the truth for future generations. There would be no more ambulance chasing for me. No more trying to hang politicians like Charlie Wolfe. No more energy wasted looking for chinks in the armour of people like Chris McDermott. This was meat. History was about to be recreated and I would stand in its glory, as I pointed my finger at the evil that Dallas called Mr. Smith. Over forty years ago, a movie star was murdered and a great man was gunned down in front of a nation. The world would soon have an answer as to why. The world would also learn who was behind the murders. The name Terry Hartree would be remembered in the same light as Woodward and Bernstein. Dallas would become as enigmatic as Deep Throat. Life was good.

I looked over the piles of paper on my desk. I turned my wrist and checked the time. Ten hours was enough. My brain was threatening to shut down, and I knew if I didn't go home now that the bottle of whiskey in my bottom drawer would find its way into my hand. The last thing I needed at this point was a bellyful of Scotch. I reached out and shut down the monitor on my computer. Time to hit the road.

⌘

A moderate dose of rain was falling again. That certainly wasn't unusual for Vancouver at this time of year. It was well past dinner and rush hour was officially over. I drove past the Fourth Avenue exit from the Granville Street Bridge and took my place in the line of cars heading south. It was cold, and I turned the car's heater up a notch. A thin blanket of mist had formed on the driver's door window and I wiped through it with the back of my hand. As I approached the intersection at Broadway, my ears picked up a warning signal. I reached for the control console and turned down the radio. A siren wailed in the distance.

The traffic light turned to green and the Chevy in front of me nosed into the intersection. The cry of the siren drew closer. I stopped my car, but I was still too far back from the crosswalk to get a good look up and down Broadway. I recognized the sound—an ambulance racing to someone's aid. The police, fire, and ambulance services all had sirens of distinctly different pitches. I could always tell them apart. I crept nearer the crosswalk. A horn blared behind me. I looked in my rear-view mirror and tried to locate the moron who was urging us forward. Someone was in trouble. The last thing I wanted to do was put my car into the path of a speeding emergency vehicle.

The wail echoed through the buildings. It was always so hard to tell the direction that the sound was coming from. I knew the ambulance was nearing. What if it was coming from behind me? The echo was deceiving. The idiot to my rear leaned on his horn a second time. The siren screamed. I hunched over my steering wheel and tried to get a better look down Broadway. I zeroed in on the sound. I had it—an ambulance was approaching from the west. I slid my foot from the brake pedal and moved slowly forward. My eyes searched the street to my right for signs of the ambulance's flashing lights. The clown in front of me was now a full car length into the intersection.

The siren sounded so close. It was definitely coming from my right, but I still couldn't gain enough of an angle to spot the ambulance. The eerie warble of the siren reverberated through the street. The echo bounced from building to building and, again, I wasn't sure exactly from which direction the sound was coming from. Maybe I was wrong. Now it didn't seem like the siren was coming from the west at all. The car in front of me made a dash through the intersection. His tires broke loose on the rain-slicked pavement and he fishtailed into harm's way. An air horn cut through the night air like a machete. My head jerked to the left. A fire truck barged into the intersection from the east and my heart skipped a couple of beats. The big red truck swerved to miss the Chevy and careened past the nose of my car. I watched the flashing red of the fire truck disappear around the corner onto Fir Street.

My heart was pounding. The fire truck had missed hitting me by mere inches. I wondered how many times motorists had panicked and driven straight into the path of an emergency vehicle because they couldn't tell what direction it was coming from. I gripped the steering wheel with both hands and took a deep breath. The goof with the horn behind me decided that I needed a third reminder to go. I flipped him the bird and proceeded through the intersection.

As I neared the light at Sixteenth Avenue, I thought back to what Dallas had said. The encounter with the fire truck had made things crystal clear; sounds and echoes could certainly be deceiving. I pulled into the left hand turning lane at Sixteenth. I switched on my turn signal and took my place in line. I tried to put myself in Dealey Plaza. I'd seen the pictures many times: a winding street that meandered through a series of tall buildings. The echo of one gunshot could sound like many. Hell, three gunshots could end up sounding like a dozen. The car in front of me cleared the intersection. I nosed forward. I wondered how my cubs would make out searching for the acoustical studies of the Dallas police recordings.

There was a break in the traffic. I swung through the intersection and headed east on Sixteenth.

# Chapter Thirty-One

THE SOUND OF a horn drew my eyes to my rear-view mirror. The Jaguar had appeared out of nowhere. I wouldn't have spotted it at all, if it hadn't pulled into the path of a car heading east on Sixteenth. By the time I'd reached the intersection at Sixteenth and McRae, the Jaguar was fast approaching. I swung a hard right onto McRae and accelerated. The driver of the Jag forced his way into the curb lane and made the turn less than a minute behind me. I reached the Crescent, a one-way circular boulevard ringed by some of Vancouver's finest homes. I turned right and punched the gas pedal. The Jag pulled around the corner moments behind me. I gripped the steering wheel as my car leaned into the curve of the road. I quickly glanced into my rear-view.

I had a good half a block on the Jag as I spun the corner onto Osler Street. I screamed past the old-growth Oak trees that lined the street and the wide centre median that ran down Osler. I skipped the stop sign at Mathews and glanced up again to check on the Jag. I'd managed to put a block between us, as I slid around the corner onto Balfour Street. I sped toward the traffic light at Oak and Balfour. My eyes bounced back and forth between my mirror and the road ahead. I had the green light and the intersection was clear of oncoming traffic. The light turned to amber. I glanced up again. The Jaguar had closed the gap and was now only half a block from my tail.

I shot into the intersection as the light turned from yellow to red. My tires fought for traction on the wet pavement, as I made the left onto Oak heading north. A patron leaving the Starbuck's on the corner made a hand gesture in my direction, as my back tires lost their grip on the road and the rear of my car slid toward the line of cars parked on Oak. I was pumped. My heart was racing; I glanced back at the Jag stuck at the red light on Balfour. I turned right into the alley on the other side of Twenty-first. My tires spun in the loose gravel as I raced toward

Laurel Street. I slid to a stop at the end of the alley and the entrance to Douglas Park.

I hesitated for a moment and then decided to turn left. I looked up at my rear-view. All was clear behind me. I swung onto Laurel. I slowed to cross the traffic control speed bumps that guarded the playground at the Douglas Park rec centre. I checked my mirror again. No sign of the Jaguar. I made my way around the traffic island at Twentieth and accelerated. There was still no sign of my tail. I drove through the intersection at Nineteenth. My hands were sweating and I gripped the steering wheel because my very life depended on it.

A long parking lot ran off Laurel to my left, just past Nineteenth. I turned into the lot and headed for the last apartment building in the row. My eyes scanned for an escape route. A row of garbage containers sat in the centre of the parking lot. A small access road led through the complex of buildings and out onto Eighteenth Avenue. I turned the nose of my car toward the trash bins; there was still no sign of the black Jag. I pulled in behind the big blue waste cans. My hand trembled as I cranked my window down. I sucked in deep breaths of cold evening air. The smell of rotting garbage made me gag.

I killed my headlights, cranked up my window, and shut the motor off. I stepped from my car into the rain and the night. I crept to the end of the row of trash bins and peeked around the corner toward Laurel Street. I cursed at myself. I should have gone a few more blocks up Oak before making my turn. I was still within sight of the intersection at Balfour, but panic told me I had to get off the main drag and find a place where I had room to run. Was Joker behind the wheel? Could he have seen me turn into the alley? I made myself a promise never to cuss at a red light again.

All was silent, except for the humming of the mercury vapour streetlights in the parking lot. I cautiously moved through the rows of cars to the corner of the apartment facing onto Laurel. I turned about face. My car was well camouflaged behind the dumpsters. I felt for my keys. I wouldn't have time to fumble if I needed to make a run for it.

I heard a vehicle approaching from the south on Laurel. I crouched down behind a row of shrubs. My eyes darted over the parking area, searching for a place to hide if Joker turned my way. I watched as the black Jag moved slowly up Laurel and past the entrance to the lot. The tinted windows protected the driver from view. As the car disappeared from my sight, I stole up beside the apartment building and peeked around the corner. The driver of the Jag sat at the intersection, deciding whether to continue his hunt to the right, the left, or straight ahead. The smoked-out windows concealed the man behind the wheel, but there was one thing that couldn't be hidden. He paused at the corner long enough for me to get a good look at the license plate number. As he made a right on Eighteenth, heading east, I pulled my pen from my shirt pocket and wrote the tag number on the back of my hand—OEE844.

⌘

I'd sometimes wondered who had first coined the phrase *knocking knees*. If Joker's intention was to put the fear of God into me, he'd certainly managed to accomplish that. I hustled back through the parking lot to my car. I stood next to the dumpster and fumbled with my keys. I chuckled nervously under my breath. Good thing I was wearing my lucky green tie. I'd managed to evade the black Jaguar—possibly even a bullet to the back of my head—and at the same time I had kept the presence of mind to lock the door of my car, I wouldn't want some young hoodlum rifling through my collection of CDs.

I leaned my head back and looked up at the sky. I closed my eyes and let the rain fall on my face. I pursed my lips and sucked in a lungful of cold night air. The clink of a fire escape door opening jarred me back to full alert. My head snapped to the right. An old woman approached the trash containers, a white plastic sack in each of her hands. I opened my car door and slid onto the cold leather seat.

I started my engine and placed my left hand on the wheel. I stared at the license plate number scribbled in ink on the back of my hand. Joker had made his first mistake. Identifying him would be the first step toward putting a name to Mr. Smith. You can't hide from me now, I said to myself.

I shifted into drive and cautiously made my way between the buildings. I eased out of the parking lot and scanned the area for signs of the black Jag. I pulled out onto Eighteenth and headed west toward Oak.

⌘

I was scared. It wasn't the kind of fear that you experience when you run a yellow light in front of a traffic cop. It was different from the adrenaline rush that you get when you open the cupboard under the laundry room sink and a big hairy spider leaps out at you. This was true fear—the kind of instant terror that charges through every cell of your being—this was the fear that comes when you are face to face with the spectre of death.

The tables had been turned. Instead of being the hunter, I was now the hunted. In this jungle of a city, I was the antelope and Joker was the leopard. Terror oozed out of every pore of my body and I had to use both hands to steady my key enough to insert it into the lock on my front door. The rain on my forehead felt especially cold in the crisp March evening air. My hands trembled as I pushed the door open and stepped into the darkness. I held the door ajar and searched the street for signs of the black Jag. My heart seemed to be hammering its way out of my chest. I'd somehow managed to shake the tail, but the possibility was strong that Joker knew where I lived. He'd know that I would seek out the safety of my home. I needed a drink.

I was a creature of habit. I held my favourite glass under the tap and rinsed the remains of last night's Scotch down the drain. I fixed on the water rushing from the faucet. I liked order in my life. You turn on the tap and water comes out. You flip the light switch and the darkness goes away. I missed Sandra.

I opened the freezer door and pulled out the remains of my bag of ice. I stared into the sack. One lonely ice cube, a handful of ice shards, and a whole bunch of snow. I carefully fished out the slivers of ice and dropped them into my glass. I thought about Mr. Smith, and about how the license plate number would lead me to Joker. This information would allow me to go on the offensive. I dragged my fingers through the snow and salvaged the last few chunks of frozen water.

I leaned my weight on the kitchen counter and hung my head. My mind wandered. I was facing a challenge that few of my peers ever would. I'd been given the chance to right a terrible wrong. I'd been chosen to fight an evil that went by the name of Smith. I would have to be strong. Dallas was right. Even though Smith never pulled a trigger himself, he was still a dangerous and lethal force. He used his words to incite an army of people to carry out his dirty deeds. He had drawn innocent people into his web of lies and half-truths and convinced them to kill. The license plate number would eventually lead me to him. Together, Dallas and I would draw him into the open and expose him to the world. People would learn exactly what suffering this man had caused with his lies. They would soon know the truth about Marilyn's death and the assassination of JFK.

The first ring jerked me out of my trance. I looked at the phone. I knew exactly what type of a game Smith and his army were playing. It rang a second time. My heart began to race. Each pulse of the ringer sent a rush of adrenaline through my body. Should I give him the satisfaction of answering? Would he get a charge out of hearing the fear in my voice when I said hello? It rang a third time. After last week's fight, I knew it was far too soon for Sandra to be calling. A fourth ring. I raised my hand toward the phone. I hesitated—a fifth ring. One more ring and the call would go to my answering machine. A sixth ring—and then silence.

Did I do the right thing? Would it have been better to confront the phantom breather and prove to him that I wasn't going to be intimidated? Should I have grabbed the call immediately, and showed Mr. Smith that the game he was playing wasn't going to scare me into abandoning my search for his true identity? Next time I would laugh in his face. I'd muster my courage and, with all the confidence I could gather, I would show him that I was not afraid.

I didn't have long to wait. Within moments of the first call, the phone sounded again. It was time to put a stop to this childishness. My hand jumped at the receiver and the cuff of my arm hit the glass and sent it crashing to the floor. I picked up the handset and placed it to my ear, expecting no more than the sound of heavy breathing. If Mr. Smith thought that he could scare me off with a couple of hang up phone calls, he had another thing coming. Soon I would have the upper hand.

"What exactly do you want?" I yelled into the phone.

"Mr. Hartree?" the voice on the other end of the line asked.

"Who is this?" I demanded.

"I was wondering if you had a couple of minutes to talk about your long-distance provider?"

I felt the skin of my face flame with anger. I pulled the phone from my ear and held it at arm's length. I wanted to climb through the phone line, grab the little bastard by the throat, and shake the living daylights out of him. I held the mouthpiece in front of my face.

"Fuck off!" I screamed and slammed the phone back onto its cradle.

⌘

I dropped to my knees on the ceramic tiles. My treasured piece of crystal was smashed to smithereens, and bits of glass and ice were scattered across my kitchen floor. I stared at the mess. At first glance, you couldn't tell the glass from the ice. Like a story laced with both truth and lies, each piece would have to be carefully examined. On the surface, they both looked the same. Each was clear and wet and shimmered in the light. Only by picking every fragment up individually could I determine the frozen water from the razor sharp crystal. Looking at the mess, I realized that there was only one thing I could resolve as fact—I'd be drinking warm Scotch tonight. Like the articles I'd penned on Ball and McDermott, things weren't always what they seemed.

⌘

The mess in my kitchen was dealt with, and I was coming back to my senses. Fear had taken control for a time, but I was not about to surrender to a black car or a coward on the other end of a phone line. What was I made of? How would the old boys from the newsroom have felt if they knew I was hiding in fear in my kitchen? Would a man like John Kennedy have been afraid to fight? Where would the world be, if brave men didn't stand up to evil men like Mr. Smith? How could I hold my head up in public, if I let Dallas do battle with him alone? How could I look at myself in a mirror, knowing that a man who recruited a secret army with lies and half-truths had sent me scurrying like a frightened child? Where would Chris McDermott be today if a challenge had been mounted and my series of articles had been exposed for what they really were—suggestions of wrongdoing built on a single truth?

There were things in life that were worse than death; one of them was warm Scotch. I would have to be cautious. Mr. Smith had killed many times and he certainly wouldn't hesitate to put one more person in a grave. I had to prove to myself that I was strong enough to face the phantom Smith. I had to know in my heart that when the time came, and it was clear to me exactly who this spinner of lies was, that I'd be strong enough to face him and put an end to him. I wouldn't allow him to send me into hiding. I wouldn't be kept prisoner in my own home. The gas station was only two blocks away; and Joker or no Joker, they had plenty of ice.

# Chapter Thirty-Two

**MY EYES OPENED** and my head jerked forward. I focused and turned to the window. The pale light of dawn was peeking through the black cotton shades in my den. I could see the silhouette of the trees across the street through the semi-transparent curtains. Their branches swayed in the morning breeze. I glanced over at the clock on the fireplace mantel. It was early—just before five. I lifted my feet from the ottoman and placed them on the floor. I leaned forward and rubbed the ache in the back of my neck. The remains of last night's supper sat on the table next to my chair—a half-empty bottle of Scotch, an ice bucket, and a single glass. A puddle of condensation had dried into a ring at the base of the glass. A rumble from my stomach informed me that it was best not to have whiskey for dinner.

I stood and yawned and stretched my arms above my head. I steadied myself and then turned in the direction of the bathroom. I stopped in my tracks. The thought of the previous night's encounter with the phantom Jaguar came accompanied by a surge of adrenaline. I walked to the window and opened the drapes a crack. I peered out onto the street. A drizzle of rain was falling and the wet greyness of the morning made the deserted street seem more depressing. I searched the street in both directions. There was no sign of the Jaguar.

⌘

I leaned on the counter of the bathroom and stared into the mirror. The face that stared back at me was tired and drawn. I studied the bags under my eyes. I could almost see myself aging like the portrait of Dorian Grey. I rubbed my hand over the stubble sprouting from my chin. I thought about my second encounter with the black Jag. I realized that both times I had seen the car near the corner of Sixteenth Avenue and Granville. Joker obviously knew my schedule and my route home.

What could have led him to me? I could understand him tracking Dallas down again, but how could he have learned that the woman and I were talking? I was certain that word of our conversations had not left the boardroom—or was I? Amanda was smart enough to keep her mouth shut. I had to admit, I was more worried about Grant.

I turned on the faucet and splashed my face with cold water. I needed a shower, but I couldn't stand it any longer. First, I had to do something about the sewer-like taste in my mouth. I grabbed my toothbrush and squeezed a line of toothpaste from its tube. I held my toothbrush in my hand and stared into the mirror. A pair of bloodshot eyes stared back. A sense of fear took over my body.

Was it really Joker behind the wheel of the black Jaguar? Perhaps Mr. Smith had recruited a younger version of Dallas. Maybe he'd spun a new web of lies and convinced some poor young person that I had to be dealt with. How could he have learned that Dallas was spilling her guts to me? Someone must have talked—it was the only logical explanation. I stuck the toothbrush into my mouth. Minty fresh—my ass.

⌘

"Good morning," I said.

Dallas wheezed.

"How are you feeling?" I asked.

"The cancer is eating me alive," she replied. "How do you think I feel?"

I hesitated. "I found information on the acoustical tests of the Dallas police recordings," I said.

"And?"

I sifted through the piles on my desk and reorganized my notes. "A Dr. Lawrence Kersta, of Bell Telephone's acoustics and speech research laboratory, analyzed the tape and concluded that there were six non-voiced noises."

"Bell Telephone?"

"That's right," I said. "I couldn't find any record of the FBI or any other government agency doing its own investigation."

"That's odd, don't you think?"

I turned a page in my notebook. "There doesn't appear to be any mention of the recording in the Warren Report either," I said. "And something else is very strange."

"What?" Dallas asked.

"The original tape seems to have vanished from the National Archives."

"How do you know that?"

"It's mentioned in a book I've been reading on the assassination."

"Don't trust writers. Just because you read it in some book, doesn't necessarily make it true."

I let the comment pass. "In 1978," I said, "a Dr. James Barger, of Bolt, Beranek and Newman, converted the sounds into digitized waveforms. He filtered out the sound of the motorcycle's engine and broke the recording down into sequences of impulses."

"Sequences of impulses?"

"Yeah," I said, "a sequence of impulse is a loud noise—like a gunshot—followed by the echoes of that noise. He identified six from the Dallas police recordings."

"So," Dallas said, "you're saying that there were six shots fired at the president?"

"I'm not saying anything yet. I'm getting a little suspicious about the Warren Commission's conclusion that the only shots fired were the three shots from the sixth floor of the School Book Depository."

"*Suspicion always haunts the guilty mind.*"

"*Hamlet?*" I asked.

"You bet," Dallas replied. "I already told you that Crystal fired once."

"Right," I said. "According to Robert Blakey, chief council of the assassination committee, based on Dr. Barger's study he concluded that one impulse originated from the grassy knoll."

"Uh-huh."

"And it was followed less than a second later by another impulse."

"It would be pretty tough for Leon to do that on his own, don't you think?"

"It would be impossible," I said. "Based on the Zapruder film of the assassination, there were 5.6 seconds between the first and the last shot that hit the president."

"How did they establish that?"

"They started the clock at Kennedy's first reaction to being hit—when he grabbed for his throat."

"And?"

"They stopped the clock when the final shot hit the president's head."

"The fatal shot," Dallas said, "from Crystal's rifle."

"Crystal fired the fatal shot?"

"Come on, Hartree," Dallas said, "you've seen the Zapruder film. Kennedy's head was violently thrust backward. Do you really believe that the head shot could have come from the rear?"

"No," I said, "it doesn't seem very likely."

"Let's think about this for a moment," Dallas said. "Put yourself on the sixth floor. You're perched in the window, waiting for the motorcade. The limousine comes into view. You have a few seconds to carefully take aim, and then you fire."

"OK," I said.

"Now you have 5.6 seconds to get off two more shots. You have to pull the bolt on the rifle back, eject the cartridge, load another round, aim and fire, and you have to go through the sequence twice."

"OK," I said again.

"Which shot do you think would be the most accurate, and which shot do you think would be the least?"

I paused. "I would imagine the first shot would be your best."

"Right," Dallas said. "But according to the Warren Commission, the first shot missed entirely; the second shot caused the wounds to both Kennedy's back and neck, as well as all the wounds to Governor Connally; and the third shot struck the president's head."

"It doesn't make sense," I said.

"Of course it doesn't. Can you imagine the state that Leon would have been in? Do you really think he could have calmed himself down enough, after he missed completely with his first shot, to be that accurate with his last one?"

"Probably not," I said.

"Leon bought the rifle from Klein Sporting Goods, a mail order house in Chicago. Guess what he paid for it?"

"How much?" I asked.

"$19.95," Dallas replied, "must have been a fine piece of equipment, huh?"

"For twenty bucks?"

"Yeah," Dallas said, "and that included the cost of the telescopic sight. It was a 6.5 mm Italian-made surplus army rifle—a Mannlicher

Carcano. It was nicknamed the humanitarian rifle by the Italian soldiers."

"The humanitarian rifle?"

"Yeah, because it never killed anyone. Apparently they weren't very good."

"Then how could Leon have—"

"He couldn't have," Dallas interrupted. "The FBI had to put shims under the scope of the rifle before they could test-fire it."

Dallas began to cough. I waited until she caught her breath.

"A historian by the name of Martinez did a documentary on the assassination. He hired a marksman named Yardley. They constructed a reasonably accurate set to match the height of the sixth floor, and the road configuration through Dealey Plaza.

"Go on," I said.

"Yardley was given a duplicate Carcano rifle and was instructed to fire three shots at a cardboard figure in a limousine that was towed down the street in front of him."

"And?" I asked.

"They did a total of seven tests."

"And was this marksman able to hit the target three times within the 5.6 seconds?"

"He was—when the gun decided to work."

"Huh?"

"Out of the twenty-one shots attempted, the Carcano misfired five times."

"Five times!"

"Uh-huh. Almost 25 percent of the time the gun didn't fire. I told you the Carcano wasn't a very reliable weapon."

"But still," I said, "he *was* able to get off three shots within the allotted time."

"He was," Dallas replied, "but don't forget—Leon was no expert marksman."

I leaned an elbow on my desk and propped my head on my hand.

"Have a close look at the acoustics reports. Do you know about the magic bullet theory?"

"No," I said.

"That's your next assignment. You and your cubs need to dig up what you can on the single bullet belief."

"OK," I said, "but first—"

"What?"

"We've got trouble," I said.

"What's wrong?"

"Last night—on my way home . . ."

"My God," Dallas replied, "let me guess—a black Jaguar."

"Right," I said. "It's the second time I've seen it."

"Are you sure it was following you?"

"One hundred percent. There's no doubt about it."

I listened to strained breaths. "Dallas?" I asked.

"I'm here," she said.

"Someone must have talked. It *has* to be Joker behind the wheel of the Jaguar."

"Agreed."

"I got the license plate number. I looked up a cop I know—Freddy Weller—at the police department this morning. He's checking into it for me."

"Are you sure you haven't said anything to anyone about our conversations?"

"Positive," I said.

"Then there are only two other places the leak could have come from."

"I know."

"Talk to Grant and Amanda again."

"It's on the meeting agenda this morning."

"I told you about Crystal. You have to be careful."

"Uh-huh."

"Crystal had a passion for orchids."

"What are you telling me?"

"She told me she received a gift—an orchid packed in a red box. It was left on the doorstep of her apartment. There was no card with it. She had no idea where it came from."

"I don't understand."

"A few days later, Crystal fell to her death from her balcony—twelve floors."

I listened to Dallas fight for each breath.

"Hartree," she said, "who do you think sent Crystal that orchid?"

"Mr. Smith?" I asked.

"And why?"

"Maybe it was a final gift—his way of saying goodbye."

"Look after yourself, Hartree. I'll talk to you tomorrow."

"Dallas," I said after a moment's pause, "there's something else."

Silence.

"Are you there?"

"Yes."

"Someone's been calling my house. When I answer the phone, they just hang up."

More silence.

"Did you hear me?"

"I was just thinking about Crystal."

"What about Crystal?"

"It was a long time ago now. I'll have to check my journal."

"For what?" I asked.

"Hang up phone calls, Crystal starting getting them too, a few days before she received the orchid."

# Chapter Thirty-Three

I PULLED MY chair away from the meeting room table and rested my foot on the seat.

"I've found some information on a study done on the Dictaphone recordings of the assassination," I said. "The study was by a Dr. Barger, with a company called Bolt, Beraneck and Newman."

The woman advanced a page of her notebook. "Right," she said. "I found that as well. Plus, I've taken it a step further."

I turned to her.

"Dr. Barger's findings were evaluated by a team from the computer science department of Queen's University in New York, a Professor Mark Weiss, and his associate, a Mr. Ernest Aschkenasy. They worked on sonar-related programs—you know—echo location—for the military. They testified before the Senate investigation committee on the assassination in 1978. I have the transcript."

"Go on," I said.

Amanda turned another page of her notebook. "They were asked to perform a refined analysis on the data relating to the presumed shot from the grassy knoll."

"And what did they find?"

"I'll read it to you," she said. *"It is our conclusion that as a result of very careful analysis, it appears that with a probability of 95 percent or better, there was indeed a shot fired from the grassy knoll."*

I leaned forward and rested my elbow on my knee. "Crystal's shot," I said.

Amanda nodded.

"The impulse patterns had to fit a certain set of criteria before they were considered. First, they had to have occurred during the 5.6-second time period. Next, the shape of the impulse had to resemble the shape of the impulse patterns produced when the sound of a gunshot was recorded through a radio system similar to the one used by the Dallas police. Then, the amplitudes of the impulse patterns had to be roughly the same as well." She turned to Grant. "All six patterns passed the screening process."

Grant leaned his head to one side and tapped his temple with his finger. "Why wasn't the tape recording analyzed back in 1963?"

I shrugged my shoulders. "I don't know," I said. "Maybe they didn't have the technology."

"Not according to Professor Weiss," Amanda said. "Chairman Stokes asked him that same question."

"And?"

"He told the committee that it basically boiled down to high school physics and geometry. That the principles of sound speed and echoes have not changed and that they never will. They are based on everlasting and relatively simple basic mathematics. All Weiss and his team used were a surveyor's map, a ruler, and a piece of string."

Grant scratched his head. "Do you think the fifth column could have had some influence on the Warren Commission? Do you think that maybe that's the reason they never had the tape analyzed?"

"It's a possibility," I said.

"We have to look at the facts," Amanda said. "Even though the sounds and echoes would travel at a constant speed, the location of the microphone would be a critical factor. What if the police motorcycle wasn't where they thought it was? Wouldn't that mean that the shot might not have come from the grassy knoll?"

"True," I said, "but the fact of the matter is that there were six impulses—not three."

"And," Grant said, "I think it's fairly obvious from the Zapruder film that the final shot didn't come from behind the motorcade."

"When the acoustical evidence was synchronized with the film, the shot from the grassy knoll aligns with the shot that hit Kennedy's head."

"My God," Grant said, "then what Dallas is telling us is true."

"Right," I said. "Crystal fired the fatal shot—not Oswald."

Amanda looked up. "Then Oswald *was* just a patsy," she said.

I turned to her. "There's something about the whole Oswald thing that really bothers me," I said.

"What?" Grant asked.

"The bullets," I replied. "There were three spent cartridges on the floor next to the sixth-floor window and one round still in the magazine of the rifle."

Grant's eyes looked into mine for an answer. "I don't think I understand what you're getting at."

"Four bullets," I said. "That's all he had."

Grant was obviously still confused.

"You're right," Amanda said. "That doesn't sound logical."

I turned to her. "Wacko or not," I said, "November 22nd was the most important day in Oswald's life. Don't you think he would come a little better prepared?"

Amanda nodded her head.

"The police and the FBI went through everything Oswald owned after his arrest. I'm sure they probably even analyzed the lint from the pockets of his jeans, but they never found a box of 6.5 mm ammunition. Doesn't that seem strange to you?"

"It does," Grant said.

"If he was acting alone, I'm sure he would have brought more than just four rounds. Nobody would be that confident."

Amanda smiled and, with irony in her voice, said, "Not necessarily. The bullets that he did use had magical powers."

I glared at her. This was no time to be cracking jokes.

"Have you read anything on the single bullet hypothesis?" she asked.

"No," I said, "Dallas mentioned it in our last conversation. She called it the magic bullet theory."

"It's amazing," Amanda said. She turned through the pages of her notebook. "According to the Warren Report, the second shot from Oswald's rifle struck the president in the upper right area of his back."

I pulled my chair back and sat.

"Then," Amanda continued, "it traveled up through his body and exited his throat."

"How could that be?" I asked. "Bullets aren't known for changing direction like that."

"There's more. When it left Kennedy's throat, it allegedly struck Governor Connally in the back just below his right armpit."

I raised an eyebrow.

"Then it changed direction again. They say the bullet went through Connally's chest cavity, exited just below his right nipple, and then it shattered the radius bone of his right wrist and ended up in his thigh."

"Impossible," I said. "How many times would that bullet have had to change directions to do all that?"

"That's not even the best part," Amanda said. "The truly magical properties of Oswald's alleged bullet were discovered later at Parkland Hospital."

"Where they took the president and Governor Connally?"

"Yeah," Amanda said, "it's interesting. Next to bone, skin causes the most damage to a bullet's exterior. Now remember, this bullet not only went through Connally's rib cage and shattered his wrist, but it also went through seven layers of skin."

"And?" I asked.

"It was found lying on a stretcher at Parkland Hospital, in virtually pristine condition."

"Lying on a stretcher?"

"Yup," Amanda replied, "Warren Commission exhibit 399. Apparently it just fell out of Governor Connally's leg."

I leaned back in my chair and stared at the woman. If I didn't know how carefully she did her research, I'd have sworn she had concocted the whole story.

"I can't believe that," I said. "Even if by some stroke of luck—"

"Magic," Amanda interrupted.

"OK," I said, "even if it was magic, a bullet couldn't travel through all that flesh and bone and still come out intact."

"Do you think it was planted?" Grant asked.

I turned to him. "I'll tell you what I don't think," I said. "I don't think one bullet could have caused all those wounds and survived."

Amanda leaned onto the table. "The weight of the fragments, recovered from Governor Connally's wrist, exceeded what was lost by the magic bullet found at the hospital."

"Mr. Smith," Grant said. "He must have planted the bullet."

"It sure looks that way," I said.

# Chapter Thirty-Four

I PUSHED BACK from my desk, spun around in my swivel chair, and leaned back and rested my elbows on the armrests. "How's it goin', Freddy?" I asked.

Fred nodded and answered my question with a roll of his eyes. He pulled Amanda's chair away from her desk and sat.

"You know," I said, "the talk among your fellow cops is that you've got some sort of arrangement with God and that he charges you by the word. Would it kill you to say good morning or something?"

Fred cocked his head slightly. "Good morning," he said. "Feel better? Do you need a hug, too?"

"Nope," I replied. "I just wanted to make sure you could still talk."

"Nothing," he said.

"Huh?"

"There's nothing on your license plate. It doesn't exist."

I stared at the floor.

"Suppose you tell me what you're up to?"

I kept my gaze to the ground. "I'm not up to anything," I mumbled.

"Look at me when you talk."

I glanced up. "Nothing's going on," I repeated.

Fred stood up from his chair. "How long have I known you, Hartree?"

I leaned my weight on my elbows and hunched forward. "Let's see," I said, "I'm thinking the early eighties. We met at the Press Club. You'd just earned your gold shield and a group of us spent the night trying to figure out who'd shot J.R. Ewing."

"Right," Fred replied, "it was May of 1980. Mount St. Helens had just erupted again."

"I remember," I said.

"And in all that time, have you ever told the truth?"

I tilted my head back and fired a glare his way. "I always tell the truth," I said.

Fred rested his butt on the edge of Amanda's desk and folded his arms across his chest. "You know, Hartree, I've spent the last twenty-five odd years asking questions, first in the military and now in the police force. I was in the intelligence corps, you know."

I nodded.

"After a while, you develop a sense. A little bell goes off in the back of my head when someone's not being honest with me."

"Maybe you should go see a doctor. There might be a pill for that."

"That little bell, it starts going off the second I lay eyes on you. You don't even have to open your mouth."

"Did you just come up here to insult me?" I asked.

No," Fred replied. "I've never liked you, Hartree. I just wanted to find out whose bedroom window you've been peeking into this week."

"Look," I said, "there's nothing sinister about this. I'm trying to chase down a story, and I was given that license plate number by a fairly reliable source—that's all."

Fred cupped his ears with his hands. "Christ," he said, "can't you hear that? It sounds like the bells at St. Mary's cathedral."

"Maybe it just means recess is over and you should get out of here and go find some criminals to harass."

"You're right. I haven't pistol-whipped anyone in close to three weeks. Why don't you just tell me what you're working on so that I can get back out there and beat up on a few low-lifes."

I aimed my stare over Freddy's left shoulder. "I told you," I said again, "it's nothing."

"You're a marvel of biological science, Hartree."

"Huh?"

"A cross between a vulture and a snake."

I looked up at him. "That's a nice thing to say to someone."

"You're right. It's not really fair to the vultures and the snakes of this world, is it? Who's Mr. Smith?"

I couldn't believe what had just come out of Freddy's mouth. I tried not to show a reaction. "I don't know what you're talking about."

"You're full of shit, Hartree. I know you're looking for a man named Smith." He reached into his back pocket, pulled out a notebook, and flipped it open. "And an ex-cop named Clemmons," he added.

"Are you deaf?" I said. "I don't know what you're talking about."

Freddy waved his finger in my face and smiled. "You're lying to me, Hartree," he said.

"Is that bell going off again?"

"No," Fred replied. "Sometimes I don't need the bell. I saw your lips move. That's always been a pretty good indication that you're not telling the truth."

I looked into Freddy's eyes. There didn't seem to be much sense in keeping the tail end of the cat in the bag. "OK," I said, "you're right. I am looking for a man called Smith."

Fred leaned back on Amanda's desk. "That's better," he said.

"How did you find out?"

"That little dweeb you've got working for you. What's his name again?"

"Shaw," I said, "Grant Shaw."

"He was nosing around the station looking for information on this cop named Clemmons. He was strutting around like he knew the winning numbers to next week's lottery. I knew he was packing some kind of a secret. I just couldn't resist doing a little interrogating."

"What did you do? Take him downstairs and beat him with one of those rubber hoses?"

"No," Fred replied, "I didn't need to be that extreme. I just gave him a doughnut and a cup of coffee."

"Police station coffee?" I asked. "No wonder he talked."

"A little coffee and a little massaging of his very large ego was all it took. That kid really thinks highly of himself, doesn't he?"

"Yeah," I said, "he does."

"Teaching him all your dirty tricks, are you?"

I looked down at my shoes.

"Teaching him how to lie without lying and how to hang a person by telling only the parts of the truth that you want the public to hear."

I looked up.

"Alan Ball and I have known each other a lot of years," Weller said, "back to the days when we were in the military together. I know you lied to your readers about him and McDermott."

"Ball was in the army?"

"I spent a lot of time south of the border. We worked together a number of times—before he left the army and emigrated to Canada."

I raised an eyebrow.

"You didn't know Alan was a Yank?"

"No," I said, "I didn't."

"So answer my question. Who's Mr. Smith?"

I paused for a moment and looked over the stacks of file folders on my desk. I turned to Fred. "I need your word that you won't talk to anyone else about this."

Fred nodded, preserving what was left of his quota of words for the day.

"I don't have a lot of answers at this point," I said. "Mr. Smith may be a man that ordered a series of murders."

Fred stood. "Murders?" he asked.

"Yeah," I said, "very high-profile murders."

"You'd better start talking to me."

"They happened over forty years ago," I said. "Not here. They happened in the United States."

"And how did you stumble across this?"

"One of the killers he recruited. She lives here in Vancouver."

"She?" he asked.

I nodded my head. "She's dying," I said. "She only has a short time left, and she wants to tell her story before she goes."

"We'll have to contact the authorities in the States. Where did these murders take place?"

"It's not that simple," I said. "I told you—these were very high-profile murders. I've only been given a few names so far. She said the killings went on for years. I can only guess how many victims there were."

"Where is this woman? I'll need to talk to her myself."

I shrugged my shoulders. "I don't know," I said. "All of our conversations have been by telephone."

Freddy leaned toward me and raised a finger.

"It's the truth," I said. "She's afraid Mr. Smith will find out we've been talking. She wouldn't be the first one of the killers who was silenced by the son of a bitch."

"She wouldn't?"

"No," I said, "her partner—a woman named Crystal—was killed for talking too much."

"In Vancouver?"

"I don't know," I said. "There were others that were silenced as well. One was in Dallas, Texas."

"Then we should contact the Dallas police."

"No," I said. "It's too soon, I need more answers first."

"Do you know the name of the person that was murdered in Dallas?"

The time for truth was over. "No," I said. Fred looked into my eyes. I though for a split second that I'd heard a tiny bell go off.

"What about this mysterious black Jaguar?" he asked. "Who gave you the plate number?"

I forked two fingers at my face. "I saw it myself," I said. "He was following me. And it wasn't the first time."

"Better think about a new pair of glasses. There's no such license plate number."

I stared over Fred's shoulder again. I thought back to my last encounter with the dark coloured Jaguar. The feeling of terror came thundering back. I remembered the waves of panic that had overcome me that night. There was only one logical explanation. I was scared half to death. I must have made a mistake reading the plate.

"Could you be wrong about the number?" Weller asked.

"I was scared. It was dark."

"But you've seen the car more than once."

"Yeah, it's followed me home a couple of times."

"This man knows where you live?"

I stared at the floor.

"Are you being careful, Hartree? Do you have any friends that you could stay with?"

I looked up.

"Sorry," Freddy said, "that was a stupid question."

"There's a nice little hotel up on Broadway—the Chelsea Arms—I stayed there for a few days while Sandra moved her things out. They have a nice little suite on the tenth floor."

"Maybe you should call them and see if they have a weekly rate."

# Chapter Thirty-Five

THE CLOCK ON the coffeemaker read 8:45.

"I need to speak to you before Grant gets here," I said.

Amanda looked at her watch. "He'll be at least twenty minutes," she said. "What's on your mind?"

I slumped down into my chair and let out a sigh. "We've got trouble," I said. "There's been a leak."

Amanda's eyes shifted away.

"Freddy Weller dropped in to see me last night. He asked me who Mr. Smith was."

Amanda looked up.

"Someone's been talking," I said, "and I know for a fact that it's Grant."

Amanda avoided my eyes.

"A car's been following me," I said, "the same car that's been staked out in front of Dallas's house."

"I should have told you," Amanda said. "I'm sorry."

"Told me what?"

"Grant," she replied. "I didn't think it would go this far. I know he's said things to people about Dallas."

"What people?" I asked.

Amanda shrugged her shoulders. "His sister," she said, "and his mother, too, I think."

"Jesus Christ," I groaned. "Wasn't he listening? Doesn't he know he could get us all killed? What if they told even more people about this?"

"It's a game to him. I don't think he honestly believes that anything could really happen to us."

"Well, the game's over," I said, "and Grant's out. I'm cancelling this morning's meeting. I want you to start digging up everything you can on the single bullet theory. I have to get back to my desk. When that prick decides to show his face, you tell him I want a few words with him."

⌘

"I've found our leak," I said.

Dallas cleared her throat.

"It was that son of a bitch, Grant."

"What are you going to do with him?" she asked.

"I don't know," I said. "Maybe I'll hand off his home address to the driver of that black Jaguar."

"Seriously, Hartree," Dallas replied, "you can't let this go. It's crucial. You need to do some damage control."

"Don't worry. I'll deal with him."

"I want you to look at the whole situation. I want you to think about the lies and the cover-ups regarding both Marilyn's murder and the assassination of John Kennedy. I want you to be honest with yourself. Who do you think would have the power to kill a president, hang the entire blame on an insignificant player like Leon, and manage to keep a lid on the whole mess for over forty years?"

"The CIA?"

"You're not as dumb as I thought you were. And what would be the safest way for the CIA to carry out an operation of this magnitude on their home turf?"

"A fifth column?" I asked. "A splinter group from within the intelligence community?"

"And Mr. Smith—are you getting an idea of who he could be now?"

"A rogue agent?"

"I told you. Mr. Smith is a power—a force personified. And he's here in Vancouver right now."

"What would bring him to Vancouver?"

"He's been after me for some time now. He almost got me once, but I managed to slip past him at the last minute."

"My God!"

"I didn't even realize that I had let my guard down. I made a simple mistake. I exposed a weakness, and that was all it took for Mr. Smith to come gunning for me."

"He tried to kill you?"

"He's relentless. Once he's made up his mind to destroy a person, he won't allow anything to stand in his way."

"Grant," I said. "I should have known this was too big a secret for him to keep."

"You have to deal with him."

"I will," I said.

"He may have signed our death warrants, you know."

I felt a shiver run up my spine.

"I told you," Dallas continued, "the killings lasted for years. The count may be more than fifty."

"Fifty!" I exclaimed.

"Or more," Dallas replied, "and I'm not even including Leon and Crystal."

"This is unbelievable," I said.

"There's even a United States congressman on the list."

"No!" I said.

"Hale Boggs—he represented Louisiana, I think. He was one of the seven members of the Warren Commission."

"Mr. Smith had him killed?"

"He was travelling; the plane he was on disappeared—without a trace. Check it out."

"I will."

"You see, Hartree, nobody's really safe from the Mr. Smiths in this world."

"A movie star, a congressman—even a president."

"How tough do you think it would be to silence another reporter?"

I swallowed hard. *"Another* reporter?" I asked.

"You heard me. You wouldn't be the first—or the second—or the third. Be careful, Hartree. He's got *you* in his sights, now."

"What do you think I should do?"

"He's stalking you—he's lining you up for the kill. That's how it all starts with him. He'll find out as much as he can about you; he'll look for a weakness and, when he finds one, he'll strike."

"What can I do to stop him?"

Dallas laughed. "How could you ask such a stupid question, Hartree? Why do you think I've spent the last days of my life leading you down this path? The only way to stop him is to understand completely how he works, and then show the world what a spineless coward he really is."

"But you stopped him."

"I delayed him," she replied, "that's all. You can't just hold up your hand and stop Mr. Smith. He's like death and taxes—they are inevitable."

"But you said that you managed to get away from him at the last second."

"I got a reprieve from my execution—that's all. Mr. Smith has already destroyed my life; he just hasn't managed to end it yet. But he will. If he's not able to kill me, at the very least he'll have stopped me from living any kind of a meaningful life until the cancer eats me up."

"Again," I asked, "what do you think I should do?"

"Try your best to hide until we're ready to execute the death blow. This whole Dallas charade has kept me safe from him for longer than I expected. Now that Grant's started blabbing—well, who knows what he's told people about me."

"But," I said, "Grant doesn't really know anything about you—none of us do."

"Fact," she replied.

"That bothers me," I said. "I can't go public with a story this big, unless I know all there is to know about my source. I'll get torn to shreds if I can't prove that you're more than just a voice on the other end of my telephone line."

"I know that. Don't worry—it's handled."

"What's handled?" I asked.

"My true identity. Do you think I don't know how important it is for you to be able to prove to yourself and to the world—exactly who I am?"

"As long as you're prepared to tell me at some point."

"After I'm gone. Trust me, once I'm dead you'll know who I am, and more importantly, you'll know who Mr. Smith is."

"OK."

"I'll give you a clue."

"A clue?" I asked.

"To *my* identity," Dallas replied.

"OK."

"No one must know. You have to swear you won't repeat this to anyone."

My vicious streak surfaced briefly. "Not even Grant?" I asked.

"You're a poor excuse for a human being," Dallas said. "You always have been, and you most likely always will be."

I kept my mouth shut.

"I assume you've been reading up on the House Committee investigation into the Kennedy assassination?"

"Everything I can get my hands on."

"Good," Dallas said. "Go over your notes. My real name will probably be in there somewhere."

"It will?"

"More than likely," she said. "It came up briefly in the committee's hearings in 1976—just before I came to Canada."

"The committee was on to you? Is that why you fled the country?"

Dallas let out a breath. "It was only a few days after Crystal's murder," she said. "For years, Leon had been referred to as a lone nut. By the time 1976 rolled around, too many people had come forward with stories and too much evidence had been uncovered about an additional shot fired from the grassy knoll. All of a sudden the talk shifted to two nuts. Crystal wasn't fond of being called a nut. I think that's why she started to talk."

"I remember," I said. "There were people that testified that they either saw a puff of smoke, or that they actually saw the shooter behind the stockade fence on the grassy knoll."

"Poor Mr. Bowers. He was so young."

"Who?" I asked.

"Bowers," she said, "Lee Bowers."

"And who's he?" I asked.

"Who *was* he, you mean."

"All right then."

"He was working in the railroad control tower the day the president was killed. The tower is behind the grassy knoll."

"And?" I asked.

"He saw us. Mr. Smith was furious."

"He saw you?"

"Crystal, Joker, and I," Dallas replied. "He tried to offer his testimony to the Warren Commission."

"What happened?"

"What do you think happened?" she asked.

"You're kidding."

"No. Mr. Smith arranged it. Bowers' time on the witness stand was cut short before he could tell his whole story to the Warren Commissioners. He didn't live long enough after that to convince the world that he'd seen Crystal fire the fatal shot."

"Mr. Smith had him erased?"

"He died when he was forty-one years old, in a single-car accident in some remote part of Texas. The medical examiner said he was under the influence of some sort of a shock-inducing drug at the time."

"My God."

"Hartree?"

"Yeah?"

"Who do you think kills like that?"

"The CIA?"

"You said it, not me. Doesn't it remind you, just a little bit, of the way Marilyn died? Bowers was only one of the people connected in some way to the assassination who died mysteriously. The Senate committee took it very seriously."

"That's when your name came up?"

"And that's when Mr. Smith decided that I was a liability, too. He had already dealt with Crystal, and he had to make sure that I wouldn't start talking as well. It wasn't the first time one of the cells failed in their mission. I remember it like it was yesterday. The car seemed like it was doing eighty miles an hour when they threw me out."

"When they what?"

"You heard me. They left me for dead on the side of the highway. I'm surprised they tried it again after the first woman lived through it."

"The first woman?"

"Her name was Rose Cherami."

"Mr. Smith had her thrown from a moving car, too?"

"He did his best to make as many of the deaths as he could look accidental. I'm not really sure who could fall out of a speeding car by accident, but I guess Mr. Smith thought differently. Rose survived the fall too, but she wasn't as lucky as I was. Mr. Smith managed to get her in the end. How did the police make out with the plate number off the Jag?"

"They didn't. Fred Weller dropped by last night. There's no such plate number—it doesn't exist."

"Jesus, Hartree, how could you be that stupid? You have the opportunity handed to you that would put us on the offensive, and you get the plate number wrong?"

"I've been thinking. I was scared, but I'm not stupid. I can't see how I could have made a mistake. The car was sitting right in front of me."

A gasp for breath.

"What?" I asked.

"What if you weren't mistaken?"

"Huh?"

"What if this cop is lying to you? How well do you know this guy?"

"Not well at all. We met back in the early eighties. We've shared information the odd time, but only when the situation forced us to. We've never really liked one another."

"Mr. Smith doesn't know borders. There's no reason why he couldn't be recruiting in Canada, too."

"Jesus," I said. "Weller spent a lot of time in the States during his stint in the army. He was CIC."

"Canadian Intelligence Corps?"

"Right," I said, "he was a spook."

"Put this guy under a microscope, Hartree. He's a man you need to know more about."

My attention was drawn away from the woman on the other end of the phone. I watched Grant zigzag through the cubicles in the newsroom.

"I have to go," I said. "My young friend Grant has just arrived."

# CHAPTER THIRTY-SIX

AMANDA DROPPED A box of pastries next to the coffeemaker and poured a dose of caffeine into her mug. "Have something to eat. I don't imagine you had any breakfast this morning."

"Thanks," I said and reached into the carton. "What have you managed to come up with on the single bullet theory?"

She leaned back on the counter top and took a nibble of her Danish. "Plenty," she said. "We know that the Warren Commission came to the conclusion that Lee Harvey Oswald fired three shots at the motorcade."

I dragged a chair from the conference room table and sat. "Correct," I said.

"And we know that one bullet missed entirely."

I nodded my head and took a bite of my doughnut.

"A man by the name of James Tague was struck by debris when the stray bullet hit a concrete curb."

"Go on," I said.

"So if three shots were fired—and one missed completely—then all the wounds to both President Kennedy and Governor Connally had to have been caused by two rounds."

"If Oswald was the only shooter."

"Analysis of the Zapruder film tells us that Kennedy was already clutching his throat when he came back into view from behind a highway sign."

"Fact," I said. "He had obviously been hit by the first bullet."

Amanda picked up a napkin and dabbed at a trace of sugar on her lips. "But Governor Connally didn't show a reaction until a number of frames later," she said as she took the seat across from me.

"Right," I said. "That concurs with what I've learned as well. In his testimony to the Warren Commission, even Connally himself was certain that he was not struck by the first bullet that hit the president, the one that supposedly exited from his throat."

"I'm having a real problem with the commission's summation that Oswald acted alone. They had three expert marksmen try and recreate the task of getting off three shots from the Carcano rifle in 5.6 seconds."

"And?" I asked.

"Only one out of the three managed to do it, and they weren't firing at a moving target."

"Interesting," I said. "And according to Oswald's military records, he was far from being an expert marksman."

"Right. He was second rate—at best."

"There was a study done on the Zapruder film. At the speed the camera was running, 1/18th of a second elapsed between each frame. Based on Connally's reactions, they came to the conclusion that he was hit between half a second and one and a half seconds after the president."

Amanda looked up at me. "Too late to be from the same bullet, and far too soon to be from a second bullet fired from the same gun."

"Then there had to be more than one shooter."

"Dallas said there were three—a primary and two backups."

I nodded. "I believe her," I said.

"I've been thinking about what you said—about Oswald only having four bullets. That just doesn't make any sense."

"No," I replied, "it doesn't. I've been doing some more digging on the whole bullet thing. It just gets better by the second."

"What do you mean?"

"OK," I said and advanced a few pages of my notebook. "Figure this out. Oswald has four bullets—right? According to the Warren Report, they were manufactured by the Western Cartridge Company of East Alton, Illinois. Do you know what a full metal jacket is?"

"No."

"A full metal jacketed bullet is a bullet that's entirely encased in a hard shell—usually copper. It was agreed at the Geneva Convention that all military ammunition would be full metal jacketed."

"OK."

"A bullet with a full metal jacket doesn't disintegrate when it enters flesh. It does far less damage to a human body than a soft jacketed or a hollow point bullet. They tend to almost explode into a shower of lead fragments when they hit their targets."

"And?"

"They're called frangible—or exploding—bullets. They do a tremendous amount of damage."

Amanda tapped her lip with her pen.

"Oswald," I continued, "appears to have had fully jacketed bullets. We know that from the round left in the Carcano's magazine and from the pristine bullet recovered at Parkland Hospital."

"I see."

"Kennedy's head appears to have been hit with a frangible bullet. You can tell by the Zapruder film. His head virtually blew apart on impact of the fatal round."

"You're right," Amanda said. "I see your point. It's odd enough that Oswald would only have four rounds. Why would he have a mixture of frangible and metal jacketed bullets as well?"

"Right," I said. "If Governor Connally had been struck by a soft jacketed or a hollow point bullet, there's no way he would have survived his wounds. If Oswald was bent enough to use one frangible bullet on the president, why not all four?"

"Dallas told us that Crystal only fired once."

"Right," I said. "Think about it. If you were going to kill a president, what would your choice be? Three shots fired from the sixth floor of a building where your view is blocked by road signs and trees? Or a straight, level, unobstructed shot from behind the fence on the grassy knoll?"

"It was only a hundred yards or so."

"Your Aunt Gertrude could have hit the president from there with a wadded up dishrag."

"And a frangible bullet would pretty much guarantee that one shot would do the job."

"I was thinking the same thing."

"What about Grant?" Amanda asked. "How did you handle that little mess?"

"We won't be seeing him for a while. We'll call it a medical leave."

"A medical leave?"

"Yeah," I said, "he was making me sick."

"So it's just you and me now?"

I nodded again.

"What do you need me to do?"

"Well," I said, "the first thing I need you to do is to start watching your back. Grant has obviously said enough things to enough people to put us all in danger. Watch out for a black

Jaguar. I've spotted it following me a couple of times, and Dallas has seen it more than once as well."

"I'll be careful."

"Then I need you to start looking into some names."

"Some names?"

"Dallas gave me some names of people Mr. Smith had erased."

Amanda turned to a fresh page of her notebook.

"Lee Bowers," I said. "You can start with him."

Amanda scribbled the name into her book.

"Then you can see if you can find anything out about a woman named Rose Cherami."

Amanda added the woman's name to her list.

"Next," I said, "look into the disappearance of Congressman Hale Boggs."

"Hale Boggs?"

"Right." I nodded at her. "I thought you'd recognize his name—he was one of the seven members of the Warren Commission."

I leaned across the table and looked into Amanda's eyes. "And finally, I want you to keep your eyes peeled for the names of any reporters."

"Reporters?"

"Yeah," I said, "Dallas figures that Mr. Smith has me in his sights. She asked me whether I thought he'd have any problems ordering the death of *another* reporter."

"Good lord."

"As you're doing your research, keep your eyes open for the names of any reporters who were either killed, or who maybe vanished mysteriously."

"I'm on it."

⌘

I jumped for the phone and grabbed it before the second ring. "Dallas?" I asked.

"You seem a little impatient today."

"I've been waiting for your call. I need verification on the bullet Crystal fired at the president."

"OK."

"It was a frangible bullet—an exploding bullet—right?"

"I know what a frangible bullet is."

"Then verify it for me. Is that the type of round Crystal fired?"

"Ask yourself this, Hartree: If you were Mr. Smith, and you were out to kill the president, what kind of ammunition would you use?"

I leaned back in my chair. "I'd use the deadliest ammunition possible," I said.

"Then you've answered your own question, haven't you?"

"What about Oswald?" I asked. "Why would he use metal jacketed rounds?"

Dallas paused. "I've told you before, Hartree. Leon was set up to take the fall. His only true assignment was to be arrested, and to take a bullet in the gut before he could prove his innocence. He wasn't exactly a crack shot. He blew his first assassination attempt as well."

"His first attempt?"

"One of the key people in the fifth column was getting a little too vocal. He was drawing too much attention to the group. Mr. Smith ordered Leon to kill him."

"And he missed?"

"I just told you that Leon wasn't a very good shot. I'm not so sure that Mr. Smith counted on him hitting anything from the sixth floor of the Schoolbook Depository. That's why he had three shooters on the job that day. Leon was simply recruited to take the blame."

"How could he have had that much control over Oswald?"

"Haven't you been listening? How many times have I told you how strong this power called Smith is?"

"I've got Amanda looking into Bowers, Cherami, and Hale Boggs."

"Good."

"I've also told her to keep her eyes open for the names of any reporters who died or disappeared while they were investigating the assassination."

"Good. I have to tell you, Hartree, you've done well."

"It hasn't been easy."

"You need to take a night off. What's your poison?"

"Scotch," I said, "the older the better."

"You should put your feet up tonight and have a couple of belts."

"I can't," I said. "I need to find the names of those reporters."

"Trust me," Dallas replied, "it won't be hard. Look for a woman. She'll be the easiest to locate."

"A woman?" I asked.

"She was a nationally known columnist and TV personality. She was at Jack Ruby's trial in November of 1965. She told a friend she was going to blow the lid off the assassination cover-up. She was found dead a few days later."

"Jesus Christ!"

"You need to be extra careful, Hartree. I've made arrangements to stay at a hotel until we can put a permanent end to Mr. Smith's reign of terror. You might want to give some thought to doing the same."

"Done," I said. "I'm moving into the Chelsea Arms up on Broadway tonight."

"Good. Your next assignment will be to look at Leon, and his connection to the whole assassination plot."

"OK."

"What do you know about Lee Harvey Oswald?"

"Just what the history books tell us," I said. "After he killed the president, he left the School Book Depository and was arrested later that day in a movie theatre."

"Right. That was after he killed the police officer."

"I remember," I said. "He shot a cop on his way to the theatre."

"The officer's name was J. D. Tippet."

I scribbled the name on my pad.

"I have to sit down and think," Dallas said. "I'll need to go through my journal as well. I'll give you more information on Leon the next time I call."

I hung up the phone. The volume of cassettes was growing. I dropped tape #18 into my drawer with the rest.

# CHAPTER THIRTY-SEVEN

AMANDA STOOD UP from the meeting table, stretched her arms and arched her back. "I'm beat," she said. "I was up half the night doing research on the names you gave me yesterday."

"What did you find?" I asked.

"Dorothy Kilgallen," she replied, "she was one of the reporters Dallas was talking about."

I leaned back in my chair and stared up at the ceiling. "That name rings a bell," I said.

"Did you ever watch *What's My Line* on TV?"

"I did," I said. "I used to watch that with my mother on Sunday nights. It was one of her favourite shows."

"Dorothy Kilgallen was one of the panellists."

"I remember."

"She also wrote a nationally syndicated newspaper column. She was granted an interview with Jack Ruby during his trial. It looks like she was the only reporter that was ever given the opportunity to talk to Ruby alone."

"And?"

"She apparently told a friend that she had uncovered some information that was going to open some new doors on the assassination. She was found dead a few days later. Her death was ruled a suicide."

"Bullshit," I muttered. "Can you imagine a reporter latching onto a story like that and then killing herself before she could bask in the glory?"

"Not a chance," Amanda replied. "A story like that would come around once in your life—if you were lucky."

"Find out everything you can about her."

"Same time tomorrow?"

"Nine, sharp. Now you get to work on Dorothy Kilgallen."

⌘

"Good morning," Dallas said.

"It's a great morning," I replied. "Everything is falling into place."

"And how's your hotel?"

"It's fine," I said. "It's a little noisy. I'm on the tenth floor right across from the elevator doors and the ice machine, but I actually managed to close my eyes for a few minutes last night."

"I've put some information together for you."

"On Oswald?"

"Yes. I spent a few hours yesterday afternoon going through my journal."

"What have you got for me?" I asked.

"The Warren Commission established the location of the window on the sixth floor where Leon allegedly fired at the president."

"Fact," I said. "That's where they found the three spent cartridges."

"And the police found Leon's rifle hidden behind a stack of boxes two hundred feet from the window."

"Fact," I said.

"A motorcycle cop, by the name of Marian Baker, entered the School Book Depository immediately after the shots were fired. He located the building's manager, and together they began to search the warehouse."

"OK," I said.

"They found Leon in the lunchroom on the second floor drinking a Coke."

"They did?"

"The cop swore it was no more than a minute and a half after the shots were fired that he confronted Leon. He actually held him at gunpoint until the building manager verified that Leon was an employee."

"Drinking a Coke?" I asked.

"Yes," Dallas replied. "The whole city was reacting to the shooting and Lee was sitting alone in the lunchroom drinking a soda."

"That's a little odd."

"Think about it," Dallas said. "The cop claimed that Leon was not out of breath and that he seemed calm and collected."

"After shooting the president?"

"Right. Figure it out. Leon had no more than ninety seconds to walk two hundred feet to the spot where he hid the rifle, climb down four flights of stairs, and buy himself a Coke from the vending machine on the second floor."

"And he wasn't out of breath at all?"

"Not according to the cop or the building manager. He didn't show any signs of being nervous or agitated either."

"That's hard to believe."

"He was seen leaving the building a few minutes after that and he arrived at his rooming house a half an hour later. He left the boarding house and walked to the corner of Tenth Avenue and Patton Street. That took roughly another fifteen minutes. That's where he shot and killed Officer Tippet."

"There were witnesses that saw him shoot the cop."

"Right," Dallas said. "The police found a woman that claimed to have seen Leon walking eastbound on Tenth Avenue toward Patton Street, minutes before Officer Tippet was shot."

"Oswald's whereabouts after the assassination are pretty well documented."

"Are they?" Dallas asked. "Did you know that an equally credible witness swore that he saw Leon walking westbound on Tenth Avenue toward the intersection at Patton?"

"That's not possible," I said. "He couldn't have approached Patton Street from two different directions."

"Not unless there were two Oswalds."

"What are you saying?"

"I'm not saying anything. It's just that two credible witnesses saw Leon in two completely different locations, minutes before the policeman was killed."

"One of them had to have been lying."

"Or one of them was simply mistaken. A citizen took Officer Tippet's gun and followed Leon to the movie theatre."

"Where he was arrested?"

"Yes."

"I don't have a problem believing that."

"When the police officers entered the movie theatre, they went directly to where Leon was sitting. They were on him so fast that he didn't have a chance to use his revolver. Guess what he said when he was arrested."

"What?"

"Remember, everything was staged so that Leon looked like some crazed lunatic who decided to kill the president. You would think that once he knew the jig was up that he'd make some sort of a political statement."

"What did he say to the cops?" I asked again.

"He said, *'Well, it looks like it's all over now.'* Don't you think that was odd?"

"In light of the fact that once they got him to the police station he denied knowing anything about the assassination of the president or the murder of the police officer."

"What have you managed to find out about Dorothy Kilgallen?"

"Nothing much yet," I said. "Amanda's working on her and the other names you gave me."

"Good," Dallas replied. "I want you to read everything you can find on Kilgallen. Look for her account of a meeting at Jack Ruby's bar in Dallas prior to the assassination. You'll be amazed."

"I'm working on it."

"Your cop friend—Freddy Weller—what have you learned about him?"

"Nothing yet, I've had my hands full."

"Listen to me, Hartree. Do you think there might be a reason he lied to you about the license plate number?"

I let out a sigh. "I was scared. Maybe I just made a mistake that night."

"Hartree, you didn't make a mistake."

"I could have—I told you, I was literally shaking in my boots."

"The Jaguar was outside my house again last night. I saw the tag myself—OEE844. You weren't wrong about the plate number. That cop is lying to you."

# CHAPTER THIRTY-EIGHT

"THIS IS HARD to believe," Amanda said.

"What now?" I asked.

"The three names that Dallas gave you," Amanda replied. "They all died mysteriously."

"What did you find out about Dorothy Kilgallen?"

"Wait," Amanda said, "I'll save the best for last. First I want to tell you about Lee Bowers."

"OK," I said, "the man who saw Crystal fire the fatal shot?"

"He died on August 9, 1966, in a single-car accident near a place in Texas called Midlothian. He actually made it to the hospital. The doctor that examined him said he was in some kind of a strange shock before he died. He said that he'd never seen a person go into shock like that before."

"Dallas told me that. I think Mr. Smith had Bowers injected with some sort of drug that would induce a heart attack or something."

"Not according to his family. They said that he suffered from severe allergies, and that it was an especially bad time of year. They thought that he had maybe gone into a sneezing fit and crashed his car."

"Bullshit," I said. "Even if he was doped up on antihistamines, the doctor said he'd never seen anyone go into shock that way before. A hay fever medication wouldn't cause that."

"But driving into a concrete bridge support would. No wonder he was in shock."

"We have to go on what Dallas told us. She said that Mr. Smith was furious when he found out that someone had witnessed Crystal shooting the president."

"I guess," Amanda replied.

"I can only imagine how angry he was when Bowers went before the Warren Commission. Mad enough to kill, I would think."

"Probably. I found out who Rose Cherami was, too."

"Who?" I asked.

"She worked for Jack Ruby. She was thrown out of a moving car near Eunice, Louisiana, on November 20th, 1963."

"Two days before the assassination?"

"Right," Amanda said. "She lived through it, though; at the hospital she apparently told her doctor that the president would be killed during his visit to Texas."

"And?" I asked.

"They thought she was crazy. She was a drug addict. She was going through withdrawal *and* trying to recover from her fall from the car."

"What did the doctor do?"

"Nothing. Everyone at the hospital thought she was nuts."

"And two days later the president died. Dallas told me that Mr. Smith had *her* thrown from a moving car as well."

"Cherami told the police that Jack Ruby and Lee Harvey Oswald were friends, and that she'd seen Oswald at the nightclub many times."

"Ruby denied ever knowing Oswald."

"Right," Amanda said. "Remember what the Dallas chief of police told the media after Ruby shot Oswald?"

I nodded my head. "He said he thought he'd seen a glimmer of recognition in Oswald's eyes."

"Then it must be true. This Rose Cherami woman must have found out about the plot to assassinate the president, and Mr. Smith tried to kill her before she could talk."

"But she lived. Dallas told me that Mr. Smith caught up to her in the end."

"True," Amanda said. "Someone accidentally ran over Cherami's head with his car."

I couldn't hold back the laugh. "What?" I asked.

"September of 1965. Someone ran over Rose's head by accident."

"How in the hell do you run over someone's head by accident?"

Amanda shrugged. "I don't know," she said, "but it happened. Rose was lying on some back Texas road at two in the morning and a car ran over her head."

"Preposterous," I said.

"It's not that preposterous. What if the tire squashing her head wasn't the real cause of her death?"

"What are you suggesting?"

"One theory was that running over her head was just a way of hiding a bullet wound."

"Well," I said, "knowing the lengths Mr. Smith went to disguise the other murders, that whole concept probably makes more sense."

"That brings us to Congressman Hale Boggs."

"What did you find out about him?"

Amanda stood from the table and walked to the coffeepot. "It looks like there may have been a little dissension in the ranks of the Warren Commission."

"Explain," I said.

She filled her mug. "It seems there were three members of the commission that had some doubts about their findings." She walked back to her chair and placed her mug next to her notebook. "Congressman Boggs was probably the most vocal. He had more than a few doubts about the magic bullet theory."

"What reasonable person wouldn't?" I asked.

"Listen to this," Amanda said and turned through the pages of her notebook, "it's a quote from a speech he made to Congress: *Over the postwar years, we have granted to the elite and secret police within our system vast new powers over the lives and liberties of the people. At the request of the trusted and respected heads of those forces, and their appeal to the necessities of national security, we have exempted those grants of power from due accounting and strict surveillance.*"

"The Kennedy brothers felt the same way. That's exactly what they were saying about the CIA that they had too much free rein, and they were abusing their powers."

Amanda nodded. "It looks like Boggs felt the same way about the FBI," she said. "Listen to what he had to say about J. Edgar Hoover."

I leaned forward.

"He apparently told an aide that Hoover consistently lied to the Warren Commission. That he lied about Oswald, about Ruby, about their friends, about the bullets, about the gun, about everything."

"Jesus," I said, "talk like that wouldn't exactly get him on the intelligence community's Christmas card list. Dallas told me that he disappeared."

"He was touring Alaska. The plane he was on vanished somewhere in the wilderness."

"They never found it?"

"At the time, the search was the largest ever undertaken by the United States. It lasted thirty-nine days. After that, all airplanes were required to carry emergency location transmitters."

"And no trace was found?"

"Nothing," Amanda said. "A few years back, a Washington-based newspaper found documents under the Freedom of Information Act that stated that the FBI had received a tip and that they actually knew where the plane had gone down."

"And it was still never found?"

"Not to this day."

"Strange," I said.

"None of this is as strange as Dorothy Kilgallen's death."

"Tell me," I said.

"She died on November 8th, 1965, from a lethal mixture of alcohol and barbiturates."

"Where have we heard that one before?" I asked.

"She was found fully dressed, sitting upright in her bed."

"Any signs of foul play?"

Amanda looked up at me. "You mean other that the fact she was dead as a doornail?"

My face went red.

"She had just returned to New York from Dallas, where she had her interview with Jack Ruby."

"OK."

"Kilgallen said she had learned of a meeting a few weeks prior to the assassination at Ruby's night club. She wrote an article about the gathering for the *Journal American*. It made the front page."

"What kind of a meeting?"

"Four men," Amanda said, "Ruby, a man named Bernard Weismann, a cop, and an important member of the Texas oil industry."

"Who's Bernard Weismann?" I asked.

"He was the person who placed the 'Welcome to Texas, Mr. Kennedy' poster in the Dallas newspapers on the morning of November 22nd."

"I remember reading about that," I said. "It was a full-page ad, surrounded by a black mourning border."

"Right," Amanda replied. "It directed twelve questions at the president. It was basically an accusation that Kennedy was going soft on communism, and that he was leaning more and more to the left. It was signed by Weismann, who called himself the chairman of the American Fact-Finding Committee."

"I wonder if they were the same people who were circulating the wanted poster of JFK around Dallas that week?"

"The 'Wanted for Treason' poster? I don't know. I did manage to find us a copy. It's not signed by anyone."

I reached across the table and took the reprint from Amanda's hand. "It looks just like a wanted poster you'd see hanging in some old western saloon or something."

"It's a typical sheriff's poster and it's accusing the president of betraying the Constitution of the United States."

"So," I said, "Kilgallen wrote an article about this meeting for the *Journal American*?"

"Yes," Amanda replied, "apparently she was scared. She told her friends that she had uncovered some frightening new information about Jack Ruby. She told them she was going to blow the lid off the assassination cover-up. She gave her notes to a friend for safekeeping—a lady named Florence Smith."

"She was scared?"

"Two other reporters—Bill Hunter and Jim Koethe—had managed to arrange to get into Jack Ruby's apartment. Nobody knows what they found."

"Let me guess," I said. "Something happened to these two men?"

"Right, on April 23, 1964, Hunter was shot and killed in a police station in Long Beach, California."

"In a police station—by a cop?"

"He claimed that he dropped his gun, and that it went off when he picked it up."

"What about the other man?"

"Jim Koethe, he died a few months later—on September 21. Someone broke into his apartment and killed him with a karate chop to the throat."

"Jesus Christ," I said. "No wonder Kilgallen was scared."

"She was just being careful. She must have thought that if anything happened to her, that her friend would pass the information about Ruby along."

"And what happened, to the notes on Ruby, after Kilgallen died?"

"Gone," Amanda said, "disappeared."

"And the copies that she gave to her friend?"

"Florence Smith died two days after Dorothy Kilgallen, of a cerebral haemorrhage."

I couldn't think of anything more to say. My mouth went out of sync with my brain. I couldn't process. My brain had blown a fuse. What I'd just been told was far too unbelievable. Coincidence was one thing, but this bordered on the ridiculous."

"The meeting," Amanda said, "at Jack Ruby's club."

I looked into her eyes, still unable to put words into a sentence.

"According to Kilgallen's article in the *Journal American*, she continued, "the cop at the meeting was none other than J.D. Tippet."

"Do you think—"

"That Mr. Smith could have recruited a police officer into the fifth column?"

"We've got another problem."

"What now?" Amanda asked.

"I told you about the black Jaguar—about the license plate number."

"Freddy Weller said it doesn't exist."

"Weller's lying, Dallas saw the plate, too. We need to find out what we can about my old pal Freddy's past."

# CHAPTER THIRTY-NINE

MY BRAIN SEIZED. It was locked up tighter than the vaults at Fort Knox, and I could tell that it wouldn't function normally until tomorrow, at the very least. It was time to call it a day. The circuits were overloaded. I couldn't believe what I had stumbled upon. The body count was rising by the minute. And after all these years, the evil that Mr. Smith represented was still actively destroying people's lives. He had to be stopped and, with the help of my anonymous caller, I was the man who would put an end to his reign of terror.

The whiskey in my bottom drawer was calling me. I pushed my coffee mug to the side. I had to focus and the last thing I needed was a drink. It was time to go to my hotel, get some food into my belly, and try again to get some sleep. How could Mr. Smith have gotten away with all of this? Why was the public so ready and willing to listen to his lies? How could the world have believed that Lee Harvey Oswald acted alone? That the murder of President Kennedy was the act of a man with a scrambled brain and a twenty-dollar rifle? How could the story that Marilyn had taken her own life survive for almost half a century? Nobody wanted to hear the truth. It was far too titillating to read about the fact that she was found naked in her bed clutching a telephone. People didn't want to hear about the bruises on her body. And Mr. Smith was powerful enough to mask the truth and hide the real facts—to hide what actually happened that August night in 1962. It wasn't as much Mr. Smith's fault for being a liar, as it was the public's fault for listening to him.

A voice from my bottom drawer called out again, but this time it wasn't the whiskey that wanted to find its way into my hand. It wasn't the numbing Scottish elixir that wanted my attention—it was the equalizer: precisely machined pieces of steel that would put me on a level playing field with Mr. Smith. The pen was still mightier than the sword, but until the day came when I could vanquish Smith with my words, I would have to defend myself.

Obviously, there was no protection in being a public figure. Well-known people like Monroe, Kennedy, Boggs, and Kilgallen had fallen prey to his evil as easily as the Oswalds, the Cheramis, and the Bowers of this world. Mr. Smith was gunning for me, and my notoriety in this town offered no more protection than a wall made of pillows.

I'd carefully planned an alternate route to the hotel. I would avoid the main streets and make sure that I had plenty of room to run if the black Jaguar picked up my trail. I'd parked my car at a public lot two blocks away. If Mr. Smith was staking out the parking garage at the *Tribune* building, he'd have a very long wait ahead of him. I reached up to the coat hook at the end of my cubicle and grabbed my old grey hat. I placed it snugly on my head and pulled it down to conceal my eyes. I turned in the direction of the elevator.

The voice from my bottom drawer called out again. Was I strong enough to go face to face with Mr. Smith? Did I have the courage to stand up to the evil and put a stop to him for good? And if I did, would it only be a matter of time before someone else took on the name and took up the task of destroying people and masking his deeds in a shroud of lies and half-truths? The voice called out once more. Was I committed enough to put my life on the line? Fuck that nonsense, I whispered to myself. All the help I needed was lying next to my bottle of Scotch, and I decided to take every advantage I could. I opened the drawer and reached for the gun.

⌘

The trip to the hotel was uneventful. No black Jaguars chasing me through the streets and no trained assassins lurking in the parking garage.

I gathered my dinner dishes together and stacked them on the room service tray. The steak was nice and tender, and the peas weren't mushy at all. I placed the tray on the table next to the door and pressed my eye to the peephole. The hallway was clear. No hired killers were lying in wait. No hit men were preparing to bushwhack me if I dropped my guard. I threw back the deadbolt, released the security chain, and opened the door a crack. I peered down the hallway then cautiously opened the door wide and placed my tray on the carpet. A bell sounded and the light above the elevator doors came on. I stepped back into my room and shut the door. I picked up my gun and stared through the peephole and watched as the room service attendant pushed his cart out of the elevator.

⌘

I filled my ice bucket and walked back to the room. I tossed a couple of ice cubes into a glass and covered them with a good two fingers of Scotch. I rearranged the pillows and propped myself against the headboard of my bed. I needed a break, so I picked up the remote and turned on the television. The evening movie was just starting. The *Manchurian Candidate*, the original version filmed back in 1962, starring Frank Sinatra and Laurence Harvey. I'd seen it before. Harvey played a Korean War hero who was captured and brainwashed by the enemy. On his return to the United States after the war, the hero, turned programmed assassin, was ordered to kill a presidential candidate. The film was withdrawn from the theatres after the murder of JFK. It was locked away for 25 years, until 1987. The story behind this was that Sinatra had purchased the rights and had the film shelved out of respect for John Kennedy. A second version of the story had also circulated that Sinatra axed the movie in a dispute over profit-sharing with the film's producers. I took a sip of Scotch and made myself comfortable.

⌘

I woke with a start. For a moment I wasn't sure where I was. The room seemed strange; the hum from the air conditioner told me I wasn't at home in my own bed.

The phone rang a second time. I reached over and turned on the bedside lamp. The clock next to the lamp read 2:14.

The phone rang a third time. I picked up the receiver and held it to my ear. "Hello?"

I listened to the deafening silence. I cleared my throat. "Hello?" I said again.

"Hartree?" the voice on the other end of the line whispered.

"Who is this?" I asked.

"Did you think you could hide?"

I sat up and swung my legs off the bed. My senses were coming back and I wasn't prepared to put up with any nonsense.

"I asked you a question," the voice whispered.

The coarseness of the voice burned into my brain. A man's muted rasp—cold, angry and threatening. It was time to go on the offensive. I glanced at my gun on the table next to the phone. "Smith?" I asked.

"No," the voice whispered. "You must have learned by now. Mr. Smith doesn't like to get his hands dirty."

"Then who are you?"

"I'm just one of the many whose life he's turned upside down. You're my new assignment."

"I'm not afraid of you *or* of Mr. Smith," I said.

"Really?" the man whispered. "That's not the feeling I get. I can hear it when you speak. I know that sound. It's the sound of terror."

I summoned all the courage I had left in me. "Tell him to come and face me," I said. "We'll see who's scared then." I looked over at my gun. "Tell him to stop being such a coward. How much fortitude does it take to call a man in the middle of the night and breathe into the phone?"

Laughter.

"What's so funny?" I asked.

"You," the voice whispered. "I don't like you very much. Do you really think you're a better man than he is?"

My turn to laugh. "Of course, I am," I said.

"What makes your lies any better than his?"

"I don't lie."

"I read the stories you wrote about that property developer—Alan Ball. What was his partner's name again?"

"Why am I wasting my time talking to you?"

"I'm like a car crash. You don't really want to look, but you just can't turn away. I know you've been talking to Dallas. We were partners once upon a time."

"I don't know who you're talking about."

Another laugh.

"What's so funny?"

"You reporters," the voice whispered. "You're always the most fun to toy with."

"What do you mean by that?"

"I'm sure Dallas has told you some terrible things about Mr. Smith. Don't believe everything you hear. She knows all about reporters, too."

"I still don't know who you're talking about."

"Tell her that I said hello. I drove by her house earlier this evening. Her car was gone. It was a little late for her to be out. I think she's on the run again. Remind her that she can't hide from me for long. Let her know that I'm close, and that it's only a matter of time before I find out where she is. Don't believe everything she says about Mr. Smith. Ask her if she remembers the thrill he got out of feeding misinformation to the press—especially that reporter from New York."

"What reporter?"

"Her name was Kilgallen. It was a long time ago now."

"Dorothy Kilgallen?"

"She wrote a story about a meeting in Jack Ruby's club. It wasn't the first time Mr. Smith had managed to put Ruby in the spotlight. The cop was a last minute addition. I thought it was brilliant, didn't you?"

"The cop?" I asked. "J.D. Tippet?"

"That's right. Smith had already managed to link Ruby and Oswald. He just fed the information about the cop into the rumour mill, and before you could blink your eyes, it was front-page news. You can't imagine how wild the conspiracy theorists went when they read that Jack had known Officer Tippet."

"Good God," I muttered.

"I hope you understand," the voice whispered, "he can't allow you to go on talking to the woman. There's been too much work put into this. He can't stand back and watch you two destroy all that he's done."

"Is that a threat?"

"It's more than a threat, Hartree. I've been ordered to put an end to you both."

I reached over and picked up my gun. Its weight gave me the courage I needed. "You tell him that when he's ready to stand face to face, he knows where to find me."

"He *does* know where to find you. He knows everything about you."

"He does?" I asked. "Then he also must know that I'm not going to rest until I stop him."

"Bring it on, Hartree, but be careful. We're very good at this."

I listened to the phone line go dead.

⌘

I pushed my fear aside and dialled the number for the front desk.

"Reception—Alex speaking."

"Alex," I said, "this is Terry Hartree in room 1026. You just put a call through to my room."

"I did," the night clerk replied. "I hope that was all right. He said it was urgent. He sounded very sincere."

"What else did he say?"

"He apologized for calling so late. He said it was an emergency. He told me it was a matter of life and death. Is everything all right?"

"I'll be checking out immediately. I just need to pack up my things. Can you please wrap up my bill?"

"Of course."

"If he phones again, don't put the call through. Tell him I've asked not to be disturbed for any reason."

"OK."

"I'll be down in a few minutes."

# CHAPTER FORTY

MY BLADDER WAS empty, my face was washed, my bag was hastily thrown together, and I was ready to go. The clock on the bedside table now read 2:56. I dropped my suitcase next to the door and had a last look around. The butt of the gun in my waistband chafed against the skin of my belly.

The first ring of the phone almost stopped my heart. I hustled to the bedside table and grabbed at the receiver. "What?" I asked.

A grating laugh.

"You again?" I asked.

"I just needed to check," the voice whispered. "It *is* the tenth floor that you're on, isn't it?"

I slammed the receiver down. My blood was boiling. How could Alex be so stupid? I specifically told him, in no uncertain terms, *not* to put through any more calls. I picked up the phone and dialled the front desk.

"Alex," I barked, "this is Mr. Hartree in 1026. I told you not to put any more calls through to my room."

"I didn't."

"Alex," I said, "don't lie to me. I just got a second call from the man that phoned a few minutes ago."

"I swear," Alex replied, "I didn't put through another call."

I hesitated for a moment. "Is there another person on the switchboard?"

"No, sir, not at this time of night."

"Then how—"

"Wait," Alex said, "if the call came from another phone in the hotel, it wouldn't go through the switchboard."

My heart was in my mouth. I dropped the phone and reached for my gun. They were here—in the hotel—and they were coming for me.

⌘

I kicked my bag to the side. If this was to be my confrontation with Mr. Smith's fifth column, I couldn't be weighed down with a few pairs of socks and a half bottle of aftershave.

I leaned into the peephole and checked the hallway. I released the deadbolt and fumbled with the security chain. I cracked the door and checked the hall again. My heart was pounding. I raised the gun and bolted across the hall and punched the button to call the elevator. I darted back into the safety of my room. I hid behind the door and watched the hallway for signs of the assassins. I checked my gun again. A bell toned and the light above the elevator doors came on. The steel doors rolled open.

How stupid was I? They would expect me to make a run for the parking garage. What if they were waiting for me downstairs? Once those elevator doors opened up, I would be totally exposed. I'd have no cover at all. I'd be a sitting duck with nowhere to run. I was smarter than that. I'd use the fire exit stairs. At least if Smith's men chose to meet me in the stairwell, I'd have some room to manoeuvre.

⌘

The stairway was cold. I took one last look down the hallway before closing the door and beginning my descent to the parking level. I hustled down the first bank of stairs. I leaned over the railing and checked the landing to the ninth floor. All was clear. I made my way down the next bank of steps, past the door to the ninth level, and down the next set of steps to the eighth floor.

⌘

I stood on the turnaround and looked down the last bank of stairs at the door marked parking. I leaned against the iron railing and tried to catch my breath. My age was showing. Too many years of riding a desk and too many glasses of Scotch had made me soft. I looked up at the zigzag of stairs and groaned. Ten flights had done me in. Too bad for Mr. Smith, I chuckled to myself. If the parking area had been on the roof, and if I'd had to go up ten flights instead of down, it would have saved him the trouble of killing me. I was sure that after three or four flights, his men would have found me flopping around on the floor like a wounded seagull, clutching my chest as my heart burst. When this was all over, I'd have to do something about my twisted sense of humour.

I cracked the door to the parking garage and peered out. I propped the door with my toe and shifted the gun to my left hand. After that many stairs, the weight of the pistol had doubled. I flexed my fingers and rolled my wrist back and forth. I scanned the row of parked cars in front of me. The coast looked clear.

I gingerly stepped into the garage and made my way past the elevator doors. My head jerked from side to side as I checked every nook and cranny for signs of Mr. Smith's hired guns. I stopped for a moment to get my bearings. I turned to the right and headed in the direction of my car and freedom.

The garage was silent, except for the low humming sound of the ventilation system. I crept along the side of a Toyota van. My hands were sweating. I stopped for a moment and placed my gun on the hood of a car. I wiped the sweat off my palms onto my pant legs.

Like a bullet from an assassin's gun, the sound of the elevator bell dropped me to my knees. I crouched on the ground behind the van and listened to the elevator doors rumble open. I checked my watch. It was shortly after three. Who would be cruising the garage at three in the morning? Panic seized me. My gun was still resting on the hood of the car. I turned in the direction of the elevator.

I could hear voices. I concentrated on the sound. Two voices—both female. They spoke softly—just above a whisper. Who did they think they were going to disturb at three in the morning in a hotel parking lot? I crawled up next to the car and reached for the hood. I kept my head turned in the direction of the voices as I felt around for my gun. I located the weapon and dragged it down across the fender of the car. I huddled up next to the side of the van. I cocked the hammer of my pistol. The voices drew closer. I listened to the sound of their heels on the concrete floor as they neared my hiding spot next to the Toyota.

The footsteps were determined. Steady and rhythmic, the sound of the steps drew closer. A new cell—I thought to myself. Another pair of young women recruited to do Smith's dirty work. Just like Dallas and Crystal, two young innocents drawn in by a web of lies and convinced to kill. I got down on my hands and knees. I lowered my head and looked underneath the van. Through the maze of tires, I could see their feet. The women were only one row of cars away from me and were advancing quickly. Each pair of feet was followed by a small set of wheels.

Travelling luggage, I said to myself. A perfect cover—and a perfect place to hide their weapons after the deed was done.

My heart was racing. What would I do if they spotted me? Should I take the offensive? I was in a perfect position to get behind them. I could easily gain the upper hand. I watched their feet until they were directly opposite me. I crawled to the rear of the van and prepared to make my move. My hands were trembling. Sweat was gathering on my forehead. My heart was again threatening to pound its way out of my chest. I crawled on my hands and knees across the aisle of cars. I was in position. I could jump up and get them both from behind.

I checked the gun again. My hands were shaking uncontrollably. The footsteps came to a stop. I could hear the women talking. I heard the sound of metal sliding against metal. They must have sensed I was near and they were loading their weapons. The showdown was about to begin. I heard more hushed voices, as I moved from my knees to a crouched position. I propped my free hand on a bumper and slowly raised myself to a place where I could see them over the fender of the car. I heard the sound of a trunk lid pop open, then more metal on metal. I watched one of the women collapse the handle of her suitcase and place it in the trunk. I recognized their uniforms. Air Canada flight attendants. Relieved, I sank to the concrete floor, while the two women got in their vehicle and backed out of the parking stall.

I leaned against the bumper of the car and tried to pull myself together. I listened as the flight attendants drove through the garage and up the ramp to the street. I wanted to vomit. The fear had torn me apart. I had to regain control. The fifth column was here in the hotel, and I had to get out. I released the hammer of my gun.

I had to get back in the fight. I wasn't prepared to die alone and afraid on the floor of some oil-stained parking garage. I wouldn't give Mr. Smith the satisfaction of adding another reporter to his long list of conquests. I had to get to my car. I pulled myself to my feet and cautiously began my trek across the garage.

⌘

It's a very distinct and recognizable sound. There's no mistaking the opening of a fire exit door. The clink of the bar being pushed, followed by the sound of the bar springing back into position. The few moments that elapse as the hydraulic piston eases the door shut, and the hollow *thunk* as the steel door slams closed. The footsteps that followed were definitely those of a man. The heels hit heavy against the concrete floor. Once again, I was not alone in the parking garage. I crouched down and focused on the sound. They were the footsteps of a man with no particular place to go. They weren't the determined steps of someone heading to a car; a couple of seconds at least, between each sound of a heel hitting pavement. These were the footsteps of a man who's searching; the slow and methodical gait of a man on the hunt. I cocked the hammer of my pistol again and crouched in the aisle. I had to think. Mr. Smith was clever, but today he'd met his match.

I reached into my pocket and fished out a quarter. I focused again on the sound of the footsteps. I had to draw the gunman out into the open. I had to get a good look at this man. I leaned out from the safety of my hiding place and threw the quarter as far as I could.

The ping of the coin hitting the ground echoed through the confines of the underground garage. The footsteps stopped briefly. The pace started up again. This time the steps were quick and driven. Now this man *had* a place to go. I readied my gun. When he reached the driveway, I could spring to my feet and strike without warning. I held my arm straight and aimed the pistol at a spot on the floor.

The footsteps came to a stop. I heard the sound of static and the crackle of another voice, this time over a radio. I thought he must know I'm in the garage and he's calling the rest of his cell members. I gripped the pistol with both hands—combat style. I had to do something to steady the shake in my arms. I had to drop him with my first shot. I would have to cut off the head of the snake, if I was to survive the night. I couldn't afford to miss.

The footsteps started once more. Again, the pace was slow and calculated. He was back on the hunt, and I could tell by the echo of his heels that he was headed my way. I drew in a deep breath through my mouth. I had to control my breathing if I was going to make the first shot count. The radio crackled again. I could hear his voice from where

I was hiding. Was it the same voice I'd heard on the phone earlier? Even though my mind was clouded with fear, I knew it had to be the same man. The radio crackled once more. He was close enough that I could make out his words. I'll be right there, he'd said. Where, I asked myself? Had his partners spotted me? Was he being called to a better position? Were they closing in on me?

The sound of the footsteps began again. This time, they headed away from me, back toward the elevator. He must be trying to flank me. I dropped to all fours and looked underneath the row of cars. I could see his feet—he *was* heading in the direction of the elevator. I grabbed a car door handle and discreetly pulled myself up and peeked over the trunk lid. I could see him standing by the elevator. The hunch of his shoulders told me he was an older man; he was dressed in a security guard's uniform.

"Christ," I whispered to myself, as the steel doors opened up and the man stepped inside. I let out a gasp and sank to the floor. I was being played. Only minutes before, the voice on the phone had told me how much Smith enjoyed toying with reporters. I had almost turned my pistol on two flight attendants and a night watchman. I released the hammer of my gun, picked myself up off the floor, and sprinted across the garage to my car.

# CHAPTER FORTY-ONE

MORNING HAD FINALLY arrived. The ordeal in the parking garage had taught me a bit more about Mr. Smith and my skin was still crawling from the experience. The mystery caller had played me like a prize trout. He'd placed ideas in my head, and then sent me scrambling about the parking garage of my hotel in search of a hired gun. He had me wound so tight that I was ready to turn my weapon on anything that moved. How could he have known where I was staying? How could he have tracked me down so quickly? I reached across my desk for the ringing phone.

"How are you doing this morning?" Dallas asked.

I leaned back in my chair and let out a sigh. "Mr. Smith's men were at my hotel last night."

I heard a gasp.

"Are you sure?"

"No question," I said. "One of them called my room—twice. I spoke to him."

"You spoke to him?"

"He asked about you. He knows we've been talking. He told me that you were partners once."

"Jesus Christ. Do you think—?"

"That it could be Joker?"

"It must be. He's the only man I ever directly partnered with."

"He told me that he drove by *your* house last night as well. He knows you're on the run, too. He's on the hunt for you again."

"I'm not worried. I'm comfortably stashed away in a nice little hotel downtown. The whole Dallas charade is working very well. Trust me on this—I'm well hidden. It's crucial that Smith doesn't figure out my game plan until after I'm dead. We're in a race against time. This whole thing will collapse if he realizes what we're doing. It's a delicate game we're playing. You know that Smith exists—and now you understand a little better how he works."

"I do."

"It's close."

"What?" I asked.

"The end."

"The end?"

"The end of life for me and the end of Mr. Smith's reign of terror. If we handle this properly, not only can we put a stop to this man, we can make it more difficult for the world to breed any more like him."

"But I still don't know who Mr. Smith is."

"Every major country in the world has an organization similar to the one that spawned Mr. Smith. They're generally a dedicated group of people facing difficult tasks—but every so often, one person breaks away. Every now and then a rogue comes up with his own set of rules and his own idea of what's right and what's wrong."

"The CIA was already out of control in the sixties. I imagine once Kennedy started to reduce some of their powers—"

"Sometimes it doesn't take much to steer men like Mr. Smith toward the dark side. And if you take a man like that, throw in a dash of charisma, and then present him with an audience of people willing to listen to his lies, it's not long before he has an army behind him."

"An army prepared to do anything."

"An army that's so blinded by the lies that it can't think for itself. An army that would end a person's life before standing back and asking themselves why."

I lost myself for a moment.

"Are you still there, Hartree?"

"I was just thinking."

"About what?"

"Nothing," I said. "Just an article I was preparing to write the day you first contacted me."

"Tell me about it."

"Like I said, it was nothing. It was a story that was beginning to take shape. There really weren't any concrete facts to base it on. It was all speculation."

"Not like the McDermott/Ball series then. You still don't realize what you started when you wrote those articles, do you?"

"What?" I asked.

"It was only after I read your attacks on those two that I decided it was time. It would have been much easier for me to take my story with me and go quietly to my grave. It took a special something to write a series of articles like that. I told you that I chose you for a reason."

"You're right. It took a lot of guts to go up against a veteran politician like Chris McDermott."

"*Guts* wasn't the word I had in mind."

"What?"

"You've done a good job of piecing things together. You've taken what I told you, and you've laid the whole story out."

"Except for the ending—stop playing with me, tell me who Smith is."

"You're closer than you think. Remember—I made you a promise."

"You don't have that much time left. What if—?"

"Don't worry. A flood begins with a single drop of rain. An avalanche starts with the roll of a solitary pebble. Have faith in me. Once the pieces start to fall into place, nobody will be able to stop the process."

"What's the next step?"

Dallas paused. "A quick review of what you've learned. Then we need to have a closer look at two of the key players in this whole dance of lies."

"Who?" I asked.

"Leon and Jack."

"Oswald and Kennedy?"

"No, Oswald and Ruby."

"How will that lead me to Mr. Smith?"

Dallas paused again, then she drew in a deep breath. "You've learned a lot over the last few days, Hartree."

I slouched back in my chair. "No kidding," I said.

"I'd be willing to bet that you've had a chance to look at yourself, too."

"I have."

"I'd also bet that you didn't always like what you saw."

"I've got to be honest with you. I've done some things that I'm not exactly proud of."

"Chris McDermott?"

"Among others."

"Let's look at Marilyn again."

"What?" I asked.

"We'll play another short round of fact or fiction. Out of all the information you've gathered about Marilyn's supposed suicide, how much of it is fact and how much of it is fiction?"

I thought for a moment.

"Are you still with me?"

"I'm here," I said. "I was just thinking. The only thing about Marilyn's death that can't be disputed is the fact that she died of an overdose of barbiturates."

"Right. Everything else is either speculation or opinion."

"And Kennedy," I said. "The only thing that was proved without question was that he died of a gunshot wound to the head."

"Exactly. A famous man once said: *History is the lies that historians agree on.*"

"Shakespeare?"

"Napoleon."

"Joker told me about Dorothy Kilgallen's article, about the meeting between Jack Ruby and J. D. Tippet. He said that Smith just fed the information into the rumour mill."

"That was his style. Then he'd just stand back and let human nature take its course."

"But if it had been true, think of the ramifications."

"Exactly," Dallas said. "If Oswald did in fact know Ruby and if Ruby did in fact know Tippet."

"Then it would be pretty hard to believe that Oswald shooting Tippet, or Ruby shooting Oswald, could be coincidence."

"Right. It would look like a massive conspiracy."

I leaned forward onto my desk. "That one little bit of information—whether it's the truth or not—changes the whole scope of the story."

"You're right."

"But now we know. Joker told me that Smith was the one that fed the press the notion that Ruby knew Tippet."

Dallas laughed. "Another unsubstantiated comment. How could you fall for that again? The only way we'll know for sure is by resurrecting Oswald, Ruby, and Tippet and asking them ourselves. What do you think the chances of that are?"

"Pretty slim, I would think."

"I'm going to tell you something that will clearly show you how Mr. Smith works."

"What?" I asked.

"I know this for a fact—Ruby *did* know Tippet."

"But we just went over that."

"Do I have to tell you again? Tippet and Ruby were friends."

"Then why did Joker tell me that Smith fed the notion that they knew each other to the press?"

"It's a fact—check it out. Let me see—I know I have it in my notes."

"What?"

"Here it is. See if you can find a record of Warren Commission exhibits 1620 and 2430. There were two Dallas police officers named Tippet in 1963. Ruby knew the other one. The Warren Commission clearly established that Ruby's friendship was with a cop by the name of G.M. Tippet—not J.D. Mr. Smith just let the press assume it was J.D. that he was referring to."

"I understand. He was telling a slice of the truth, versus telling the whole truth."

"I knew you'd be able to relate to that. All Mr. Smith did was say that Ruby knew Tippet. He wasn't lying."

"And he wasn't telling the truth either."

"He just stood back and let the press assume that he was referring to J.D."

"So tell me," I said, "when it's time for me to expose Mr. Smith, how will I prove that any of this is true? How will it be any different? What will make it more than uncorroborated statements made by a dead woman?"

"Believe me. He won't be able to hide from you. You'll have a flesh and blood person, and you'll have enough on him that he won't be able to deny the fact that he is Mr. Smith. Do you think you'll be strong enough?"

"I know I'll be strong enough."

"Every end also marks a beginning."

"What do you mean?"

"The end of Mr. Smith may also mark the beginning of a new Terry Hartree, one that doesn't have to lie."

"I don't lie."

Dallas chuckled. "You don't?" she asked. "Maybe I should call up Alan Ball and ask him what he thinks."

"Alan Ball and Chris McDermott are ancient history. I wish you'd get off that subject."

"But don't you see, Hartree? What you did to Chris McDermott was the same thing that Mr. Smith did to Leon. He took someone who was vulnerable and set him up to take the fall. Feeding the information that Ruby knew Tippet to the press—it was the same as you suggesting that Ball and McDermott had prior knowledge of the location of the new Skytrain station. You didn't come right out and lie, but the damage was done just the same."

"I don't think Oswald was all that squeaky clean."

"Of course he wasn't. You and Amanda are going to learn a few things about Leon that will make your heads spin."

"When?"

"Soon. I have to go through my notes. It was a long time ago. November 22 wasn't the first time Leon used his rifle on someone. Mr. Smith needed to know if Leon was capable of planning and executing a job of this magnitude. He failed the first time, too. The important thing for now is to stay clear of Mr. Smith. This is how it all started with Crystal. First the hang up phone calls, then the gift—the orchid—in the red box."

"And then—"

Dallas finished my thought: "Then came her swan dive off her apartment balcony."

"I've already instructed Amanda to start digging into Oswald's life."

"Good. You need to concentrate on the time directly prior to November of '63. You need to look at the few years of his life before the assassination. I told you how much work went into grooming him for his role in all of this."

"We're on it."

"Be careful. I'll check on you again before the end of the day."

"OK."

"Hartree?"

"I'm still here."

"It sounds to me like Amanda has been the backbone of this search of yours—the probe for the truth."

"She has," I said. "It's incredible, the amount of information that she's managed to gather."

"So, you don't miss Grant then?"

"Yeah"—I chuckled—"like I'd miss a toothache."

"Have you told her?"

"Told her what?"

"Have you told her what a good job she's been doing?"

"She's a big girl. She doesn't need a pat on the back every time she comes up with an answer."

"Good," Dallas said. "I can't have you going completely soft on me. It's good to know that you're still the same self-centred, arrogant son of a bitch that did in Chris McDermott. You're going to need every ounce of that attitude when it comes time to put an end to Mr. Smith."

# CHAPTER FORTY-TWO

AMANDA MESHED HER fingers together and hunched over her notepad.

I poured myself another coffee and leaned on the boardroom table. "Any information on Oswald's past, yet?" I asked.

"I'm putting together some notes. I'll have more for you tomorrow."

"We have to pull out all the stops. We're running out of tomorrows. Dallas hasn't got much strength left."

"Oswald was a pretty strange person. Did you know that there's a story floating around that he actually asked a New Orleans district attorney whether it was legal to import LSD into the United States?"

"LSD! The CIA did experiments with LSD in the early sixties. I wonder if that's how he came in contact with it."

"It wasn't until much later in the sixties that the use of LSD flourished."

"I knew it. That suggests there was a link between Oswald and the intelligence community. We have to concentrate on Mr. Smith. The end is coming, and we still can't positively identify him."

"She said we were closer than we think."

I dragged out a chair and sat.

Amanda drew a deep breath and then let out a long sigh.

"I have a theory," I said.

"What is it?"

"Fred Weller. There's more to that man than meets the eye."

"What?"

"I have a number of sources on the police force. I wasn't able to find out much about Weller's time in the military through any of the usual channels."

"And?"

"We know he was CIC."

"Canadian Intelligence Corps?"

"Right. And we also know he spent time in the United States."

Amanda nodded. "Late sixties and early seventies: the cold war years."

"And that's when he first met up with Alan Ball."

"What are you suggesting?"

"Think about it," I said. "I'm almost certain that Alan Ball is in this up to his eyeballs. And we also know that Weller worked in the intelligence community."

"But you don't know in what capacity. He could have been a clerk or a messenger or something."

"Not according to the scuttlebutt around the police station. He was a spook."

"That's hearsay. You can't verify that just from chatter around the watercooler at the police station."

"But if he was a spook, and he first met Ball through his travels to the States, don't you think it's possible that Ball was a spook, too?"

"It's possible, but there's nothing to prove it."

"There's nothing to disprove it either. What if Ball was CIA?"

"Sure," Amanda said, "and what if the moon really is made of green cheese?"

"Don't you see? It all fits. Weller's ready for retirement and Ball must be past sixty."

"He sure doesn't look it."

"Back when this whole mess started, they'd have been in their primes. That would have placed them both smack in the middle of the cold war."

"So, what's your point?"

"If Weller and Ball were both part of the intelligence community, there's a possibility that they might have been recruited by Mr. Smith into the fifth column."

Amanda held up her hand. "Wait a minute," she said. "You're spinning out of control. Remember, this is just another theory. You haven't got any proof that either of these men was involved with Mr. Smith."

"But you have to admit—it's a possibility."

"OK. I'll admit that it *is* possible."

"Good," I said. "You see my point at least. What if Mr. Smith came to Vancouver to hook up with Weller and Ball again? What if he's using them to help search for Dallas?"

"But your conversation with Freddy, he asked *you* who Mr. Smith was."

"What if he was testing me? What if he was just fishing around to find out how close I was to identifying Smith?"

"You're out of control. Next, you'll be accusing one of *them* of being Mr. Smith. You don't still believe in Santa Claus and the Easter Bunny too, do you?"

I leaned back in my chair and folded my arms across my chest. "Why would that be out of the question?" I asked. "Why couldn't either Ball or Weller be our Mr. Smith?"

"That's ridiculous."

"Why?" I asked.

Amanda hesitated.

"You said it yourself. We both know that Alan Ball's a player and that he's got some skeletons in his closet."

"Who doesn't?"

"Think about it," I said. "Ball moves to Canada and hooks up with a crooked politician. Doesn't that sound like Mr. Smith's style to you? He would want to have control over some powerful people."

"Chris McDermott didn't hold a public office when the two of them partnered up. They were just a pair of property speculators."

"Perhaps Chris McDermott was *placed* in office. Maybe Mr. Smith was building a power base in Canada, like he did in the United States."

"You're putting two and two together and coming up with twelve."

"Dallas told us that the fifth column was everywhere. Why couldn't Mr. Smith be here to recruit cells in Canada?"

"You're putting pieces of the puzzle together the way you want them to go together."

"I am not," I said. "It makes perfect sense that either Ball or Weller could in fact be our Mr. Smith."

"Look at it this way. Let's take everything we know about Lee Harvey Oswald and throw it into that old grey hat of yours. A lone-gunman believer could take every one of those pieces of information and turn it into a perfectly plausible explanation for what really happened on November 22, 1963. On the other hand, a conspiracy theorist could take the same data and turn it into some wild story that involved everyone in Texas playing a part in a concerted effort to kill the president."

"I know I'm on the right track. Now, what else have you got on Oswald?"

"He joined the Marines when he was quite young."

"Uh-huh."

"In 1957, he was posted to the Marine air control squadron one. He was stationed in Atsugi as a radar operator."

"Atsugi?"

"It's about twenty miles from Tokyo. It's the air base where the U2 spy planes flew from. That's where the surveillance flights over Russia originated."

"Sounds like it would be a fairly high-security assignment."

Amanda nodded. "Right," she said. "It's odd, Oswald was a self-confessed Marxist. His fellow marines called him Oswaldskovich."

"That makes a lot of sense, doesn't it? At the height of the cold war, you assign a marine who's a self-confessed communist to a top secret air force base in Japan."

"He wasn't a very good soldier. He was court-martialled twice."

"He was kicked out of the Marine Corps?"

"No. He finished his tour and was given a dishonourable discharge in September '59."

"Dallas told us that Mr. Smith spent years grooming him for his part in all of this. I wonder—?"

"Are you thinking that Mr. Smith was powerful enough to have the Marines turn a blind eye to Oswald's affinity for the communist way of life?"

"It makes sense, doesn't it? Look at it this way. Prior to Mr. Smith recruiting Oswald into the fifth column, what if he was being prepped to go to the Soviet Union and spy for the CIA? Wouldn't it be likely that they would want him to appear sympathetic to the communist way of life and also have some kind of history that the Russians would think was valuable?"

"He applied for a visa to visit the Soviet Union on October 12, 1959, at the Russian embassy in Helsinki."

"And?"

"What if I told you that his visa was approved and issued within the space of two days? What would you make of that?"

"Two days!" I said. "That's unbelievable. During the height of the cold war—an ex-marine, fresh out of a top secret Air Force base in Japan, gets issued permission to visit the Soviet Union within forty-eight hours? Dallas told us Mr. Smith was everywhere. He must have had his fingers in the embassy in Sweden."

"Helsinki's not in Sweden. It's the capital of Finland."

"She told us that Mr. Smith spent years grooming Oswald for his role. What if Smith arranged for Oswald to be fast-tracked into Russia? What if he knew that the minute Oswald set foot on Russian soil, the KGB would pick him up and brainwash him? What if Mr. Smith had agents in the Soviet Union as well? What if he had the Russians program Oswald to assassinate the president?"

"I saw that movie the other night, too. It was nominated for two Academy Awards."

"Look at the facts. At the height of the cold war, Oswald is granted entry to Russia in less time than it takes to fry up a couple of eggs. Don't you think he had some help somewhere along the line?"

"It looks pretty sinister, doesn't it?"

"You're damned right it does. It's almost like the Soviets were expecting him."

"If Mr. Smith was recruiting rogue agents out of the CIA, why couldn't he be drawing from the KGB as well?"

"Exactly, and that could explain Fred Weller, too. He was Canadian Intelligence Corps. There's no reason why Smith couldn't have enrolled Canadian agents, too."

"What about the British Secret Service? What about the Mossad?"

"You're right," I said. "Dallas told us he was everywhere."

"This is amazing. And you came up with all of this just by analyzing the fact that Oswald was granted a visa to Russia in only two days."

I grinned. "It adds up."

"So we know that Oswald was issued a visa from the Soviet Embassy in Helsinki."

"Fact."

"And we know that it only took two days to be processed."

"Fact," I said again.

"Now—what if I told you that from the embassy in Finland, two days was well within the average waiting time for a visitor's permit to Russia?"

I looked into Amanda's eyes.

"It's true," she said. "Helsinki wasn't a very busy embassy. Oswald didn't show up on any Russian security watch lists. His application was just rubber-stamped through."

"Are you sure?" I asked.

Amanda nodded. "From the information I've been able to gather," she said, "two days was the average time for a visa approval."

I looked down at my shoes.

"Telling the whole truth, instead of just half of it, certainly blows your theory, doesn't it?"

"I need to get back to my desk," I said. "Dallas said she'd call again this afternoon."

# CHAPTER FORTY-THREE

"**How did you** and Amanda do this morning?"

"Good," I said and looked over my notes. "She's found out some interesting things about Lee Harvey Oswald."

Dallas laughed. "I'm sure it will be nothing compared to what I'm going to tell you about him."

"When?" I asked.

"Soon, I haven't had much energy the last few days. I've been sleeping a lot. I need another day, at least, to finish going through my journal."

"Time is not something we have an abundance of, I can tell by your voice. You're not doing very well, are you?"

"I'm weak. The end is near. My doctor's insisting that I check myself into the hospital."

"You have to hang on. I still don't know—"

"You're close," Dallas interrupted. "A lot closer than you think. I have a confession to make."

"What?" I asked.

"I haven't been totally honest with you."

"About what?"

"When it came time for me to choose who I was going to tell my story to—When it came down to a choice between you and Sharon Halter."

"What?"

"It was more than just that series of articles you wrote on those property developers."

"Ball and McDermott?"

"It was more than the fact that you weren't afraid to take on powerful people."

"Tell me," I said.

198

"Mr. Smith is clever. I needed someone who could spot him when the time was right. I told you—he's hidden himself behind a veil of respectability. To the naked eye, he appears to be an upstanding member of the community. It's only when you look past that veil. It will take a keen eye to see the monster behind the mask. Remember, I won't be here to point him out. That's why it's so important that you follow the clues yourself and find him on your own."

"But I still don't know—"

"You *do* know. You have a shock awaiting you. You've crossed paths with the monster before. You've looked into his eyes."

"I have?"

"So has Amanda. You both know this man. Hartree, be careful, he's dangerous, and I don't think he likes you very much."

I swallowed a lump in my throat.

"Why do you think your cop friend lied to you about the license plate?"

I hesitated.

"We both saw the number. We know it exists."

"I've been asking some questions about my old pal, Freddy Weller."

"And?"

"He spent a number of years in the Intelligence Corps. I think he was a spook."

"A spy?"

"An intelligence agent. In the sixties the Canadian Intelligence Corp was Canada's equivalent to the CIA. Weller apparently spent a lot of time in the States."

"Working with the Americans? Doing what? Do you know what his assignments in the U.S. were all about?"

"No," I said. "But he did let an interesting bit of information slip out."

"What's that?"

"Alan Ball. He was in the army too—the American army."

Silence.

"Are you there, Dallas?"

"You discovered the truth about Mr. Ball quicker than I thought you would. Now you need to sit down and ask yourself some questions, Hartree."

"What questions?"

"Alan Ball. What do you think he did in the military? Do you think he could have been Army Intelligence?"

"It's possible," I said. "If Freddy Weller was CIC, he probably didn't spend his time in the States learning how to polish the treads on a tank. He must have worked with U.S. Army Intelligence."

"And you think that's how he first met Alan Ball?"

"How else could it have happened?"

"Maybe Alan Ball worked in the mess hall. Maybe he was just the guy at the end of the chow line slinging the mashed potatoes."

"I've been thinking. I didn't even tell Amanda that I was staying at the Chelsea Arms."

"What are you getting at?"

"Weller," I said. "I made a comment to him when he was here the other morning."

"When he came to see you about the license plate?"

"Yeah, I've been thinking about that, too. We both saw that plate number. We know that it exists."

"What are you saying?"

"Figure it out. We know Weller lied to me about the license plate number, and I didn't tell anyone else that I'd be staying at the Chelsea Arms."

"You told me."

"Besides you, I mean."

"Then Weller must be fifth column."

"Both him *and* Ball—I think I know who Mr. Smith is."

A quick laugh.

"What's funny now?" I asked.

"Are you sure this time?"

"I'm sure."

"It wasn't that long ago that you were certain that Gino Morazzo was Mr. Smith."

"That was early in the game. I didn't have all the facts then."

"You have to be positive this time. Remember, you'll only have one shot at him, you have to make it count."

"I need to dig up more on this man."

"Get back to work on Leon's history. I'll have lots more information for you as soon as I can finish going through my journal."

"Something's fishy about this whole visit to Russia thing. Did you know it only took two days for Oswald to be granted an entry visa?"

"I did know that. On his second day in Moscow, he informed the Soviet officials that he wished to defect."

"And?"

"They turned him down. They weren't interested in having him stay in Russia."

"But he lived in Russia for some time."

"Fact. Why do you think they turned him down the first time he tried to defect?"

I leaned on my elbow. "Maybe the Russian officials knew he was a CIA plant."

"Or maybe they knew he was a nut case and they didn't want anything to do with him."

"But they *did* grant him the right to stay. Something—or someone— must have changed their minds."

"Two weeks after the Soviets rejected Leon's offer to defect, he stormed into the American embassy in Moscow. He told the staff at the embassy that he was not only going to renounce his citizenship, but that he was going to give the Russians everything he had learned as a Marine radar operator at Atsugi."

"And how do you think that got back to the Russians?"

"Come on, Hartree. You remember the stories about the cold war. That embassy probably had more bugs in it than the pile of firewood under your back porch. Everything that was said in that building probably went straight to some radio receiver in the Kremlin."

"It was an act?"

"Put on for the benefit of the Soviet listening devices. Mr. Smith knew all about the hidden microphones in the embassy. Only a few months after that, the Russians shot down a U2 spy plane over Moscow."

"Francis Gary Powers. Then the information Oswald gave the Russians must have been pretty valuable."

"That's one way to look at it. Or maybe the Soviets were just getting better with their radar tracking and their missile development."

"But it *is* another rather an odd coincidence, don't you think?"

"He lived in the Soviet Union for almost three years. He spent most of his time in Minsk, and he lived quite well, compared to the average Soviet citizen."

"He only stayed in Russia for three years?"

"Almost three years."

"Mr. Smith must have decided that that component of his grooming was complete."

"Wait a second."

"What?" I asked.

"I know I have it written down here somewhere. Here it is. It cost $435.71 for him and his new Russian bride to return to the United States. See if you can find out who paid the bill for his transportation home. I'll talk to you again tomorrow."

# CHAPTER FORTY-FOUR

AMANDA LEANED AGAINST the back of her desk. "You'd better sit down for this," she said.

I spun my chair around and sat. "What?" I asked.

"Dallas told us that November 22nd wasn't the first time Leon had used his Carcano rifle."

I nodded my head. "And that he'd failed in his first assassination assignment from Mr. Smith."

"The man's name was Walker—Edwin Walker. He was a general in the U.S. Army. He led the 24th Army Division."

"And?"

"Kennedy relieved him of his command in 1961—for distributing right wing propaganda material to his troops."

"Jesus Christ," I mumbled.

"He resigned from the army and took up residence in Dallas. He actually ran for Governor of Texas. He lost out to John Connally."

"And?"

"This guy leaned so far to the right that he could probably have touched the ground with his nose."

"And Oswald tried to kill him?"

"Uh-huh. He stalked him for weeks. He took pictures of Walker's house, he studied Walker's movements, he even prepared a location to bury his rifle, and he had a map of a planned escape route."

"That's incredible."

"He snuck into Walker's back yard one night. The general was working at his desk."

"And?"

"Oswald fired one shot, from less than one hundred feet."

"And he missed? He really was a lousy shot, wasn't he?"

"It was just pure luck on Walker's part. Apparently the bullet grazed one of the wooden slats that held the glass panes in the window. That deflected the shot enough, so instead of hitting Walker in the head, it actually passed through his hair."

"You're right. Walker must have had a guardian angel watching him that night."

Amanda hunched forward. "There's something else that's really odd," she said.

"What?"

"Oswald left detailed instructions for his wife about what she should do if he was either captured or killed."

"That is strange."

Amanda reread her notes. "He even instructed her how to dispose of his clothes. He was adamant that she keep all of his papers, but he was equally insistent that she throw away every stitch of clothing that he owned."

"Dallas told us that Mr. Smith was preparing Leon and that the Walker shooting was just a warm up for the Kennedy assassination. Do you think—?"

"He was preparing him, right down to the part of his taking a bullet in the gut afterward?"

"How could Mr. Smith have had that much control over the man?"

Amanda shrugged her shoulders. "I also found out who picked up the tab for Oswald and his wife's passage back to the U.S. when they left Russia."

"Who?" I asked.

Amanda turned a few pages back in her notebook. "$435.71," she said, "paid in full by the U.S. State Department."

"Jesus," I muttered. "That kind of thing has CIA written all over it."

Amanda nodded. "And, even though the intelligence agencies knew that he had threatened to give the Soviets everything he had learned about the U2s, he wasn't even debriefed when he returned to American soil."

"I knew that Oswald was connected in some way to the intelligence community."

"And the fifth column."

"Keep working on him. I'll see you tomorrow morning at ten."

# Chapter Forty-Five

I LIFTED THE stack of file folders off the top of my filing cabinet and slapped them onto my desk. Above all else, at least I was organized. I placed my hands palms down on the tabletop and leaned forward and closed my eyes. I was exhausted. Who would have thought that after all the years of telling lies that it would be the truth that kept me from sleeping? I stood and arched my back and tried to force the grogginess from my head. I sorted through the folders and added Amanda's notes to Oswald's file. I placed the folder to one side. Dallas would need to verify a few details and I was still waiting for her to finish reading through her journal. The phone rang, I reached for it.

"Hartree?" the man whispered.

I recognized the voice. I opened my desk drawer and punched the record button on my tape machine.

"I know who you are," I said.

A laugh.

"There are two in every deck," I told him.

"I guess that means you've been chatting with Dallas again. Did you remember to say hello for me?"

"What do you want?"

"I'm just checking up on you. I enjoyed talking to you the other night at the hotel. You'll have to excuse my poor manners. I should have invited you downstairs to the lounge—they make an excellent martini; maybe next time. Where are you staying now?"

"Wouldn't you like to know?"

"Never mind, you weren't that hard to find the last time. I'll track you down soon, I'm sure. That's my specialty."

"I'll ask you again," I said. "What is it that you want?"

"Come on, Hartree. I don't really need to answer that, do I? It's *you* that I want. We like to tease our victims a little first—that's all."

"You know where I am right now. Why don't you hop in your Jaguar and come on over?"

Another laugh.

"What's the matter?" I asked. "Are you afraid to go face to face with me?"

"I helped to kill a president. Do you really think that a man like you could scare me?"

I felt a cold finger touch my heart.

"Besides," he whispered, "that would take all the fun out of it. We have a couple of ideas, but we still haven't decided what to do with you. I'm sure the woman has filled you in. We always try to make these things look like accidents. Though sometimes, we just can't help being a bit theatrical."

"What are you going to do? Toss me out of a speeding car?"

"That wasn't one of Mr. Smith's better plans. It doesn't work quite as well as, say—falling off a balcony. Does the woman still quote Shakespeare?"

"What woman?"

"Don't play games with me, Hartree. Ask her if she remembers how Claudius killed King Hamlet. It's an interesting concept; I've often wondered how it would work. Do it soon, though. She won't be around much longer."

"Son of a bitch," I muttered.

"Tell me. What's it like?"

"Huh?"

"What's it like to know you're being hunted? What's it like to know that the next time you step into an elevator, one of our agents could be waiting for you? What's it like to know that the next time you turn the key in your car's ignition, the shaped charge under the seat could blow you to smithereens? What's it like to know that I'm after you, and there's nothing you can do to defend yourself?"

"Maybe you should ask Mr. Smith that same question," I said. "After all this time, how does it feel to know that I'm on to him, and that his days are numbered?"

"I guess we'll just have to see about that. I'll make you a deal. When this comes to a head, I'll buy the martinis at the Chelsea Arms—a toast to the victor, whoever it may be."

"I can tell you who it will be. I'm close."

"You *are* close. A lot closer than you think. I'd prepare myself for a shock, if I were you."

"My—uh—source tells me that I know him."

"You *do* know him."

"I'm a powerful man," I said. "He won't be able to stop me."

"You *are* a powerful man. I'll tell you, there's nothing Mr. Smith likes more than to destroy a man with clout. I know he's looking forward to this."

"I'm looking forward to it, too."

"I have to admit, I'm going to enjoy watching this fight. And I have a confession to make."

"What's that?"

"Mr. Smith destroyed a lot of lives. Ask Dallas the next time you speak to her. He ruined her life, just like he ruined mine."

"You want me to win?"

"Let's just say that I agree with Dallas that the man should be stopped. A little taste of revenge might be sweet."

"Dallas walked away from him. Why didn't you?"

"A different set of circumstances. I was on the periphery. Once I was drawn into the web of lies, it was impossible for me to get out."

"Why is that?"

"My sense of loyalty, perhaps. I knew what I was doing was wrong, but I was in too deep."

"So you're hoping that when I stop Mr. Smith, you'll be set free."

"I guess that's a good way to explain it. If Smith was out of the picture, I could end this charade. I wouldn't be hanging around hotels in the middle of the night or chasing people like you down Oak Street in my Jaguar."

"You son of a bitch."

"I just hope you've got enough strength to continue your pursuit, even after your fountain of information suddenly dries up."

"What?" I asked.

"The woman—Dallas. I have an advantage over you. I know *who* she is, and I also know *where* she is."

I drew a breath.

"Does that surprise you? Did you think I'd have trouble finding her?"

I held my tongue.

"She's an intelligent lady, but she just doesn't understand the world we live in today. People leave trails."

"You're bluffing," I said.

"Am I? Next time you speak to her, ask her how she paid for her room. I can give you her credit card number, if that helps to convince you."

"Jesus Christ," I muttered. "She wasn't careless enough to use her credit card, was she?"

"Like I said, she grew up in a different time. It probably didn't occur to her that one swipe of that card through the hotel's reader was all I needed to pinpoint her."

"And have you passed this information on to Mr. Smith?"

"Not yet."

"Are you going to?"

"I don't know. My actions have been scripted, and I'm not yet entirely sure what's on the next page."

"You mentioned loyalties. What about your loyalty to Dallas? You were partners for how long?"

"Twenty years or more."

"Then how could you turn her over like that?"

"It's more complex than that. If I can help it, Mr. Smith won't find out where Dallas is hiding until it's too late. But there are other people involved."

"Other people?"

"Mr. Smith is out there searching for her, too. We'll know if he finds her. We'll know when he's ready to strike."

"How?"

"He'll send her a gift."

I closed my eyes and shook my head.

"He always likes to send a gift just before the end."

"Your other partner—Crystal. It was Smith who sent her the orchid."

"Who do you think sent it? I felt bad about Crystal. She was a good operative. She always came through for us. Not like Leon and some of the others."

"Don't lie to me. Oswald did exactly what he was programmed to do."

"You just don't understand what Mr. Smith had to deal with. Really—the egos of some of those people—and the incompetence! It was almost too much to bear sometimes. Have you learned about General Walker yet?"

"I have. Smith ordered Leon to shoot him."

"Right, but he missed. I couldn't believe it when I heard the news. I should have handled Walker myself."

"Maybe you should stand in front of a mirror when you talk about people and their egos."

"We could stand side by side. You've come up with some twisted idea that just because Mr. Smith has had a few people killed that he's some kind of master demon. What about you? You print lies and distortions of the truth, to get what? A pat on the back from your boss or a little framed certificate to hang on the wall of your study? Let's call a spade a spade, Hartree. Why do you think it was so easy for Mr. Smith to convince Leon to wrap that cheap Italian army rifle of his up in a blanket and run around Dallas shooting at people? How do you think he talked Jack into strolling into a police station less than forty-eight hours after Kennedy was killed and putting a bullet in Lee's belly?"

"How?" I asked.

"He offered them a page in the history books. They both wanted to be someone special. They weren't much different from you."

"This is nonsense," I said. "Don't try and paint me with that brush. The cat's out of the bag. His days are numbered, and you know it."

"I can hardly wait."

I switched the phone to my left hand and wiped the sweat from my right. "For what?" I asked. "For me to expose him? You want this nightmare to end?"

"No, that's not what I meant. You haven't won this battle yet. I can't wait to see the look on your face when you finally put the pieces of the puzzle together. That's if you and Dallas last that long."

I pulled open my desk drawer and checked on my gun. "We'll see about that," I said. "I'm stronger than you think."

"Smith has a lot of people under his spell. As far as they're concerned, everything that comes out of his mouth is pure gospel. All he needs to do is tell them that you have to go. There are legions of them standing in line—ready to believe whatever he tells them, and do whatever he wants them to do. You know how he works. That's why it was so easy to eliminate Leon. He just planted the idea in Ruby's mind, and then he whipped him into a frenzy with a bunch of lies, and the suggestion that his actions would earn him a place in the history books and save the country from the torment of going through a trial."

"I read that," I said. "Ruby made a statement that the reason that he shot Oswald was to save Mrs. Kennedy from the pain of coming back to Texas to testify at the trial."

"All Mr. Smith had to do was to plant the seed. You work much the same way he does. Take Ball and McDermott. You fed the public the idea that the two of them had done something wrong. Once that notion was firmly embedded in their minds, people were blinded. They couldn't see the whole picture. They only saw the version of the truth that you wanted them to see."

"While we're on the subject of Alan Ball—"

"Never mind Alan Ball. It's you I want to talk about."

"I know that somehow he's involved in this."

Laughter.

"What's so funny?" I asked.

"Look at the whole forest, Hartree. Not just the trees."

"You're an American, aren't you?"

"I could be. Nationality really has nothing to do with this."

"You were in the military, weren't you?"

"Lots of people my age got their start in the military. There weren't as many opportunities for young people back then."

"I know who you are."

"Are you sure?"

"Almost," I said. "The list is down to two names."

"Then you'd better start writing your story. We'll start the clock now, let the games begin. Be careful, though. Stand back and look at everything you've learned, not just the parts you want to believe are true."

"I've already started. I'm just waiting for a little more from my source."

"Dallas? You'd better hurry. She hasn't got much time left."

"Is that another threat?"

"It's a fact. I have to go now. I have some things to do. Get some rest tonight; you're going to need it. And I'd sleep on my back if I were you."

I shut off my recorder as the line fell silent.

# Chapter Forty-Six

I LEANED ON the counter and stared at a splatter that stained the wall next to the coffeemaker. Amanda stood at the window of the meeting room and gazed out at the morning rain, completely lost in her thoughts. I'd come to see her in a different light over the last week or two. She wasn't the bundle of misdirected energy that I had pegged her for in the past. She wasn't just a millstone hung around my neck by my editor—a way to break up the old boys' club in the newsroom. Despite the way I'd treated her, she always produced quality work. She made the best out of each situation, regardless of what she was handed or the roadblocks that were placed in her path. The woman both had a gift and was a gift.

I thought about her story of the Russian woman. I'd dug it out of my bottom drawer again last night and reread it for the fifth or sixth time. I couldn't put it down. The image she presented of the old lady was so vivid and precise that I'd swear that I would recognize every wrinkle on her face if she walked into this room. I didn't deserve to have an apprentice like Amanda. I wondered, sometimes, what she really thought of me. She was close enough to see through the facade, close enough to see the type of man I'd become.

Joker was right. Smith and I were a lot alike. I hadn't killed anyone, but I'd created a niche for myself by turning a blind eye to the truths that didn't fit my agenda. I'd hung Chris McDermott out to dry, for no other reason than to earn a shot at a Ceejay. I'd be burying Charlie Wolfe right now, if Dallas hadn't stumbled into my life.

"Come on," I said. "Let's get to work." I pulled my cassette recorder from my briefcase and placed it on the table. "I got a call from Joker this morning."

⌘

I switched the recorder off and pushed it to one side. I turned in Amanda's direction.

"What do you think?" I asked.

She lifted her head and looked into my eyes. She held my gaze for a moment and then turned away.

"What is it?" I asked.

"I'm scared," she said, "scared for you. Joker really is coming for you."

I ran my hand through my hair. "I'm being careful. Remember, we're just as close to nailing Mr. Smith."

"Are we? We really aren't any closer to putting a name to him than we were last week—or the week before that."

"I disagree. We've got two strong possibilities."

"Alan Ball and Freddy Weller?"

"Right," I said.

"We still don't have anything concrete on either of these men. I agree, with what we know, and with the information that Dallas has given us, they both look pretty suspicious. But we still have nothing that proves that either one of them could be Mr. Smith."

"Let's look at the facts. We know Weller lied to me about the license plate number."

"And how do we know that, for sure?"

"Dallas saw the plate number, too. We know that I didn't get it wrong."

Amanda looked down at the table. "And then there was the night that Joker showed up at your hotel."

"Right," I said, "I didn't tell anyone but Weller where I was staying."

"Joker said he tracked Dallas down by her credit card. You didn't—"

"Of course I didn't. I know better than that. I paid cash for my room."

"Then I guess we have to look at who could have access to credit card information."

"Right," I said, "a bank employee, or—"

Amanda looked up. "A cop," she said.

I nodded my head. "I'll have to stay close to the phone. I have to warn Dallas that Joker knows where she is."

"I hope she calls this morning."

"She will," I said. "She hasn't got much time left. Every day might be her last."

"You know that Joker has made a direct threat on your life, don't you?"

"What do you mean?"

"When he mentioned King Hamlet—when he told you that you'd better sleep on your back."

"Explain."

"The belief was that the king went to sleep in an orchard, and that he was stung by a serpent."

"Huh?"

"Bitten by a poisonous snake."

"OK," I said.

"Prince Hamlet met his father's ghost one night on the battle platform of Elsinore Castle. King Hamlet asked his son to *revenge his foul and most unnatural murder*."

I nodded.

"The ghost revealed that it wasn't a snake bite that killed him. It was Claudius who poured a *leperous distilment* into his ear while he was asleep."

"*Leperous distilment?*"

"Poison. I think that's how Mr. Smith intends to kill you, and that's why Joker warned you to sleep on your back."

"Don't worry," I said, "I'm being careful."

# CHAPTER FORTY-SEVEN

I LUNGED AT the phone and swung the receiver to my ear before it had a chance to ring a second time.

"Hartree?" the woman asked.

"Dallas," I said, "I've been sitting by this phone for hours waiting for your call. You've got major problems."

"Let's see," the woman answered, "I have cancer raging through my body, I'm confessing to crimes that would turn a goat's stomach, I have a monster trying to track me down and if he finds me he's going to destroy me. What on earth could my problem be?"

"It's Joker. He knows where you are."

"And how did you come across that little bit of information?"

"He called me again," I said. I turned my wrist and looked at my watch. "About four hours ago."

"And he told you that he knows where I am?"

"Did you use your credit card when you checked into your hotel?"

"I did. I thought about it afterward; I guess that wasn't the smartest thing for me to do."

"No," I said, "I guess it wasn't. You have to leave—now. Don't bother to pack up your things—just get out."

"I'm not going anywhere," she said. "I just don't have the strength to run any further."

"Tell me where you are. I'll come and get you."

Dallas let out a weak laugh and then began to cough.

"Enough games," I told her. "Give me the name of the hotel."

"So you can do what?" she asked after she caught her breath. "If he gets us both, he's won the contest, hasn't he?"

"You can't just sit and wait for him."

"Why not? You have almost all the information you need to carry on without me. Anyway, I still have a little time left."

"Are you crazy?" I asked. "Joker could be on the way to your hotel as we speak."

"No," she replied, "he can't come for me yet."

"And why is that?" I asked.

"My gift—I haven't received my gift yet. Mr. Smith always sends a gift first."

"Please. Tell me where you are."

"I've had a chance to do some reading. I'm surprised at how many things that I'd forgotten about Leon."

"What things?"

"Mexico, for one. Did you know that before Leon moved to Dallas, he ran the New Orleans chapter of the Fair Play for Cuba organization?"

"I read that he was involved with that group, but I didn't know he ran his own chapter."

"Get Amanda to look into it. Mr. Smith thought it was important for Leon to have some high-profile and subversive activities in his past."

"I will."

"I've noticed a bit of a change in you over the last few calls."

"What kind of a change?" I asked.

"You're not being as hard on Amanda. I can tell by your voice."

I drew a breath and looked down at the floor. "I have to admit," I said, "she's been a godsend."

"Hartree?"

"Yeah," I said.

"I need to ask you a question."

"Go ahead," I told her.

"I want an honest answer."

"OK."

"Chris McDermott: Have you ever had any regrets?"

"About the stories I wrote?"

"Yes."

I leaned my elbow on the desk and dropped my head and scratched the back of my neck. "Yeah," I said, "I've had regrets. Lots of regrets."

"About destroying an honest and hard-working politician's career?"

"About the lies, mostly," I mumbled.

"Could you speak up a little?"

"About the lying," I repeated. "There—are you happy now? I've said it. I lied."

"And do you feel better about yourself now that you've confessed it to me?"

"You aren't going to get all religious on me, are you? You're not going to ask me to drop to my knees or anything?"

"No, but you have to admit, you do feel better."

"I do."

"I needed to hear you say it. I needed to hear you admit to yourself that you lied. It will make things a lot easier for you a few days down the road."

"What?" I asked.

"When it comes time to point the finger at Mr. Smith; at least you'll be going up against him with a clean conscience."

"You mentioned Mexico a minute ago."

"That's right. I dug through some old notes. You have to understand how Leon was set up. You need to know how Mr. Smith convinced him to pack his rifle to work with him that morning."

"How?" I asked.

"It was just like the Walker shooting. Leon was given instructions— right down to his escape plan."

"I don't imagine he knew that his only part in the assassination was to be the fall guy."

"Of course he didn't. He even made a dry run."

"To Mexico?"

"Right. In September of 1963."

"A few weeks before the assassination."

"Yes, Leon took a bus to Mexico City. He went to the Cuban embassy to apply for a visa."

"The Cuban embassy?"

"That was the escape plan. Fly to Cuba, and then to the Soviet Union."

"What happened?"

"Mr. Smith convinced him that the Cubans would lay out the red carpet for him. Leon showed them his Fair Play for Cuba and his American Communist Party membership cards."

"And?"

"He even took his Russian residency papers and some newspaper clippings of the time he was arrested for starting a fistfight with some anti-Castro demonstrators in New Orleans."

"The Cubans turned his visa request down?"

"Leon was furious. I think the worst part for him was that someone he trusted completely had lied to him. Do you know what that feels like, Hartree?"

"Let's get on with this. What did he do after the Cubans turned him down?"

"He went to the Russian Embassy next. He thought that they could put some pressure on Havana."

"And?"

"No go. They told him he'd have to go through the application process like everyone else. He had to submit five copies of his visa request, along with five passport-type photos."

"And he was running out of time."

"So was Mr. Smith, he still had some work to do on the frame he was building."

"What kind of work?"

"The rifle mostly."

"The Carcano?"

"Mr. Smith knew that Leon would be smart enough not to leave prints on the gun. And he already knew what the results of the paraffin tests would show."

"The paraffin tests?"

"It was the first thing the police would do if they got their hands on Leon."

"*If* they got their hands on him?"

"I told you that Leon's purpose was to take the blame, and that he had to die before he could prove his innocence. I didn't say that it had to happen in the police garage in front of all those TV cameras. Leon made one big mistake that day. If only he hadn't crossed paths with Officer Tippet."

"Tippet disrupted Oswald's escape plan?"

"Leon managed to walk a mile from his boarding house. He was only a few blocks from the Route 55 bus stop."

"To Mexico?"

"The Route 55 bus would have taken him to the Greyhound bus that was going to Monterrey in Mexico. He had $13.87 in his pocket when he was arrested—just enough to pay for his ticket."

"And we know this for a fact?"

"You'll find it in chapter six of the Warren Report."

"Let's get back to Mr. Smith. I know that Alan Ball is mixed up in this somewhere."

"I guess it's time for me to confirm *something* to you. You were right all along: Alan Ball is deeply involved."

"I knew it. And what about Freddy Weller—what about him?"

"Don't be greedy. You know for certain about Ball, now. You've taken a major step forward."

"But I still don't know for sure if Ball is Mr. Smith. It could be Freddy Weller."

"Or it could be someone else entirely. I only said Ball was a part of this."

I heard a noise in the background. "What was that?"

"You'll have to wait a minute. Someone's at the door."

"Dallas," I said, "let it go. Don't answer it."

I heard the sound of the phone being placed down. I waited for what seemed like an hour.

"I'm back," she said. "It was just the bellboy."

I heard the sound of ripping paper.

"Oh, my," she said, "it's gorgeous."

"What?" I asked

"My gift, a leather-bound edition of *Hamlet*—and it was wrapped in bright red paper—just the way I expected. I'm going to hang up now. I'm tired. I'll call you tomorrow. I'm sure Mr. Smith will give me at least a day or two to enjoy my new book."

# Chapter Forty-Eight

AMANDA OPENED HER briefcase, pulled out a stack of loose papers, and slapped them on the meeting room table. "This whole thing is getting more absurd by the second," she said.

"I know. It's hard to believe what we've stumbled upon."

"That's not what I meant. It's all the lies and the twisting of what actually is true."

"What are you saying?"

"The last call from Dallas, she mentioned that Oswald headed the New Orleans chapter of the Fair Play for Cuba organization."

"And?"

"It sounds pretty subversive, doesn't it?"

"She told us that it was part of Mr. Smith's plan—to make Oswald look like some sort of revolutionary."

"If she knew Oswald that well, why wouldn't she have told you how many members were actually in the New Orleans chapter?"

"How many?"

"Including Oswald?"

"Yeah."

"One."

"That's all? Are you sure?"

"I'm sure." Amanda nodded and pointed to her notes. "There's nothing to indicate that Oswald had any other members in his group."

"Dallas mentioned the prints on the gun."

"And the paraffin tests."

"What do you think she was trying to tell us?"

"It just led me to more lies and outrageous theories. The Dallas police apparently lifted Oswald's palm print off the rifle, but I read that the FBI was unable to find any prints on it at all."

I drummed my fingers on the table. "That must have made the FBI look good."

"And that's when the rumour surfaced about the mortician."

"The mortician?"

"From the funeral home where they took Oswald's body. He claimed that some mysterious characters showed up one night and placed the rifle in Oswald's dead hands."

"The Dallas police falsified the palm print?" I asked.

"The mortician claimed that he didn't know whether they were police, FBI, CIA, or Secret Service."

"Or fifth column."

"He said he had to wash the fingerprint ink off Oswald's hands when they left."

"Then there's the paraffin testing," I recalled. "No gunshot residue was found on Oswald's cheek. When a person fires a rifle, there's blowback of powder and residue that ends up on the shooter's face."

"Uh-huh."

"But there was no such residue on Oswald's face; therefore, he couldn't have fired his rifle."

I looked Amanda in the eyes. "Dallas was telling us the truth," I said. "Oswald didn't fire those shots from the sixth-floor window."

"Mr. Smith built the perfect frame around him."

"He was the ideal patsy. Christ, he even looked guilty. The police did find gunpowder residue on his hands—from his revolver—from when he shot the police officer."

"There were witnesses that saw him shoot Officer Tippet."

"So, how do we prove that Mr. Smith falsified the prints on the rifle? And how do we prove that Oswald didn't fire his Carcano on November 22nd?"

"Prove it?" Amanda groaned. "Listen carefully to what we just said."

"That someone planted Oswald's prints on the gun?"

"Sure," Amanda said. "Does this all sound plausible to you? Some sinister group of people show up at the funeral home with the rifle that supposedly killed the president."

"The fifth column."

"The five stooges—maybe. If they were that good at killing people, why would they leave a witness? Why would they use fingerprint ink, if they were there to place an impression of Oswald's palm on the gun? He spent almost two days in police custody. I'm sure they didn't need more prints from him. And tell me why, after all that, they wouldn't take the time to wash the ink off Oswald's hands?"

"You're right," I said, "it does sound a little ridiculous."

"It's insane. How could anyone be expected to believe a story like that?"

"But the paraffin tests—we can't dispute the scientific evidence."

"We can't?"

"Oswald never fired his rifle."

"Do you know anything about paraffin testing?"

"No," I said and looked down at my shoes.

"Warmed paraffin is placed on the skin to open up the pores. It's peeled off after it starts to harden and the cast is treated with a chemical. The wax will show speckles of blue if it picks up any trace of nitrates."

"Gunpowder?"

"It's an extremely unreliable examination. A positive test shows the presence of nitrates. It could mean that the person being tested had just scooped up a handful of laundry soap, or smoked a cigarette. Nitrates are a pretty common substance."

"Then why—?"

"Dallas is only telling us the information she wants us to hear," Amanda said.

"She's leading us to Mr. Smith. In order to do that, she has to show us how he built the frame around Oswald with his lies. This woman has an agenda. She's out to destroy Mr. Smith, and she's giving us the ammunition that we need to carry on the fight after she dies."

"There are so many stories. Oswald acted alone; there was a second shooter on the grassy knoll—"

I interrupted her: "A Dallas police officer claimed he was turned away from the grassy knoll by a man who produced Secret Service ID."

"And there were at least two people who claimed that they had filmed the assassination and that their films were confiscated by the Secret Service."

"There *were* no Secret Service agents on the ground in Dealey Plaza. Their job was to protect the president. They were all in the motorcade.

Obviously, Mr. Smith had fifth column operatives posing as Secret Service agents."

"Obviously?" Amanda raised her eyebrows. "You don't think these people could be lying? Maybe they were simply mistaken. Don't forget, their president had just been shot. Those men could have produced their library cards as ID. There must have been complete panic going on."

"Maybe," I said.

"There were so many wild theories flying around that, in 1981, they actually exhumed Oswald's body to make sure it was really him in the grave. How does the truth manage to get warped so badly?"

"It doesn't take much," I said. "There are two sides to a coin. Sometimes all you need to do is make a suggestion."

"How will we ever know?"

"We have Dallas on our side now," I said and stood away from the table. "We're going to win this fight."

# Chapter Forty-Nine

"Hartree?" the man whispered.

"Joker," I said, "I've been expecting you to call."

"How's your search going?"

"Fine," I said. "I know about Oswald's escape plan—to Cuba."

"You do?"

"I even know about the trip to the Cuban embassy in Mexico City the month before the assassination."

"That was never proven. A lot of people believe it was an Oswald look-a-like that Mr. Smith sent to Mexico that September. The CIA photographed everyone that went into that embassy. They never got any pictures of Oswald."

"It *was* proven," I said. "In 1978, the Cuban government turned the original visa applications over to the House Select Committee on the assassination. Handwriting experts verified Oswald's signature. His picture was attached to all five copies."

"Then why do you think the CIA never got any shots of him entering the embassy?"

"Mr. Smith still had ties to the intelligence community. I think he made the pictures go away."

"Are you sure about that?"

"I understand how he worked: he framed Oswald, and he only allowed the information that he wanted the public to hear get out."

"That's a pretty serious accusation."

"I also know how Oswald's palm print got on the rifle."

"You didn't believe that one did you? I thought you were smarter than that."

"It was all part of the set-up."

"The original plan was to have Oswald hijack a plane. The State Department had banned all flights to Cuba. Oswald thought that sounded like a revolutionary thing to do. Mr. Smith even had Oswald convinced that Castro himself would be waiting at the airport to greet him."

"What changed Smith's mind?"

"He had to keep Oswald in Dallas long enough for Jack to do his job. He couldn't take the chance that Leon might actually make it to the airport."

"The Dallas police were broadcasting Oswald's description less than fifteen minutes after the shots were fired in Dealey Plaza."

"And he was dead less that forty-eight hours after that."

"I know how the police were able to pin Oswald as a suspect so quickly."

"You think so?"

"Come on," I said, "admit it. There wasn't enough time to link him to the rifle that they found on the sixth floor. Someone must have tipped off the police."

"Everything went the way it was planned."

"Everything except for Officer Tippet."

"A plan has to have a glitch somewhere. Luckily, Jack had access to the police station."

"Ruby?"

"Yeah."

"Tell me," I said, "how could Mr. Smith convince a person to waltz into a police station and shoot someone in front of dozens of people and TV cameras?"

"It's not that hard. How did you convince your readers to hang Chris McDermott?"

"This has nothing to do with Chris McDermott."

"Of course it does. Mr. Smith filled Jack's head with lies; then he whipped him into a frenzy with more half-truths and the suggestion that what he was about to do was for the good of the people."

"By saving the country the pain of going through a trial."

"He convinced Jack that he'd be the hero. You remind me a little of Ruby."

"What?" I asked.

"He always wanted to be someone. He always wanted people to see him as some sort of crusader. He needed to be recognized. He was just like you."

"That's ridiculous," I muttered.

"I guess that's not really fair. You never killed anyone. You just destroyed Chris McDermott's life, that's all. I guess you're more like Mr. Smith than you are like Jack. You're a master at masking the truth, just like he is. Still, Jack should have listened."

"Listened?"

"There's a crime in Texas called 'murder without malice.' It carries a sentence of no more that five years."

"And?"

"It would have been a simple defence. He could have said, 'I saw him, I had the opportunity, I knew that he had killed my president, the impulse took hold, and I shot him.' But Jack wouldn't listen. He decided to go for an acquittal. It took the jury less than an hour to convict him of premeditated murder."

"And the sentence was death."

"Yes. He was granted a second trial on the basis that the statements he made to the Dallas police, after the shooting in the garage, should not have been allowed. He was also granted a change of venue. The second trial was scheduled for December of 1966."

"I didn't know he had a second trial."

"When the sheriff arrived early in December to transport him to the new venue, he refused to take him because Jack was too sick. That's when they discovered that Ruby had cancer. It was everywhere—his lungs, his liver, his brain. He died in January of 1967."

"And another loose end was conveniently tied up. I read somewhere that Ruby claimed he was injected with cancer cells."

"It saved Mr. Smith the trouble of dealing with him in prison. Jack liked to talk—a lot."

"I know that Ruby was programmed to kill Oswald from the very start. That was part of the master plan. Oswald had to die to cover the tracks of the others."

"It's amazing what you can make people believe with a handful of well-placed lies, isn't it?"

"It is."

"We could have used a man like you back in the sixties. What you did to Chris McDermott was brilliant. You printed only the information you wanted the public to know. You published the truth, but you presented it in a way that made McDermott look guilty as hell. Nothing that you wrote could be denied. You built the perfect frame."

"I didn't do anything that was wrong."

"You killed a powerful political figure, just like Mr. Smith did. The only difference was that you used a pen instead of a rifle."

"I don't have to sit here and listen to your crap."

"Have you spoken to Dallas today?"

"Who?"

"Don't play games with me, Hartree. Did she like her gift?"

"You son of a bitch."

"She's going to die soon, and I'll be holding her hand when she goes."

# CHAPTER FIFTY

"MORE COFFEE?" I asked.

"No, thanks," Amanda replied.

"Something's bothering you. It's written all over your face."

Amanda nodded. "There *is* something bothering me," she said. "I'm starting to wonder whether everything Dallas has told us is true. I'm beginning to think that maybe some of her facts are a little twisted."

"You don't think she's been telling us the truth?"

"Maybe it's not her fault. Maybe she's just telling us what she believes to be true."

"Be more specific."

"Jack Ruby. There's something about Oswald's shooting that doesn't add up."

"What?" I asked. "Ruby was on the street outside of the police station. The officer that was guarding the entrance to the garage was distracted for a few moments. Ruby walked down the entrance ramp to the parking garage, strolled right up to Oswald as he was being moved to a police vehicle, and shot him in the stomach."

"It sounds like the perfect plan, doesn't it?"

"Mr. Smith's timing was flawless. Oswald was in the parking garage for less than a minute before he was killed."

"So you're saying that the murder of Lee Harvey Oswald was planned down to the split second."

"Right," I said. "You've seen the TV footage. He was escorted into the garage, and Ruby was there in a flash with his gun."

"It stinks of conspiracy, doesn't it?"

"Mr. Smith knew that in order for his plan to work, Oswald had to die."

"The police announced that Oswald would be transferred at 10:00 a.m. Originally, they planned to use an armoured car. The first one they brought in was too big; they couldn't get it into the garage."

"And?"

"The second one was too small to accommodate Oswald as well as his guards. That pushed the transfer back by an hour."

"So?"

"If Mr. Smith ordered Ruby to kill Oswald, why wasn't he in the police garage at ten o'clock?"

"Smith must have gotten word that the transfer was being held up."

"He must have. One of Ruby's strippers phoned him that morning and asked to borrow twenty-five dollars. He told her that he'd wire it to her. The Western Union office was only a block from the police station."

"So he stopped to send her the money first?"

"The clocks at all the Western Union offices were synchronized with the U.S. Naval Observatory clock in Washington DC. They were checked and reset every morning at 11:00 a.m. Ruby's receipt for the twenty-five-dollar transfer was time-stamped 11:17 a.m. It's seems like the planning had gotten a little loose, don't you think?"

"But we know that Mr. Smith was everywhere. He must have had someone in the police station."

"The police investigators finished with Oswald in the interrogation room at 11:00 a.m."

"Then the plan wasn't unravelling. Ruby had to be in a position to enter the garage at precisely the right moment."

"You're right. It must have all been part of the grand conspiracy. Mr. Smith must have been informed of the *exact* time that Oswald was going to be moved."

"Someone in the police department *had* to have been involved."

Amanda nodded. "I found the name of the person that delayed the transfer long enough for Ruby to get into position."

"You what!"

"You heard me. I know who held up the transfer long enough for Ruby to make his way from the Western Union office to the police garage in time."

"Who?" I asked. "Tell me!"

"His name was Lee Harvey Oswald."

"What," I said, "that's ridiculous."

"The interrogation ended at 11:00 a.m. sharp. Oswald insisted on a change of clothes. It took more than twenty minutes to find him something else to wear. If they had left as planned, when Ruby was still at the Western Union office, Oswald would have been safely out of the police station—instead he asked for a different sweater to put on."

"But that would make Oswald part of the conspiracy to cause his *own* death."

"You're right. That *is* ridiculous."

# CHAPTER FIFTY-ONE

THE VOICE WAS weak. I strained to hear.

"I think this is goodbye, Hartree," Dallas said. "My days are done. We won't be speaking again."

"But—"

"I know," Dallas replied. "I promised that you'd be able to put a name to Mr. Smith before I died. I'm just addressing the mailer now. It will be couriered to you after I'm gone."

"Marilyn's red diary?" I asked.

"Your last clue. Trust me; everything will fall into place when you and Amanda follow the instructions that are in this envelope."

"Instructions?"

"That's right. I've learned that there's going to be a meeting in town. I know Mr. Smith will be there."

"Mr. Smith will be there!"

"That's right, him *and* Joker. I'm sure of it. I don't think there's anything that could keep them away."

"How will I know?"

"Keep your eyes and ears open. You won't have a problem spotting him."

"I can't believe this," I said "I don't know how to thank you."

"I should be thanking you. I've accomplished a lot in my life—both good and bad. When the cancer was discovered, I made up my mind that the last thing I would do was stop Mr. Smith. I couldn't have done it without you. Just promise me that you'll do what's right."

"I promise."

"You'll need to be strong," she said. "Once you see who he is, it's going to take a lot of courage on your part to finally end his reign of terror."

"I'm not afraid," I said.

"Even if it means putting yourself in harm's way?"

"I've learned a lot over the last few weeks. I've had a chance to stand back and take a good look at myself, too."

"Did you like what you saw?"

"In some cases, yes," I said. "Not in others."

"Shakespeare put it best. *To have seen what I have seen, see what I see.*"

"*Hamlet?*" I asked.

"Yes. I told you, it's my favourite. That and *Henry VI.*"

"Everyone's done things they regret. We're only human."

"That's right," she replied. "Nobody knows that fact better than I do."

"You were young. You made some horrible mistakes."

"Age has nothing to do with it. Even good people falter sometimes."

"Even great people," I said. "Look at John and Bobby."

"No one can dispute the things they managed to accomplish. The Civil Rights Movement, the Peace Corps—the list goes on and on."

"I agree," I said. "The things they did changed not only their country, but the rest of the world as well. Sometimes we forget that they were human, too. They made mistakes, just like the rest of us."

"You can find a skeleton in almost anyone's closet. It just depends on how hard you look."

"Or how you present the facts," I said. "Look at Marilyn."

"She led a troubled life—and she died a tragic death. She lived in the fast lane. She ran with powerful people, and she paid the price for it."

"The diary," I said, "that was her downfall. She knew too much."

"Perhaps. Maybe the contents of the diary were simply the details of a turbulent life. It's still only speculation that the red diary ever existed at all."

"We know it exists. You have it."

"Are you sure?"

"You told me. You said it was in a safety deposit box here in Vancouver."

"And you know for a fact that I was telling the truth?"

I hesitated.

"A statement is no more than hearsay, until it is proven."

"Were you lying to me?"

"About the diary? Or about Mr. Smith?"

"Jesus Christ," I said. "About anything!"

"I told you that we would expose Mr. Smith together. That was not a lie. You've done a good job, Hartree. You'll know who Mr. Smith is soon."

I breathed a sigh of relief.

"I have to go now, Hartree. This is goodbye. I'm counting on you and Amanda to make things right."

"But—"

"I'm going to address the instructions to her—just in case Joker gets to you first."

The phone line went dead. I ejected the tape cassette and held it in my hand. This was it. It was time for the showdown. It was time to expose Mr. Smith's and his machinations, and the final clue was on the way.

⌘

I poured the last couple of aspirin from the bottle into my hand, popped them into my mouth, and washed them down with the remaining mouthful of coffee in my mug. The contest between Mr. Smith and me was approaching its final quarter. The clock was ticking down and the score was tied at zero. Dallas was close to death, and I still couldn't positively identify Mr. Smith. I had him in my sights, but I wasn't sure whether Ball was taking his orders from Weller, or if Weller was taking orders from Alan Ball.

The fact that I actually knew the man behind the shroud, that I'd looked him in the eyes, was established early in the game. However, the only real confirmation I'd managed to get from Dallas was that Alan Ball was in this up to his slimy little neck. She had also told me that Joker was ruthless, and I knew that Mr. Smith was as cold-hearted and conniving as they came. Weller was a tough cop. He'd lied to me about the license plate number, he was the only person who knew I was bunked at the Chelsea Arms, and he had enough clout to access credit card information. Ball, on the other hand, had the reputation for ruling his boardroom with an iron hand. Both could be described as ruthless within their own arena. Weller was as fierce on the streets of Vancouver as Ball was in the office towers—or as *I* was behind a keyboard. I knew that I had both Joker *and* Mr. Smith by the balls. I just wasn't sure which one was which.

I tried to focus. I had to put a name to the man who'd ruined so many people's lives. Joker was right. I had to look at the whole forest, not just the trees. So much of what Amanda and I had been told could be interpreted in a variety of ways. Over the course of forty years, the facts regarding the Kennedy assassination had been tainted; there were so many half-truths and wild theories that the lies had *become* the truth. Perhaps Marilyn had started taking Nembutal early in the evening. If she'd taken one or two at a time, over the course of eight hours, she *could* have consumed a whole bottle. Maybe her body *could* have metabolized and stored enough of the drug that it would have only taken a tiny amount to push her over the edge. Maybe it wasn't a suicide *or* a murder. What if it was no more that a horrible accident?

And what about Jack Ruby? Amanda was right. The circumstances were just too weird. What if there had been a lineup at the Western Union office, and what if Oswald hadn't asked for a change of clothes? Jack Ruby was a dog lover—a fanatic about his pets. He referred to them as his family, and he actually called one his wife. He had his favourite dog with him in the car that morning. He must have known that the Dallas police wouldn't just let him stroll back up the entrance ramp to the garage after he shot the alleged assassin of the president. If the shooting of Oswald was an act that was months in the planning, why would Ruby bring his dog along? He must have known that the animal would be locked in the car—in the hot Texas sun—for hours afterwards.

What if Dallas was lying to me, or what if she was just speculating? I knew she'd met Jack Ruby before—the night she spent partying with the Friendship Seven. Did Mr. Smith really issue the order to silence Lee Harvey Oswald? Or did he just take advantage of what had already happened, to camouflage the real truth with more suggestions of what *could* have been the facts surrounding the shooting in the police garage. I needed more on Weller and Ball. I was certain that one of them had to be Mr. Smith. I'd listened to the recordings of Joker's calls over and over. I needed the last clue that Dallas had promised would come before she died. I couldn't decipher whether the whispers on the tape recordings were Ball's or Weller's. If I could put a finger on Joker, by process of elimination I'd have Mr. Smith. I had to give it another try. I pulled out my tape recorder.

# Chapter Fifty-Two

THE NEWSROOM WAS shutting down for the day. As darkness took over the city, the day shift began to wrap things up and head for the elevator. I held the phone to my ear.

"Hartree?" I listened to him say.

I leaned closer to Amanda and tapped her arm. "It's Joker," I whispered.

"I have some news for you," he said.

"What?" I asked.

"The woman—she's dead. It happened a few hours ago."

"You bastard," I said. "You killed her."

"I told you she didn't have much time left. I told you that I would be there holding her hand when she died. You knew this was coming."

"I know who you are, and I know who Mr. Smith is. And I'm not going to stop until the world knows as well."

"Were you surprised when you finally figured out how close you were all along?"

"I was."

"And are you sure you've got what it takes to carry on, now that the woman's dead?"

"I'm sure."

"I'm going to miss her. We spent a lot of years together. I have to admit, I cried for her when the end finally came."

"You son of a bitch."

"She spent her last day reading Shakespeare. At least I know that she had a little bit of pleasure at the end. Did you receive your gift yet?"

"What?" I asked.

"Your gift. The game's not over. You can't call yourself the victor yet. We still have a card or two to play."

I pulled open my desk drawer and checked on my gun. "Aren't you getting tired of threatening me?"

"You could still lose, you know. You just might get thrown a curveball at the last minute. We don't know for sure, if we'll be meeting for martinis at the Chelsea Arms."

"There'll be no martinis at the Chelsea Arms. You're the last person in the world that I'd sit down to drinks with."

"Really?" he chuckled. "Do I sicken you that much?"

"You repulse me."

"I've always had the feeling that you didn't like me, but I never thought I actually repulsed you."

"Well, you do."

"The end is coming, Hartree. The woman is dead now; I guess the gloves are off. Maybe this will mean the end of you."

"What's that supposed to mean?"

"There have been plenty of Mr. Smiths. You'd just be vanquishing one, and in order to do it, you might be sacrificing yourself. Maybe it will be up to your apprentice to carry on the fight. Dallas told me all about her before she died."

"Amanda's a strong person. And she's not afraid of people like you."

"Good, because *you* might not be around for much longer. Enjoy your gift."

⌘

I glanced at the clock on my computer screen. "You should be heading home, Amanda. It's almost seven, and there's nothing more we can do today."

"I'll see you bright and early then. Are you going to be all right?"

"I'll be fine," I said. "I've been sleeping on Sandra's couch the last few nights. I'm just going to clear up a couple of things before I head out."

"Then I'll see you tomorrow."

"Thanks," I said. I watched as she walked to the corner of the newsroom and held the elevator doors for Petra and her mail cart.

The young woman pushed the trolley through the maze of vacant desks and stopped at my cubicle.

"You're here late," I said.

Petra rolled her eyes and smiled. "We're swamped down there. I figured if I worked a couple of extra hours tonight, I'd have a jump on tomorrow."

"What have you got for me?"

"This arrived by courier late this afternoon. There was something for Amanda, too."

She handed me a parcel and she placed an envelope on Amanda's keyboard. "Catch you tomorrow," she said and turned her cart in the direction of the elevators.

⌘

I'd been staring at the package for the better part of an hour. The wrapping paper was a deep shade of red, closer to the colour of blood than the colour of a ripe apple. Each corner was meticulously folded into place and fixed with exactly the right amount of tape. It was obvious that a great deal of care had gone into the preparation of the gift. Every angle of the paper was precise and every crease was sharp and crisp. This offering had been prepared by someone with a keen eye for detail, a person who knew the importance of presentation. Like the stories I'd written about Ball and McDermott, it wasn't simply the lies that did McDermott in, it was how they were presented. Just the right amount of truth caused the old politician to stumble and fall. Dallas was gone now, and it was up to Amanda and me to stop the monster known as Mr. Smith. I leaned back in my chair and closed my eyes. Joker was right: Mr. Smith and I were a lot alike. So much of what we know about that November day back in 1963 could be interpreted in different ways. It was so easy to take the facts and turn them into lies.

I knew that Alan Ball was involved—it was the only thing that Dallas had actually confirmed before she died. And what about Freddy Weller? There had to be a reason why he lied to me about the license plate number.

I couldn't stand it any longer. I picked up the parcel and tore through the blood red wrapping paper. I opened the lid of the cardboard container and dumped its contents into my hand. I stared at the label on the bottle. Macallan—Fine Oak—single malt—eighteen years old—at least $250 dollars a pop. One more thing we have in common, Mr. Smith, I said to myself as I held the bottle up to the light. We both know fine whiskey.

# CHAPTER FIFTY-THREE

AMANDA NOSED HER car up to the swing arm that blocked the entrance to the underground parking garage of the Bayside Hotel. An attendant leaned out of the window of the control shack and passed her a ticket. We drove into the parkade.

"Lots of people here today," she said. "Keep your eyes open for a parking spot."

"There," I said and pointed to the ramp up to the second floor. "Let's try upstairs."

"I wonder what this is all about?"

I shrugged my shoulders. "I don't know," I replied.

"All the note said was to be in the Seymour Room at the Bayside Hotel at eleven." Amanda drove onto the ramp. "Do you think Dallas was telling the truth?" she asked.

"Huh?"

"That Mr. Smith would be here today. How will we know?"

I shrugged again. "She said to keep our eyes and ears open," I said. "She told me we'd both know who he was."

Amanda turned toward the first lane of cars on level two of the garage.

"Stop!" I yelled.

Amanda hit the brake pedal. The chirp from her tires echoed throughout the parkade. I jumped from the car.

She leaned over the passenger seat and called through the open door. "What is it?"

"Get out," I said, "come with me." I slammed the door closed.

She inched her car to the side of the lane and stopped.

"What?" she said again, as she exited the vehicle.

My heart began to race. There it was—one row over—a few stalls to the west. "Look," I said and pointed, "a black Jaguar."

Amanda joined me and together we cautiously approached the black Jag. The dark tint of the windows made it impossible to see if anyone was inside. We crept towards the rear of the vehicle. I stopped a car length away and looked at the license plate.

"It's Joker's car," I whispered. "Look at the plate number."

A wave of fear raced through my body. There it was—bright blue numbers on a white reflective background—OEE844.

Amanda walked up behind me and looked down at the number tag. "Something's not right," she said.

She brushed her way past me and headed for the rear of the car. I grabbed her arm.

"Be careful," I whispered.

She broke free of my hold and walked straight to the back of the Jag. She crouched down next to the license plate. "Come and look at this," she said.

I took a quick glance around the area, as I joined her at the rear of the car. She reached out and began to pick at the letter "O" as I crouched beside her.

"Blue pin striping tape," she said. "Look, the letter 'C' has been changed to an 'O'."

She picked away at the letters on the license plate. She stood and placed a wad of blue coloured tape in my hand. "See," she said, "OEE844 now becomes CFL314."

"Clever," I whispered. "That's why we couldn't find any record of the license plate number."

"You know what this means, don't you?"

"What?" I asked.

"Freddy Weller wasn't lying to you. OEE844 really doesn't exist."

"He's still a part of this, I know it."

Amanda looked me in the eyes, then turned her head and scanned the rows of cars. "I'm sure of one thing now," she said. "Mr. Smith *is* here today."

"There's an empty spot," I said and pointed. "Park your car and let's get upstairs."

⌘

The Seymour Room was beginning to fill. I nodded to the film crew from BCTV news as Amanda and I grabbed two seats next to the aisle.

"Reporters and politicians," I whispered, "I wonder what this is all about?"

Amanda nudged me with her elbow.

"Look," she said, "front row—left of the podium."

"Sharon Halter, Jesus Christ. I hope she's not in on this."

"Look who's sitting next to her."

I leaned over for a better view. "Son of a bitch," I whispered. "Freddy Weller. I knew it."

"Just wait. You can't accuse Weller with the information you have so far."

"Keep your eyes and ears open. We know Mr. Smith is here in this hotel somewhere. Dallas said we'd recognize him."

I rested my arm on the back of Amanda's chair and scanned the room. Most of the faces were familiar: colleagues from radio and television news, a number of political figures, reporters from our sister newspaper, the *Vancouver Herald*. I made eye contact with Charlie Wolfe. Amanda prodded me again.

"Look," she whispered, "isn't that Alan Ball?"

My heart began to pound. I turned to face the front of the room. Ball walked to the podium and pulled the microphone into place.

"Good morning," he said. "Thank you all for coming. I have a short announcement to make."

The room fell silent.

Ball paused for a moment and looked over the faces before him.

"Shortly after noon yesterday," he said, "Christine McDermott left us. She died at home. Her family and friends were at her bedside."

A buzz ran through the crowd. Ball held up his hand.

"As many of you know," he continued, "Christine and I became partners over twenty years ago, after I moved to Canada from the United States. She was an intelligent woman, whose word you could take to the bank. She worked very hard and never strayed from her strict set of principles and moral values."

I turned to Amanda. I couldn't utter a word.

"When she decided to run for public office," Ball continued, "I had mixed emotions."

He made eye contact with me. I looked down at my shoes.

"On one hand," Ball said, "I felt I was losing my right arm."

I glanced up. He was still focused on me.

"On the other hand," Ball continued, "the community that Christine grew up in gained a strong and determined voice."

I felt a sickness.

"As you are aware, Christine came under attack some time ago. Her cancer had been discovered at that point, and even though I argued with her decision, she decided to step aside. She didn't want to start a battle that might possibly drag her family, and the people that worked alongside her, through the mud. She resigned her seat and spent her remaining months with her family and friends. She will be buried at Mountainview Cemetery on Thursday. The family would like the services to be private."

"Come on," I whispered to Amanda, "let's get back to the office. I've heard enough."

Ball cleared his throat. "Christine asked me to relay a message today," he said, "to a Mr. Smith."

Amanda gripped my arm.

Ball unfolded a piece of paper and placed it on the podium. "Christine loved the works of William Shakespeare." He pulled his glasses from his breast pocket. *"I'll never pause again, never stand still, till either death has closed these eyes of mine or fortune has given me measure of revenge."*

I wanted to throw up.

Ball removed his glasses and tucked them in his shirt pocket. "That's all I have to say," he said and wiped a tear from his eye. "Thank you again for coming."

# CHAPTER FIFTY-FOUR

"ARE YOU ALL right?" Amanda asked.

I lifted my head and looked into the eyes of my female cub. I held her gaze for a few moments, then turned my head and stared at the heap of papers on my desk. "I can't believe this," I said. "The whole thing was a scam. It was all lies."

"It wasn't *all* lies," Amanda replied. "We did the research. Everything Dallas told us about Marilyn was documented. Everything we learned about the Kennedy assassination was right out of the history books, too."

I hung my head. "She picked the right story. If she wanted to draw me into a web of lies, she couldn't have found a better subject than the Kennedy assassination."

"She put a lot of work into it. She sorted through the dozens of theories and laid out a trail for us to follow."

"Then she spiced it up with enough of her own half-truths to lead us in the direction she wanted us to go in."

"Maybe Napoleon was right. Maybe history *is* just the lies that historians agree on. It doesn't take much. One good fib is enough to taint volumes of truths."

I looked up at her and smiled. "I remember," I said, "what one of the old boys from the newsroom used to tell me: You can take a bucket of horse manure, stir in a cup of fine wine, and you're still left with a bucket of horse manure. On the other hand, if you stir a cup of horse manure into a bucket of fine wine . . ."

Amanda placed her coffee mug on my desk. She pulled her chair next to mine, sat down, and took my hand. "I'm sorry," she said.

"I didn't start out like this, you know. When I was your age, I had some pretty strong ideas about what was right and what was wrong."

She smiled and squeezed my hand.

"I don't know how it happened," I said. "Time goes by so quickly. All of a sudden, I wasn't the youngest face in the newsroom anymore. Then along came the Cottonwood scandal. I showed the people of this city what Stanley Cottonwood really was—a common thief."

"He deserved what he got. That was first-rate reporting on your part."

"But then I had to face the facts. I felt that I had reached the pinnacle of my career. After Cottonwood, everyone wanted to see what I would come up with next. It's not like city hall was crawling with crooked politicians."

"So you created one."

"Somewhere along the line, what people thought of me became more important than being honest." I looked into her eyes again. "Winning a Ceejay became an obsession. And I didn't care what I had to do, or who I had to destroy along the way."

"I know," she said, "it's your curse."

"Christine McDermott was vulnerable. She couldn't deny the fact that she and Ball made a lot of money on the sale of that property."

"And there was nothing wrong with that. They didn't do anything improper when they bought that land."

"But it was sure easy to make it look like they'd done something inappropriate. I really thought she'd put up a fight."

"And you'd have hidden behind that unnamed source that you claimed to have stashed away. The battle could have lasted for years."

"She knew she didn't have years."

"So she came up with a plan, and sent us searching for the elusive Mr. Smith."

I smiled. "It didn't take us all that long to find him, did it?"

Amanda shook her head.

"Dallas—or should I say Christine McDermott—did what she set out to do. She promised we would be able to put a name to Mr. Smith before she died. She said we had to right a terrible wrong. She told us we had to put a stop to a monster."

"An evil personified," Amanda said. "Lies, half-truths, and innuendo."

"When did you realize that *I* was Mr. Smith?" I asked.

"I'm not sure," she replied. "I've had my suspicions over the last few days. Every time I listened closely to what Christine was telling us, the finger pointed directly at you. I guess I should have caught on sooner. *Hamlet*—the theme is revenge."

"I have to give her credit," I said. "She led me where she wanted me to go."

"She was a smart lady."

"And having Alan Ball chase me around town in his friend's Jaguar—that was a stroke of genius."

"She could have destroyed you. She could have let you print the story. She didn't have to get us invited to Ball's press conference. She didn't have to leave us that last clue—Ball's announcement."

"She had more class than that. I think she must have known that in order to stop the evil that was Mr. Smith, I would have to do it myself."

Amanda nodded again.

"I wonder if we'll ever learn the whole truth about that day in 1963?"

"I just finished another book on the assassination," she said. "The author made an interesting comment in his conclusion, about Lee Harvey Oswald and about why Kennedy's murder has spawned so many weird conspiracy theories."

"Why?"

"There's no balance. The criminal doesn't fit the crime."

"Explain," I said.

"If you look at the murder of six million Jews versus the Nazi Party, you have some sort of balance. The biggest crime in history was perpetrated by the biggest criminals in history."

"I see."

"Then you look at John Kennedy—"

"One of the most popular leaders of the twentieth century . . ."

"Versus a sick little man like Oswald."

"You're right. There's no balance." I shook my head at the irony.

"It's so easy to believe that there was a more sinister and complex plot, something that could explain the senseless tragedy."

I reached down and pulled open the bottom drawer of my desk. "I have something for you," I said.

I pulled a manila envelope from my drawer and handed it to her.

"What is it?" she asked as she tore open the seal.

"Your story on the Russian woman. It's going to print tomorrow. I've also sent a copy off to the Journalist's Association. There's an award category for apprentice reporters. I've nominated you. You've got an incredible talent."

Amanda's eyes lit up. "I don't know how to thank you," she said.

"I'll be handing in my letter of resignation this afternoon. It's time for me to go."

The sparkle in Amanda's eyes dimmed slightly. "It's the right thing to do," she said.

"But first I need to write an apology to Christine McDermott's family."

"And to the readers of this newspaper," Amanda added.

"Do you want to hear the good news?" I asked.

Amanda forced a smile.

"Sandra and I are going to work on getting back together. We had a long talk the other night and we're going to give it another try. I'm going to put all my efforts into making things right between us."

"That's wonderful news."

"I also need to apologize to you, too," I said. "Pass me your coffee mug."

She lifted her cup from the desktop and handed it to me.

I looked down the throat of the mug. The coffee stains were just about right. I reached into my desk drawer and pulled out my bottle of Scotch. I cracked the seal on the bottle of Macallan's and poured a splash into her mug. I poured a shot into mine and placed the bottle next to my phone.

"Here," I said as I passed her the mug—and the torch. "To a brilliant future," I said and raised my cup to meet hers.

CPSIA information can be obtained at www.ICGtesting.com
Printed in the USA
LVOW08s1006100414

381043LV00001B/25/P